A CHANGE FOR THE

BY Stephanie Drury

Table of Contents

Table of Contents

CHAPTER 1

The rain was bucketing down, hammering on the roof of the car like a demented pigeon having tap dance lessons. Katie peered through the windscreen at Tolpuddle House, of course it was raining! It was wet and gloomy, just like her mood. How had she agreed to come here? Still, no use sitting in her little sports car ruing her unfortunate position, after all, it was almost entirely her own fault that she found herself in her current predicament. It was pointless hiding here in the car, watching the rain and feeling sorry for herself, she had nowhere else to go so she may as well make the best of it. Katie carefully opened the door and promptly put her foot straight into a muddy puddle about six inches deep. "Bugger" she mumbled, still at least these were the Primark imitations and not the actual Ugg boots that were tucked away in her case. Splashing through the puddles Katie opened the boot of the car and heaved the cases out, dropping the corner of one onto her foot, which was now throbbing and wet! Carefully she turned towards the house and stopped. Katie stood in front of the old house, taking in it's familiar outline, The rickety turret at the top, resembling a tower where the princess (always herself) would be imprisoned awaiting the handsome prince to rescue her. "Not anymore" thought Katie bitterly "rescue yourself; no swashbuckling knight on a white horse or charming prince was going to come along and do it for you, no they would be cowering in the bushes or hightailing it in the opposite direction. Princes were definitely not what they used to be" The ivy was climbing up the west side of the house and it now covered almost half the house giving it a slightly sinister look like a theatrical mask concealing half its features, that was only offset by the many different shades of light beaming out of the rooms, like many twinkling eyes of soft shades of luminous pale light from the turrets to a bright vivid red light with mauve tones from the first floor window, setting the house alive.

It had been an age since Katie had been here, at least three years, but when she was a child she had spent many happy times here, staying at her grandparents, being spoiled and scolded in equal measure, living out huge adventures in the rambling garden and throughout the house in all the nooks and crannies. Katie smiled as she recalled Mo (as everyone called grandma) and granddad sat in front of the open fire in the kitchen, squabbling gently about anything and everything whilst she sat eating a bowl of plum crumble and custard or tucking into a doorstop sandwich, the only thing ever known to stop her talking for five minutes.

Katie smiled, despite its sometimes imposing appearance; Tolpuddle House was a warm and welcoming place inside and always provided a safe haven from the hostile world outside. Katie needed a haven now, she knew that, but she still wasn't sure if she'd done the right thing by coming here – but it was too late now.

Giving herself a mental shake Katie opened the gate and entered into the slightly wild garden following the slightly overgrown path to her new, if temporary, home.

It had been only two days ago when Katie had received a call from Mo in hospital. She'd had a 'slight' fall as she understated it. Actually she had clattered down one and a half flights of stairs in Tolpuddle house before ending up in a heap in the middle of the hall. Fortunately there had been someone else in the house at the time and they had, despite Mo's very vocal protests, called the ambulance straight away.

Mo, much to her chagrin, was now in hospital with a broken hip, bruised ribs, concussion and severely dented pride, but she was on the mend now. In fact when Katie had visited her she was practically back to her usual irascible self.

"I don't even know why they're making such a fuss - it was only a little tumble" moaned Mo.

"It was not a 'little tumble' Mo" Katie replied shortly "it was a nasty fall for someone half *your age.*"

"What's age got to do with it? I'm as fit as a fiddle, I've never been ill in my life I ..."

"Yes, you old battle-axe, you're indestructible I know" Katie interrupted, as Mo could run on eloquently in this theme for some time, "but either way you're in here now and you have to stay until you're fixed. Anyway it may not be so bad; it's a mixed ward you know!" Katie added with tongue firmly in cheek.

"You cheeky mare" Mo laughed in mock outrage, "but don't you go thinking I'm past it. How's that young man of yours anyway, you know the one you won't let any of us meet."

"He's history, Mo - I don't want to talk about it but he's gone and I'm officially homeless and probably jobless too." Katie sighed, this was a conversation she wasn't ready to have yet - the wounds were still raw. In addition there were so many other problems her current situation brought with it that she had no idea where to even start explaining it all. Mo saw the shutters go down on her granddaughters expressive brown eyes and saw her chin tilt up in that determined fashion she'd had since she was a stubborn five-year-old who really didn't want to go home. There'd be no confidences from Katie now. Mo sighed, she really admired Katie's determination and strength but sometimes she wished she could open up so that she could put her arms around her to help make things better. Still at least she could help with one or two of Katie's problems this time without appearing to. Mo cleared her throat and jumped in before Katie could steer the conversation completely away from herself.

"Well Katie, we won't talk about it if you don't want to, but when you do want to, you know where I am, I'm not going anywhere for a while! Anyway I need your help if I'm going to be stuck in this godforsaken place. I need you to look after Tolpuddle house for me." Mo paused and listened for any reaction in the heavy silence that followed. Katie didn't think she'd heard correctly.

"Sorry, keep an eye on it you mean?"

"No" Mo shook her head vigorously until the bandages started to wobble; "I mean look after it - move in to it and make sure all my people are ok too. Come on, you just said you had nowhere to live and no job either!" Mo looked up innocently from her bed, holding Katie in her translucent blue gaze. Anyone who knew Mo would tell you there was no escape from Mo's plan when she fixed you with those azure glinting innocent eyes. They were much more Machiavellian than innocent in the workings behind them.

Katie took a deep breath to buy herself a bit more thinking time, but Mo seizing the moment, decided to take this pause as consent and before Katie could respond in any way Mo had removed her keys from her bag along with a list of instructions from the notepad by the side of her bed and pressed them into Katie's hand. As if on autopilot Katie took them and started to rise from the chair - she knew she was already beaten.

"Ok Mo, I'll look after things only for as long as you're in here. I'll see you soon," she said kissing the top of Mo's head, "I just want to have a word with the sister before I go." Katie rose thinking she had taken control of the situation well. It wasn't until she had spoken to the sister that she realised quite how skillfully she had been stitched up. Mo would be in hospital at least a month, need a convalescence period for another two months after that and even then she may not be strong enough to look after the house and it's inhabitants. Katie had just been signed up for at least a three-month stint!

So here she was 48 hours later outside the front door of Tolpuddle

House with her case, holdall, wet feet and reference from her previous

employer who had been irritatingly eager to let her go immediately - to

save any 'embarrassing little encounters' as they put it.

Still Katie couldn't help but look affectionately at the huge, oak,

varnished door with a solid brass knocker in the middle. It had always

seemed like an invitation to adventure when she was small. Now it

seemed a bit ramshackle and certainly not the modern, up-to-the-

minute outfit she was used to, but nonetheless it was reassuring in its

familiarity. Katie slipped the key in the lock and heaved on the door. It

didn't move. "Great" she thought, Mo had said it could be a bit stiff -

but it was more like jammed. Now what was the knack Mo mentioned,

lift up the handle, kick the bottom right of the door, push the handle

down simultaneously and SHOVE. "Ok here goes nothing" Katie

mumbled to herself and shoved and kicked as instructed. A few seconds

later as she hauled herself off the hall floor and dusted down her Calvin

Klein jeans she announced to her reflection in the hall mirror, "Yes,

that would appear to be the knack!"

Katie collected her bags from the path and took a proper look around the hall. It was much as she remembered, the magnolia paint that could do with a fresh coat, the staircase heading upstairs – with a less garish carpet than had graced it during the seventies and eighties. To her right was a door leading into the front room. Mo and Granddad never really used this room although it had a beautiful big bay window overlooking the front garden. It had been impossible, despite all Granddads' efforts, to get the room warm. They had always preferred to sit in the living area of the kitchen with its oversized misshapen sofa and armchairs, the range giving off a cosy heat and always some wonderful aromas of baking bread, casseroles or roasting meats, whilst watching all their favourite soaps on the telly. On Katie's left was the door into Mo's flat and straight ahead up the hall led to the ground floor flat occupied by some of Mo's 'people'. Altogether the house had seven other occupants in the various flats and bed sits that Katie's Granddad had created over ten years before.

Katie took out Mo's list as she opened the door into the flat and dumped her bags at the side to be dealt with later. There, on the list, were Mo's acerbic details of her current 'guests' as she called them.

Downstairs - Ground Floor Flat, Mary & Ken Clackett, both 70 but think they're 40 - watch out for any DIY undertaken.

First Floor

Bed sit 1 - Guy Masters, something to do with computers doesn't't speak much - make sure he eats.

Bed sit 2 - Poppy Smith, Student at Rawlinston College studying dresses - make sure she eats too.

Bed sit 3 - Hermione Sheridan, spinster of this parish (not her choice!). A bit fussy but her hearts in the right place

2nd Floor Flat - Bradley & Tamsin Dixon, newlyweds, both very into the environment, animals, children and each other.

Below all this Mo had also written details of the various rents each of the 'guests' paid and which bank account to pay them into and how much Katie should take each week for her housekeeping role. Katie smiled as she read it - that had been an hourly amount in her last job! Still she wouldn't need much money around here. Laxley Heath was not renowned for it's wealth of activities, "Still" Katie thought "perhaps I should've tried a bit harder to save some of that money I earned instead of blowing it all on trips, holidays, clothes and gadgets which would be of little or no use to her here."

Choosing not to dwell on her short-comings at the present moment, Katie picked up her bags and put them in the first bedroom, wincing at the chintz with added chintz decor that Mo favoured in here. Deciding to unpack her things later Katie headed for the kitchen in search of something familiar, and there they were the big old range, the comfy sofa, a flat screen TV with DVD recorder (that was new Mo!) and the huge pine kitchen table. Katie felt inspired immediately and putting the range on to warm up the flat and the water she decided to see what food was available. As it turned out not much in the finished form but the ingredients for almost anything, just as she had expected. Without thinking Katie rolled up her sleeves and collected all the things she needed to make some bread. Of course in London she had a top of the range bread-maker for this, but she knew how to make it herself. Mo had spent many evenings and holidays when Katie had come to stay teaching her grand-daughter how to bake freshly made bread, tasty crunchy biscuits, melt-in-the-mouth sponges and all sorts of buns and fancies. Katie had loved learning how to bake and she had a natural instinct for it, always knowing what to add or how long to stir the mixture without spoiling it and then pulling the finished article out of the range at just the right moment. Katie loved to bake, she found the measuring, stirring and kneading, soothing and settling all to create a delicious concoction when she felt worried or stressed. It was almost as comforting as eating the creations fresh from the oven. This was just one of those times Katie reflected ruefully, her whole life had just been turned upside down, she had lost her love, her home, her job and was pitched up back where she had started out from eight years before, and she had no idea what she was going to do next, but somehow as she threw the ingredients in the bowl, mixed them and kneaded the soft springy dough she felt her nerves relax, and a calmness surround her. She might not know what tomorrow would bring but just for now she was alright.

An hour and a half later Katie was sat on the sofa eating freshly baked bread with butter dripping from the sides, accompanied by a steaming hot mug of tea, watching the late afternoon offerings on the telly. Quiz shows and talk shows, but nothing challenging or disturbing - just what she needed to keep her troubled spirits soothed. As she sat in a half trance like state sherealised there was a fairly persistent knocking on the door in the kitchen. The door opened onto the path at the side of the house leading round to the patio and the flat at the back.

Rising slowly from her seat Katie was loath to let the real world back in so soon but realised that, as the lamps were on, there was no use in pretending no one was home. As Katie opened the door lilting Irish tones reached her.

"No, no, Ken, leave that be, just put the bag in the bin like I said - Oh hello my dear, you look confused, are you tired? My goodness what a delicious smell, fresh baked bread, how wonderful" The flow of conversation never stopped as the elderly, but sprightly, lady walked through the door and plonked herself firmly on one of the kitchen chairs.

"Oh you have the range on too, lovely, I always think the range gives off a homely, proper heat, not like the central heating or those storage heater things" she said the words as if they were the work of the devil and in the short intake of breath she took then Katie decided to jump right in before getting lost in the next bit of chatter.

"Um hello, do come in. I'm Katie Collins, Mo's grand-daughter. Can I help you?"

"Well of course you are - I'm Mary Clackett from the ground floor. We've met before, you know, when you came to visit Mo a couple of years ago, though I must say you were not so skinny then."Mary cast a disapproving eye over Katie. Being thin was clearly on a par with storage heaters to Mary Clackett.

"Of course we did, Mrs. Clackett, it's been a while and I'm afraid I'm a bit shell shocked at the moment with all the things that have happened" Katie tried to defend her forgetfulness.

"But of course you are my dear" clucked Mary, "and call me Mary, what with your grandmother's fall and all - it was such a shock to all of us. It was Ken that found her, poor love; he went as white as a sheet, no use, like most men, in a crisis. He just stood there opening and closing his mouth like a goldfish, fortunately me and Hermione were there, you know Hermione in the first floor bed sit?" enquired Mary.

"Um no, I've not had the pleasure yet" Katie replied.

"Pleasure - huh!" grunted Mary, "not so much a pleasure as an endurance but, none the less, there she was and with that mobile phone thingy at least she could ring the ambulance straight away. I can tell you I was worried about her."

"Hermione?" asked Katie after getting lost in the story telling again.

"No, no, my dear, Mo - your grandma. She looked terrible and all at a funny angle. Anyway that's why I popped round as soon as saw a light on, to see how she was" Mary finally came up for air. Katie reflected that Mary must have been sitting outside waiting as she had only put the lamps on five minutes before, but she sensed in Mary a genuine concern and affection for Mo in between all the extraneous chatter and she sought to put her mind at rest.

"Mo's doing very well, I saw her yesterday she has a broken hip and some other bruises and bangs but she's firmly on the mend and already looking forward to creating havoc on the ward. I'm sure she'd love some visitors if you wanted to go over and see her." Katie moved towards the door as she spoke, hoping it might encourage Mary to get up and walk through it, but she was looking thoroughly settled at the kitchen table. It didn't seem to have the required effect, in fact, quite the opposite as Mary turned towards the centre of the table and looked around expectantly.

"Has that kettle just boiled my dear? I could murder a cuppa" suggested Mary, Katie knew she was beaten and resignedly got another mug out of the cupboard and fetched her own to refill.

17

"I really would like to go and see Mo at St Thomas's;" Mary sighed "Mo's always been so kind to us, inviting us in for tea and biscuits." Katie went straight to the biscuit tin and put it on the table, "making sure the flat was ok," Mary continued "watching out when we were away, always making time for a chat. I really would like to go and see her. I'll get Ken to check the bus timetables; we can make a little trip out of it." Mary seemed so genuinely excited by the thought of this little outing that Katie realised Mary had probably missed Mo very much over the last couple of days. She doubtless didn't get to go to many places or see many people. Katie's reserve melted as she saw the real concern in Mary's round and lively face.

"Don't worry Mary; I have my car here now I'd love to take you and Ken over to see Mo. You let me know when."

Katie was rewarded with a look of such deep thanks that it brought tears to her eyes. It was a long time since such a small thing as giving someone a lift had made Katie feel good about herself. In fact she reflected grimly, it was a long time since anything had made her feel good about herself. Katie decided to open the cream biscuits too.

CHAPTER 2

The following morning as Katie awoke to the sound of feet clattering up, down and possibly sideways in the hall, she was less bothered about feeling good about herself and more concerned with the bad feelings she had about everyone else living in Tolpuddle House. Getting out of bed, wrapping her dressing gown around her, Katie flung open the door of the flat to reprimand whoever was responsible for the unnecessary noise, but as she looked, she was greeted by an empty hall and staircase and a loud thud as the last person pulled the un-cooperative door shut as they left. Mentally making a note to tackle everyone about it later and also to see about some thicker carpet than the thin effort currently on the stairs, Katie turned back into the flat and resigned herself to an early start despite the lie in she had promised herself the night before. Moving quickly into the kitchen, she set the kettle on the range and cut herself two thick slices of the whole meal bread she had baked the day before, spreading them with a generous layer of butter and honey. Making herself a strong mug of tea Katie realised she had used the last of the milk and the butter so therefore an expedition to the shop could be put off no longer.

So it was that an hour later Katie found herself heaving shut the front door and heading into the village surrounding Tolpuddle House. Katie had decided to tackle the local shop rather going off in search of the nearest supermarket some five or six miles away on the edge of Rawlinston.

Stepping out into the winter sunshine Katie reflected that cold but sunny January days were really quite beautiful and that Laxley Heath was a quaint picture postcard village. Katie mentally painted the roofs and trees with a light dusting of snow, lit the lanterns in front of the houses and composed as pretty a scene as pictured on so many Christmas cards over the years.

Tolpuddle House stood on the lower edge of the village at the side of the main road that cut the village in two. It was the largest house in the main part of the village, although Burton Manor and Langley Farm, both about a mile out from the village were larger.

Katie headed up the street towards the small parade of shops that had been there ever since she could remember. In addition to the local convenience store where Katie was headed, there was also the Laxley Heath Souvenir store and post office run by Ted and Tanya Taylor who, despite other post offices falling by the wayside in rapid succession, had managed to keep enough business from the store and post office to keep going. Then there was Mary Allen's Ladies' Fashions and Hairdressers, fashions from when, was less obvious but Ms. Allen had been fitting out and coiffeuring ladies of a certain age to their satisfaction for many years now. Lastly there was the tackle shop, which, as its name implied, sold tackle for fishing, riding and even golf. It wasn't clear how the truculent owner Mr. Alan Kenworthy made his money but in fact he ran a successful mail order and Internet business from the shop to enthusiasts around the country which provided a very good income. Alan Kenworthy could be an awkward bugger but he was always open to an opportunity and as a result had a finger in many pies most of which, if not all, were successful to varying degrees. Of course as required in any picture postcard village there were the usual three or four antique shops alongside the village green. The green sat back from the road with a large stream tributary to the River Rawlin with ducks parading up and down and a small bridge ideal for playing "pooh sticks" under. The Rose & Crown Pub framed the second side of the green. Laxley Heath had become a very popular stop for tourists of all shapes and sizes, they walk down the quaint main street of the village, sit and relax by the green and wander in and out of the antique shops before moving on to Burton Manor or Laxley Castle a few miles further up the road. But before Katie reached this dazzling array of retail opportunities she noticed a new addition to Laxley Heath's commercial sector. One of the small terrace houses edging the main road had turned the front entrance into a very small but exquisitely set out display area for a selection of beautiful hand painted and probably hand-made pottery. Katie took a step up into the front entrance to take a closer look at the wares.

Once inside the tiny display area Katie picked up a cup decorated with brightly coloured bold strokes diagonally across its bowl drawing the eye time and again to the rim. It wasn't one of those delicate teacups favoured by mythical great aunts, but a cup for a frothing latte or a piping hot, strong tea. Katie could picture herself very clearly curled up on the sofa; fire burning, a good book in hand and a steaming hot drink in this beautiful cup. Katie rubbed her hands around the cup, very rarely could such an ordinary object inspire such a vivid daydream that Katie immediately wanted to buy it and run home to use it. Just as she was looking for a price she heard a noise behind her and turning round came face to face with a smiling, slightly wild-looking woman.

"It's a beautiful cup but it needs to be used doesn't it?" the lady said

"Oh absolutely" Katie replied "How much is it?"

"Never mind that - come on through and let's give it a test drive. I was just about to make a drink for myself. I'm Cliona by the way." She held her hand out as she spoke.

Katie shook the proffered hand "Katie Collins; I'm looking after Tolpuddle House whilst my grandmother's in hospital."

"Ah yes, I thought you must be Mo's grand-daughter, you're just how she described you. And the jungle drums, Laxley style, said you were coming to stay. How is she doing?" They chatted about Mo's progress as Cliona led the way through the house. Katie was impressed by the artistic order of the house; although there were many throws, beads and books about, the house still looked ordered and clean. Katie had an impression that most artistic types were too into their 'muse' to deal with such mundane tasks as dusting, vacuuming and polishing, but it seemed Cliona was able to set her mind to both the creative and practical aspects of life.

After passing through the relaxed and soothing living area they crossed the dining room, complete with an old, slightly marked but lovingly polished mahogany table and chairs that had clearly seen many dinners and, if they could speak, would have many stories to tell, and passed into the kitchen. Here Katie was to receive her second surprise. She had been expecting a slightly frayed but warm and welcoming kitchen with bold colours, big old pots and solid wood furniture, the sort of archetypal farmhouse kitchen. Instead she walked into a state of the art, modern 21st century kitchen, straight out of a Kensington catalogue. Beech wood units, gleaming stainless steel tops and glass intersections. The colours were muted but warm. It was a staggeringly lovely (and expensive!) room but Katie found it hard to match it with the wild and free spirited Cliona in front of her, possibly sensing her confusion Cliona offered Katie a seat and continued

"The kitchen is my partner Declan's choice, he's the chef of the house and as he cooks for me and all the little get-togethers I organise, the least I could do was let him have the kitchen he wanted. It's a little too clinical for me" she confided with a wink. Katie smiled back and took the proffered seat, thinking how the style was so like her small kitchen in the penthouse flat she had just had to leave.

"So what will it be?" Cliona's question cut into Katie's thoughts.
"Sorry, what will what be?"

"Your drink - I have coffee, decaf or caff, latte, cappuccino, mocha or tea, breakfast, earl grey. Hot chocolate, er hot water if you prefer."

"I'm sorry" Katie laughed "I didn't see the 'cafe' sign out front. I'd love a latte - decaf please."

Katie observed her new acquaintance as she poured a shot of espresso coffee into the cup they had brought through and added the foaming hot milk. It was easy to feel at ease with Cliona, she had such a warm, but not intrusive personality with a huge dollop of mischief thrown in. She was the sort of person who could make even the dullest gathering a giggle - probably when you were least supposed to. As they sat down to drink the coffee and eat the custard creams Cliona had produced from another cupboard Katie felt more at ease and calm than she had for many weeks. Cliona eyed her curiously,

"So what's the story then Katie, what's really bringing you to Laxley Heath?"

Katie smiled "Well, I really am looking after Tolpuddle House as Mo's in hospital, but you're right I needed somewhere to be and something to be for a while."

Cliona raised a quizzical eyebrow, prompting Katie to continue, not that she needed much prompting Katie needed to tell someone about what had happened.

Katie had wanted a job in London ever since she could remember, she was dazzled by the glamour of the idea, working for important people, living in penthouse apartments, earning good money and being secure for the rest of her life. Her chosen plan was to be an indispensable assistant to these important people initially and then become important in her own right later. It sounded ridiculous when you said it out loud but it was important to have a plan and know where you were going and why. Katie's plan was to be financially secure and held in high esteem by all those around her. She had gained her degree in English at Bristol University and had then done a crammer course in secretarial skills at a private college, then she had applied for every PA position at a city firm she could find. Four years later having gained valuable experience at two solicitors firms in the centre of London, when a top PA position came up at Dawson, Philips & Chamberlain Barristers, considered to be among the top three firms in London and who had many glamorous, famous and extremely rich clients on their books, Katie had put everything into her interview and secured the job as personal assistant to Marcus Chamberlain. Marcus, at 44, was a brilliant lawyer but he was also devastatingly handsome in the tall, dark tradition, a sharp thinker, extremely charming with a wicked sense of humour that made him approachable and down to earth despite all his 'god-like' qualities. He also looked after his staff in many thoughtful ways, small presents to say thanks for a job well done, always treating successes as a team effort or remembering personal details that were important to them. It took Katie all of about three months to fall in love with her new job, her new lifestyle and her new boss! It took a further six months for Marcus to reciprocate. Katie had shut out the fact that Marcus was married with two children and had planned a precise campaign to win him over which she executed to perfection. This involved being the ultimate PA, loyal, unobtrusive, one step ahead of all his needs, always on hand, never complaining and with a ready smile for him. To this she added personal touches. His favourite biscuit with coffee, a drink ready mixed at the end of a tough day in court, an ear available to listen to all his woes but never imposing any of her own and most importantly she made him laugh. Katie always tried to leave Marcus with a smile on his face, that way she figured he would associate her with good times.

Katie's plan worked like a charm, soon Marcus was relying on Katie, not only to keep his working day as trouble free as possible, but also he needed her to relax and enjoy himself in a way he couldn't't at home with his wife and children making all the everyday demands on him that families do.

It was soon a full blown affair; Marcus secured Katie an apartment in the docklands. It was exactly the sort of place she had dreamt of, a New York style loft space with polished floors, windows on two full sides, a balcony to relax on and it didn't cost her a penny. Actually it cost Dawson, Philips & Chamberlain, as Marcus put it through the firm as a place for visiting experts and witnesses to stay, not that they ever did!

Life continued in this way for three years, Katie didn't really have any friends as she made sure she was always available for Marcus whenever he was free, but it didn't worry her. She saw people at work, she e-mailed and visited a few old college friends who lived outside of London and, of course, she had Mo too. The loneliness she felt sometimes she thought was a price worth paying for all she had around her, the flat, the designer clothes, the state of the art gadgets in every room and last but definitely not least Marcus.

Then it had happened, it had all come tumbling down and exposed the fragile 'house of cards' her life actually was. Katie and Marcus had been away on another business trip, they generally kept business trips very businesslike until they had concluded work and then stayed on for a couple more nights for themselves. Apparently Sarah, Marcus's wife had had her suspicions and had employed someone to watch him, not that Katie and Marcus knew that then. No, the photos of their liaison were presented by Sarah the following Wednesday in the middle of the partners meeting when Katie was taking minutes.

Katie paused in her story, shuddering as she recalled the horror of that moment. Cliona just reached out and patted her hand to reassure her. Taking a deep breath Katie continued. Sarah had stormed into that meeting waving the photos and spreading them round for all the partners to see. She then told Marcus where to go and called Katie a few choice names in the well-worn tradition of wives to mistresses. Then she'd turned on her Jimmy Choos and left. Katie was dumbstruck, horrified and had lost the use of any of her limbs and looked to Marcus for support. That, of course, was not forthcoming. He had looked at her with disgust and then shot out of the room after his wife leaving Katie to face the other five partners who were now all looking to her for answers. It was Jed Dawson, the most senior partner who had come to her rescue. Realising she was in no fit state to answer any questions relating to her position at the moment and that she didn't have to answer the more curious ones about their relationship, he had dismissed the meeting, fetched Katie a drink of water and then once she had regained her composure he had sent her home telling her to take the rest of the week off. She was instructed to ring personnel once she was feeling better and they would take things from there. Somehow it was Mr. Dawson's kindness, despite the disapproval and disappointment that was clear in his eyes, which upset Katie the most. For the first time she really felt like the scarlet woman, the home wrecker, that no doubt, everyone in the office was branding her.

At home, in her beautiful flat, Katie waited for Marcus to ring, and waited, and waited. She had thought he would at least ring to see if she was ok but by Thursday evening there had been no contact at all. So nervously Katie had dialled his mobile, it was switched off. Then she checked her e-mails to see if he had sent her a message under the guise of doing some work, but again there was nothing. By Saturday evening when there was still no word Katie realised she wasn't going to hear from him, he was simply going to cut her out of his life as if she never existed. Katie had been asked to go in for an appointment at work on the following Tuesday where they had quietly dispensed with her services. She had gotten the call about Mo's fall on the Sunday and found herself in Laxley Heath and Tolpuddle House by Wednesday.

Katie paused at the end of her story, she looked briefly at Cliona, not wanting to see the dislike in this kind woman's eyes but expecting it none the less. But instead Cliona just patted Katie's clenched hands, smiled at her with genuine warmth and said

"You made a mistake, you've paid the price and you'll never do it again. Pick yourself up, dust yourself off and do something new - and remember security in life only ever comes from within - someone else can't give it to you, because they can always take it away again."

CHAPTER 3

A few days later as Katie was returning from what was becoming a fairly regular morning coffee with Cliona, she arrived at the front door at the same time as one of Mo's other guests. The girl was attempting to follow the guidelines for opening the door but with a folder under one arm and a long slim jersey skirt restricting her leg movements it was proving impossible. Katie arrived just in time to stop a string of expletives about to be uttered.

"Oh hi, thank god you've arrived" the girl looked at Katie with undisguised relief "this bloody door won't open - now there is a knack if you ...."
Katie had already heaved and kicked against the door and was now bowling into the hallway again.

"Oh" the girl commented "you know the knack - you must be Mo's granddaughter. I'm Poppy, first floor right side studio flat" Poppy extended her hand solemnly to Katie, which she took and shook with equal solemnity.

"Delighted to meet you Poppy, I'm Katie and yes I'm Mo's grand-daughter" Katie replied "It's nice to see another of Mo's tenants I'm afraid I've been a bit slow in getting round and introducing myself but I'm sure we'll be seeing each other around, maybe we can have a cuppa sometime."

Poppy's face broke out into a huge smile that transformed her plain features
"Oh yes please - I'd love to, me and Mo often used to have a cuppa and a natter when I was off college or on a free period you know." Poppy headed straight to Mo's door as Katie realised she intended to take up the offer right now and it was too late, without being rude, to retract the invitation.

Resignedly Katie opened the door and invited Poppy through to the kitchen. As Katie was making the tea, boiling the kettle and warming the pot, Poppy chattered on quite freely about her college course. It transpired she was a design student, specialising in jewellery design. She was in her second year and loved the course. Her ambition was to be a jewellery designer to the stars. She had already designed her own logo and name "Poppy Seeds"

"You get it" she laughed "Ideas planted and developed by Poppy"

Katie smiled back it was impossible not to be affected by this girl's raw enthusiasm and delight in her passion. Katie looked at her again with renewed interest. She was a petite size, maybe five foot two; she had a shock of black hair with bright blue flashes here and there. She was wearing what Katie called a 'goth' outfit, long black jersey skirt, a black top and black Doc Martin boots. This was complemented with lashings of black eyeliner and mascara, but most eye-catching were the intricate trellis earrings that dangled below her cropped hair and the double looped necklace interlaced with amber coloured quartz. They looked stunning and very expensive.

"Are those your own designs then?" Katie asked

"Yes" Poppy replied "I've just completed these for my second year free style project."

"They're beautiful - you must be very talented." Katie was impressed.

"Thanks" Poppy seemed a bit awkward accepting praise.

"So, how do you normally get through the door - do you just wait for the next person to arrive?" Katie asked, noticing her discomfort and changing the subject as she passed over a packet of biscuits for Poppy to open.

"Oh no, eventually I have to put my folder down and hitch my skirt up. I can get a pretty good kick going with these on" Poppy pointed down at her Doc Martins.

"I would think so" Katie laughed "but one day you might go through it all together. I think maybe I should get someone in to fix it. I'm sure I saw a card for a builder round here somewhere" Katie rooted through some drawers "Aha!" she proclaimed, triumphantly waving a small business card about.

"BW Building and Maintenance, I'll give them a call and get them round to look at the door - I don't want to be responsible for either of the Clacketts doing themselves a mischief on our door!"

"Oh don't worry about that" Poppy replied as she stood up and headed for the door "they have their own door at the back, they always use that." She pulled the door open and shouted back to Katie "thanks for the tea - it was great." and she shut the door firmly behind her. Katie collected her cup from the table and noticed that over half the packet of biscuits had been eaten and she hadn't had one. Laughing she thought, students - they're the same wherever you go. That was why she saw a lot of Mo. Mo loved feeding people.

The following day Katie decided she really would have to venture to the supermarket. There were just too many ingredients, fresh fruit and vegetables she had been doing without. One big shop should keep her stocked up for a while and she could pop in and see Mo as it was a couple of days since she had been. Mo was improving steadily the sister informed Katie when she arrived at the hospital, but they were still concerned about how long it would take the fracture to heal and they still couldn't be certain about the longer term, the injuries could well leave her weaker and with some movement difficulties.

Katie found Mo in bed with a posse of the over 65's around her indulging in an 'innocent' game of poker. As they dispersed to let Katie visit, one of the old boys winked at Katie and with a twinkling smile said "Don't look so disapproving my dear - it's only a bit of fun, no money has changed hands"

"Only because you haven't coughed up your debts yet, Bert Riley, don't think I'll forget. I'm in here for a fractured hip not a knock on the head." Mo shooed him away and Bert left laughing.

"Oh Mo" Katie asked concerned, "I'm not sure you should be playing poker - don't they need a licence for that?"

"Stop worrying, Katie Kettle; I don't think they'll throw me out for having a bit of fun and keeping five patients from going up the wall with boredom. Don't look so worried, we're all allowed to let our hair down now and again - even you!"

Katie smiled, it was a long time since Mo had called her 'Katie Kettle', it had been Mo and her Grand-dad's nick name for her when she was little as she had always been asking Mo to put the kettle on for a cup of tea. She had never wanted pop or squash, always tea, mainly because at Mo's you always got a biscuit, a bun or some other treat with a cup of tea. So 'Katie Kettle' had stuck and whenever Mo wanted to make Katie smile or relax she called her by it and it always worked, it took Katie back to a safe and innocent time in Mo's kitchen with the range lit and the kettle boiling.

"Ok Mo" Katie held her hands up in mock surrender "I'll stop nagging"

Mo laughed too "and will you do something else for me too while you're at it?"

"I suppose so, as long as it doesn't involve smuggling whiskey in to liven up your little tournament" Katie shook out her long brown wavy hair in feigned indignation.

"Now there's a thought that hadn't crossed my mind until you just mentioned it" teased Mo "but no, not at the moment. Would you make sure that you arrange a little get-together for everybody at Tolpuddle soon? I was due to have one this week and for people like Poppy and the Clacketts they look forward to it. I don't want them to miss it just because I'm stuck in here" Mo looked at Katie surreptitiously hoping she wasn't going over the top, but she desperately wanted Katie to do this, not just for her regular tenants but for Katie herself. Mo wanted her to get to know people locally again, restore a bit of confidence and colour back into her granddaughter after whatever had happened in London had knocked it out of her. It seemed she had got it right; Katie smiled and held Mo's hand

"Of course I will if you want me to -if only to stop you discharging yourself for some ridiculous party crisis. Anyway I think it might be the only food Poppy gets. She packed away half a packet of biscuits in under ten minutes the other day."

By the time Katie left Mo she had promised she would organise something for the following Thursday evening and that she would return to see Mo on Saturday to go through the guest list and more importantly the food list! Mo took entertaining very seriously and always tried to match the food to the guests, a knack that her granddaughter had inherited but one she'd put to little use over the last few years, as somebody's mistress you didn't do the entertaining or act as the hostess - you only ever did intimate little meals for two, and often they had to be abandoned early as some new family crisis loomed from down the mobile phone. As Katie remembered this she stood stock still in the corridor and another visitor cannoned into the back of her. Katie barely noticed, she'd just realised it had been over three days since she had even thought about Marcus and what's more when she had, it hadn't been to wish she was back in his arms in her flat or in a nice hotel somewhere, no, it was to be irritated with him (and herself) that she had always come second best. Maybe she was starting to get over this just as Cliona said she would.

A couple of hours later as Katie loaded her shopping into the boot of her car, her optimistic mood had passed and a black cloud had descended over her. This was due in a large part to the nightmare that was supermarket shopping. Screaming children, old ladies pushing trolleys in pairs at a snail's pace up every aisle, other impatient shoppers ramming her on the ankles at least three times and lastly some phantom shopper who seemed to have picked up the last one of at least half the things she had wanted to buy just before she got there!

Katie slammed the boot shut, jumped into the car and set off. She just wanted to get home as quickly as possible now, the guy from BW Building was coming to look at the door and thanks to the extremely large queues at the checkouts she was now running about half an hour later than she had expected.

Katie raced through the country roads in her sporty little Mazda mentally making a list of the order in which she would like to eliminate all her supermarket devils and the many and varied ways in which she would do it. As she turned another corner at probably ten miles an hour too fast she came across a cyclist towards the middle of the road. She had just enough room to pass the bike but in doing so she set the rider off balance who proceeded to roll headlong into the hedge at the side

of the road. Katie slowed and looked in the mirror as the rider picked

himself up, dusted off his jeans and blue T-shirt and started to head

towards her. She couldn't really see his face as he had a scarf wrapped

around it and a cycle helmet on but she sensed he wasn't happy from

the determined steps he was taking towards her. Deciding she couldn't

face another incident today Katie slammed her car into gear and set off

around the next bend but not before she had given a cheeky wave out

of her window to the advancing cyclist. The last thing she saw was the

less than happy rider standing flabbergasted in the middle of the road

as she disappeared.

CHAPTER 4

Katie got back in good time, the building person wasn't due until 3.30pm so she still had fifteen minutes to put the kettle on and grab a quick snack. At 3.45pm she starting to wonder if she had got the time wrong just as the doorbell to the front door chimed in the kitchen. Katie ran out to the hall getting ready to make some barbed comment about time-keeping but as she opened the door she was struck dumb. There, stood in front of her, was the cyclist she had just driven off the road. Although he no longer had the scarf or helmet on these was no disguising the mud stain halfway down his left leg and even if that hadn't given him away the thunderous look in his eyes as he looked from Katie's car back to her would have been sufficient. Katie was struck by a sudden urge to laugh and the corners of her mouth must have given her away as the man rounded on her.

"Oh I see, you think driving some innocent cyclist into the hedge and then driving off without so much as an apology is funny, do you?" His voice was deep and pleasant even though his tone wasn't and it took the desire that Katie had to laugh away completely. She had been just about to apologise for those things but his demanding, almost pompous tone, changed her mind.

"No, I don't think it's funny and neither is cycling haphazardly and in an uncertain manner in the middle of the road, springing out in a dangerous manner on cars using the road in a perfectly normal manner." Katie held her chin out obstinately, as she was wont to do when getting into an argument and awaited some pithy response from the cyclist. Unexpectedly he burst out laughing which completely threw Katie

"You're absolutely right, I was riding my bike with total disregard for other road users and I offer you my sincere apologies." He held out his hand and looked at Katie with twinkling blue eyes underneath his rather unruly sandy coloured hair. Katie got the impression that he might actually be laughing at her but decided she just wanted to put an end to this. So, somewhat reluctantly, she took the outstretched hand and begrudgingly said

"Well, I'm sorry if I startled you by using the road" she paused and then added "oh and for driving off without speaking to you." Thankful that this confrontation had come to a peaceful end Katie waited for the man to go but he didn't seem to be in any hurry, instead he started to scrutinise the house and the doorframe.

"So" he said eventually just as Katie was starting to lose patience "this is the door that's causing the problem then?"

"Yes it is - oh are you? I'm sorry, who are you?" Katie stumbled over her words. Smiling that mischievous smile again he held out his hand again,

"I'm Ben Wilson, BW Building. Is Mo in? I can go through what needs doing with her."

"Actually, Mo's in hospital at the moment" Katie replied coolly "I'm looking after things for a while, I'm her granddaughter Katie Collins."

"Katie, that's why you seemed so familiar - you're Katie Crabstick!"

Katie stopped her hand in mid air

"Katie Crabstick! How do you know I'm ... I mean, where did you hear that?" Katie looked at him suspiciously. Grinning from ear to ear Ben replied,

"If you remember I was in your class for two years at Laxley Heath Junior & Infants. In fact I used to sit right behind you in Mrs Beattie's class. I used to get the rough end of your tongue on many occasions."

Katie looked at the six foot tall, wavy haired, reasonably good-looking man with a lopsided and currently very annoying grin and tried to picture it against any of the boys in her class for the two years she had spent at Laxley Heath aged nine and ten. She had been sent there when she has stayed with Mo when her parents had gone to work abroad on a contract. She vaguely remembered an annoying boy who used to sit behind her and kick the back of her chair a lot.

"Oh God, yes Benny Wilson, it's no wonder I didn't recognise you - you spent more time standing outside the classroom didn't you?"

"Yes, but I prefer Ben now, Benny makes me sound a bit stupid." Katie simply raised a questioning eyebrow.

"Ok" he conceded "I asked for that. Look I can fix the door, it seems to have warped quite badly but I know a place I can get a replacement, one that will fit in with the character of the house. I might be able to get a reclaimed one to blend in, not look too new. I'll give you a ring once I've found it and arrange a time to come and fix it - OK?"

"Fine - I'll write the number down for you." Katie disappeared to find a pen and paper and Ben pondered the small world that had seen him bump into Katie Collins twice in one day after not seeing her for twenty years, not that he'd tell anyone but he used to have a bit of a crush on her. Still not anymore, it seemed she hadn't calmed down over the years and if her taste in cars were anything to go by she was probably a bit rich for him.

Katie watched Ben leave after she had passed over her number. He didn't seem to have achieved much over the years, working for a building company and riding a bike - didn't he have any ambition? Still he seemed competent enough and even pleasant once he'd stopped ranting, despite a habit of laughing at you a little too much.

Katie returned back into Mo's flat and decided she may as well issue the invitations for the following Thursday's get-together. Venturing up the two flights of stairs to the second floor flat reminded her of the times when she was small and had sneaked upstairs to the top of the house to play at being the princess captured by an evil king waiting for Prince Charming to come and rescue her. Katie wasn't supposed to come upstairs on her own then. That was when her Grandparents were the housekeeper and handyman for Miss Talbot-Clyde, the owner, and they had lived in the flat at the back of the house, now occupied by Mary and Ken Clackett. Miss Talbot-Clyde had passed away when Katie was eight, and much to everyone's surprise, Mo and Alfred especially, she had left Tolpuddle House to them. She had no relatives and had valued their friendship and loyalty over the years more than anyone had realised. Alfred had converted the house into flats and bed-sits over the years following their inheritance so that they were able to make an income out of it. They had briefly thought about selling it but they were every bit as attached to it as Miss Talbot-Clyde and couldn't bear the thought of leaving it. Miss Talbot-Clyde probably knew this when she left it to them. So Katie felt a slight knot in the bottom of her stomach as if she were doing something naughty as she headed up the second flight of stairs.

The flat at the top was the two bed-roomed one, although the second bedroom was little more than a box room. The flat itself had "a lot of character," as Mo said, or as Katie said "a heap of slanted ceilings and wonky walls". Its current inhabitants were Bradley and Tamsin Dixon, who according to Mo's notes were newly married and friends of the earth. Katie knocked on the door but received no reply so she eventually stuck a note under the door

Tolpuddle House Get-Together

Next Thursday 16th at 7pm

Just Bring Yourselves

Katie C

Turning round in the small landing Katie noticed that the garish carpet that had disappeared from the lower floors was still laid in all its glory up here, and as there was no sunlight reaching this part of the stairwell it was still vivid in the reds, browns and oranges of the original colours. Maybe this was all part of the character Mo had been talking about! Carefully making her way back down to the first floor Katie surveyed the landing. This was a much more restful area with a light beige carpet and magnolia walls, nothing very striking but nothing to make you feel dizzy either.

There were three bed-sits, or studio flats as the estate agent called them, off this landing. Katie knocked on flat 1A first, this was Poppy's flat and she could hear the muffled beat of music coming from within letting her know that Poppy must be at home. Sure enough she could soon hear someone moving things about inside and swearing at regular intervals until the door eventually opened.

As soon as Poppy saw Katie she grinned, "Quick come in - I thought it was Hermy come to invite me to some worthy event again or to offer me a selection of lace covers for my furniture." Katie squeezed into the flat and attempted to find a place to stand. This was by no means easy as almost every available piece of floor was covered in drawings, material, discarded clothes or boxes containing all of the above.

"Sorry about the mess but I don't work very well in a neat and tidy place. I've got a couple of projects to finish and I needed some inspiration" Poppy said by way of an explanation.

"It's fine" Katie replied "look I won't keep you long but I just wanted to let you know I'm having a house get-together next Thursday at 7pm, so I just wanted to make sure you could come."

"Oh excellent" Poppy rubbed her hands together with glee "I'm fine for next Thursday. Are you doing the cheese scones and the coffee cake?"

"Um well I hadn't quite decided what the menu was yet" Katie hesitated and saw Poppy's face fall, she really was as transparent as a five year old, with all her enthusiasm and innocence, and every bit as

49

persuasive. "But of course" Katie continued "if that's what you'd like, I'm sure I can knock something together." Katie was rewarded with that beaming smile again, transforming Poppy's features.

"Oh great, I can't wait. Are you off to see Hermy and Guy next?" Poppy asked.

"Yes, I haven't had a chance to meet them yet so I thought I should introduce myself."

"Well, Hermy's in 1B and Guy's in 1C. I didn't mean to be rude about Hermy before, she means well and she's kind hearted it's just sometimes she's a bit much. I don't really know Guy - computer geek, never really speaks; no trouble though." Poppy shut the door behind Katie, who smiling ruefully thought that most of the trouble probably came from Poppy, unintentionally of course, but she reminded Katie of a puppy bounding about with no idea of the destruction it was leaving behind in its wake but you couldn't help but love it anyway.

Looking around the landing Katie decided to try Hermione's flat first and rapped a couple of times on the door. A few seconds later the door was opened by a slightly nervous looking lady, who looked about fifty but was probably slightly younger, she had clearly taken to dressing from Mary Allen's Ladies Fashions and it added years to her appearance. She was wearing a tweed skirt, lace blouse with a bow, sensible shoes all below a very severe bun into which her hair was scraped with absolutely no chance of escape. As she opened the door wider Katie was struck by the complete contrast of Hermione's flat to Poppy's. Despite its tiny proportions the place was absolutely spotless with nothing left lying around or out of place. There wasn't a great deal of furniture in the room, a sofa, a chair, sideboard, TV and coffee table but it was all set at right angles to each other, polished and covered in cloths and antimacassars to protect it. Taking in the curtains and cushions it seemed that Hermione, like Mo, was no stranger to chintz. All her belongings seemed a little old and worn, but were clearly all lovingly cared for. The smell of polish hung in the air and there was not a speck of dust to be seen.

After introductions were exchanged and Hermione enquired after Mo's health, Katie issued the invitation to the 'get-together' and Hermione replied,

"I'd be delighted to attend. How kind of you to think of it. Of course I have a committee meeting at five, but I'll be back by seven. Thursday will be lovely."

Hermione rattled on in this vain for a bit longer and Katie listened with a polite smile. It was clear that Hermione was a kind person involved in many committees and good works, but for all that she seemed a bit lonely and a little shy which made her appear nervous and to talk rather more than required. Hermione invited Katie to numerous meetings and charity events but she managed not to commit herself to any of them without appearing rude and after twenty minutes managed to make an exit back to the calm surroundings of the landing. "Just one more to go" Katie thought, Guy Masters, computer geek, not very enticing for someone whose IT interest started and finished with surfing the net for gossip or bargain designer gear. Katie used computers all day long at work, had a Blackberry and an iPad. She loved what they could do for her to make life and work easier but she was not remotely interested in talking RAM, megabytes, pixels or networks. In the past she'd simply ask the IT department or the pale skinned assistant at the computer superstore. Still she'd promised Mo she'd invite everyone, so she would! Knocking purposefully on the door she waited as she heard an irritated sigh behind the door and then the latch turn.

"Yes" came the less than promising start from Guy as he opened the door. Katie paused, open mouthed for a minute; the man in front of her was not the stereotypical computer expert she had expected. He was over 6ft, but well built, dark hair, no glasses and fairly good looking too. In fact apart from the obligatory pale skin of the computer enthusiast, gained by too many days and nights spent in front of a flickering screen, instead of in the fresh air, he seemed a pretty regular guy, did Guy. Katie smiled at her own joke and then smiled again more purposefully at Guy.

"Hello, I'm Katie Collins, Mo's granddaughter. I'm having a bit of a house get-together next Thursday night. I just wanted to ask if you'd like to come."

"Er, I don't know, I'm not really into social gatherings" he replied noncommittally. Katie viewed this as a challenge. She wasn't going to let this man refuse, no, she would turn on the charm and soon have him eating out of her hand.

"Oh but Guy, may I call you Guy, it will only be a few of us from the house and it wouldn't be the same if you weren't there."

Guy looked slightly bewildered as she continued; "it'll just be a bit of fun for us all to get to know one another a bit better." With this Katie flashed her killer smile, to leave Guy with the feeling that it was, in fact, only him who she wanted to know better.

"Well of course, I don't want to be rude" he answered curtly and in complete contrast to his words, "I'll pop in as long as I don't get a call out or anything" with that he shut the door almost in Katie's face. Feeling a little foolish Katie took a step back, although he was no Adonis, Katie liked to think she could make an impression on a man when she wanted to and Guy's apparent imperviousness to her winning smile and slightly flirtatious manner was, in all honesty, a bit deflating. It seemed Katie was turning into a dab hand at repelling men at the moment. It didn't bode well for the future!

CHAPTER 5

The following Thursday afternoon Katie was busy in the kitchen preparing the food for the house gathering that evening. She was well organised and already a large part of the menu, approved by Mo at her hospital visit on Saturday afternoon, was ready or in the range cooking. They had finally settled on a simple finger buffet that everyone could eat without the need for sitting down or knives and forks. That way everyone could mingle around the table and through the rest of the room without being in danger of landing a forkful of food onto someone else. At many of the corporate events Katie had organized at Dawson, Phillips & Chamberlain there had often been near fisticuffs over an unexpected forkful of tomato pasta or two, landing unceremoniously on someone's Giorgio Armani!

Katie had prepared crudités of carrot, cucumber, celery and apple served with homemade dips of cheese & chive and yoghurt & cucumber, cheese straws (and scones for Poppy), brioche stuffed with cream cheese and smoked ham, freshly baked bread sliced and buttered with a variety of toppings of pate, cheese and cooked meats, but nothing too 'slippy' to land unexpectedly in someone else's lap. Katie had also made mini quiches and sausage rolls for the meat eaters, cheese & onion for the veggies. In addition she had made the promised coffee cake and added a tray of oatmeal honey flapjack. She had just put the white wine and orange juice in the fridge to chill and the red wine was on the side to acclimatise when the front door bell echoed through the house. Cursing under her breath as she really didn't want a distraction now, she grabbed a towel and rubbed her hands quickly on it, ran them through her hair to straighten it out, make it more presentable. Opening the door she found Ben Wilson on the other side crouched down inspecting the lower part of the door frame.

"Er hi, was I expecting you?" Katie asked

"Well sort of - I said I'd let you know when I found a door suitable for Tolpuddle House, which I have, and I have a couple of hours to spare so I can put it on now if that's ok?" Ben responded with what Katie presumed he thought was his 'winning' smile.

"Well I don't know, I mean I do want the door sorting out but a bit of notice would've been appreciated." Katie paused, feeling a bit ungracious, after all, the guy was doing her a favour "but sure it'll be great to get it fixed." Grinning even more broadly Ben stepped inside producing a toolbox that had been hidden round the corner

"Good, I was hoping you'd say that. I'll just get on and you can get back to your cooking." Katie's indignation rose up straight away

"Cooking, what makes you think I'm cooking, you chauvinist, just because I'm a woman at home during the day I must be cooking or cleaning or watching talk shows on TV I suppose" she snapped.

"Well yes all that of course, - and your hair" Ben replied gesturing to the top of Katie's head. Swinging round quickly to look in mirror, too late Katie realised that in running her fingers through her hair she had deposited a few streaks of flour and also had a fair sprinkling across her nose and cheeks. Quickly rubbing them away she spoke with what she hoped was dignity and disdain

"Absolutely, I'll leave you to get on. Just give me a shout if you need anything. The kitchen's just through here." She pointed through the open door on the left hand side of the hall.

"Yes, I know my way about; I've done quite a bit of work for Mo in the past." Ben informed her as he started to remove tools from his box. He looked up just as she was about to disappear he added "it wasn't just your hair you know, the smell of freshly baked bread is everywhere - it's making me quite hungry." he winked and rubbed his stomach as he spoke. Katie turned towards the kitchen but couldn't help a smile crossing her face. Ben Wilson was just as annoying, cheeky and funny as he had been twenty years ago. Never mind, she thought, I'll get my own back when he least expects it and then Katie realised she too was a lot more like herself twenty years ago - really, he definitely brought out the worst in her.

For the next hour Katie polished glasses, set the big kitchen table and finished up the food preparation for the evening, to the accompaniment of various bangs, crashes and sawing noises from the hallway and also the occasional burst of song when things were going well and a few mutterings when things clearly weren't. As she'd done everything she needed to in preparation for the house guests, she decided to put the kettle on and made Ben and herself a mug of tea. Shouting through the doorway she asked if he took sugar, just one came back the reply and just as she was about to ask if he wanted the tea bringing through Ben stuck his head round the corner.

"Is it alright if I come in? I'm not going to get in the way of anything am I?" he asked cautiously.

"No, no" Katie replied "I've finished my 'cooking' now; it's quite safe to enter."

"Wow, you've got quite an appetite then." Ben surveyed the table stacked with food. Katie pulled a face at him.

"Actually, if you must know we are having a house get-together tonight."

"A house what?" Ben queried

"Get-together - just an informal party, keep everyone on good terms and, according to Mo to make sure they're all eating properly."

Ben laughed "That sounds like Mo - always forcing food on people. Ow!" Katie slapped his hand as he tried to pinch a cheese and onion roll.

"Well, I'm not Mo, so you can leave that alone. Here have a biscuit if you're hungry" Ben took the offered packet and ate a couple of biscuits out of it.

"It does look very nice though," he said through a mouthful of crumbs "I'm sure you wouldn't miss one." he raised pleading eyes to Katie, who remained completely immune.

"Yes actually I would, but look everyone will be here in the next hour. If you want to stay you're welcome, you can keep the conversation flowing. I recall you were quite good at talking rubbish for indefinite periods." Katie teased.

"Well, after such a gracious invitation how could I refuse?" Ben answered, with mock affront, "But I would like it to be known I'm staying to sample the food on offer and in no way to help you out of any awkward social situation. OK?" Ben popped another biscuit in his mouth and smiled at Katie.

"Yeah, yeah, whatever, go and finish the door otherwise you'll be acting as security guard out there." Katie shooed him towards the door ignoring the cheese and onion roll he sneaked off the plate as he left.

Half an hour later Ben had completed the door replacement and after several test openings and closings by Katie it had passed its examination.

"Although I will miss my daily fall into the hall," Katie mused sarcastically, "Thanks Ben, how much do I owe you?"

"Don't worry about that now" Ben replied "I'll get the office to drop you a bill round next week. Can I use your bathroom to clean up a bit before everyone else arrives? I don't want to show you up."

Katie showed Ben to the bathroom and fetched him a clean towel from the airing cupboard. Then she returned to the kitchen and poured herself a large glass of white wine. She was actually pleased to have a friendly face on hand for tonight, and despite his habit of winding her up, Ben felt like an old friend. He was easy to be around and Katie was a bit nervous about the evening, although she had met them all apart from the Dixons, she was nervous of making a poor impression. Katie hadn't had much need to be around friends socially over the last couple of years. She had always been with Marcus or at a works do where she was playing the part of perfect PA. She'd never really had to be herself and she wasn't quite sure who she really was at the moment. Taking a large slurp of wine Katie checked the table once more and fiddled with glasses, putting them in strictly parallel lines. Ben returned to the kitchen just as she was checking the table again.

"Don't worry, it all looks fine" Ben said seriously, picking up on Katie's tension "Now is there a cold bottle of beer in the fridge."

Katie passed him a bottle and an opener and flashed him a grateful smile, "I don't know why I'm nervous," she laughed "it's not like I'm entertaining the Queen."

Just then there was a ring at the doorbell, Katie jumped up and looked at her watch, quarter to seven,

"Oh God, it's probably Jehovah's Witnesses or something - just what I need." Katie left the flat to open the now freely opening front door. As she pulled it open, dreading it being someone she couldn't get rid of, and at the same time, strangely hoping it might be too. She heard the familiar tones as Cliona announced her arrival.

"Hi Katie love, Dec and I came a bit early. I thought you might need a hand or a bit of moral support at the very least, it's quite strange having your house full of strangers." Katie relaxed immediately. Cliona was such a perceptive friend yet she never seemed intrusive. Katie began to wonder how she had done without such a friend before; perhaps things would have worked out differently if she'd had some wise and caring counsel. Katie made a resolution immediately that as soon as she was back in London she would put plenty of effort into finding at least one friend she could rely on half as much as she could on Cliona even in this short space of time.

Katie waved Cliona and Declan into the flat. Declan, Cliona's partner was a big bear of a man, over six foot four and nearly as wide Katie thought, but he was as gentle as he was big and although he was a man of few words, being with Cliona meant he didn't get many opportunities to talk anyway. When he did speak it was usually to the point and well observed, served up in a deep and husky voice that had retained a faint Irish burr despite leaving Ireland when he was only eight.

On reaching the kitchen Katie started the introductions,

"Um Ben, this is my friend Cliona and her partner ..."

"Dec" Ben interrupted shaking Declan's hand warmly and giving Cliona a peck on the cheek. Katie looked at Ben for an explanation and Ben obliged

"I've known Dec a good few years now; we did a renovation job on his restaurant about four years ago."

"That he did, but even so we managed to stay friends" Declan teased and Ben grinned clearly pleased to have a real friend to talk to.

"So I know how we know Ben" Cliona remarked "but how do you know Ben" she asked Katie.

"Well actually it turns out we used to go to school together but I called his firm to come and fix the uncooperative front door and in an extraordinary display of bad timing he turned up this afternoon." Katie swept her hair back as she spoke to give the impression she had been put out.

"You forgot to mention knocking me off my bike and driving off without a backward glance" Ben remonstrated and, as Katie tried to but in, added "and waved to me as I headed into the hedge" Cliona and Declan were laughing out loud now and Katie could feel the colour rising from the tips of her toes to the top of her forehead as she recalled her less than gracious behaviour.

"Katie, you never told me about that" Cliona chided her friend "tell me now exactly what happened, as I know Ben has a tendency to exaggerate on occasions."

Just as Katie was thinking how she could get out of this gaping hole Ben had dropped her in there was a loud rat-tatting on the door and shortly after Poppy came bowling through the kitchen looking as excited as a five year old going to their first party. Without waiting for any introductions she headed straight for the table rubbing her hands with glee and stuffing a whole cheese scone in her mouth at once. It was only then she turned round to see there were people other than Katie in the room.

"Oops sorry" she exclaimed through a mouthful of crumbs "I didn't see any of you here, but to be fair my attention was focused elsewhere." Poppy admitted with complete honesty "but I know for sure" she continued "that none of you live here so why are you here?" Poppy's bluntness although sometimes a bit of a surprise could never be offensive as it was always delivered with such childish naivety everyone just knew she wasn't been rude. Somehow she had never lost that childlike way of asking whatever was in her head the minute she thought of it.

Katie made the necessary introductions and left them all chatting as simultaneous knocks at the front and back doors left Katie trying to go in two directions at once. Seeing her dilemma, Ben jumped up to see to the back door which could only be the Clacketts, leaving Katie to go and meet the only house guests she hadn't met so far.

On opening the hall door Katie was met by two beaming faces who introduced each other, rather like news-readers on a breakfast TV show and they were every bit as polished too!

"Hi, this is Bradley" beamed the girl clearly extremely proud of Bradley and certain that everyone else would be

"And this is Tamsin" Bradley returned indulgently "and you must be Katie, it's so nice to finally meet, we've heard so much about you, haven't we Tams?" Bradley looked to Tamsin to take up the narrative which she was clearly used to doing.

"Oh absolutely, all good, mind. Mo loved telling us all about you and Poppy's taken over that duty since Mo's been in hospital. She thinks you're 'pretty cool' which believe me is a ringing endorsement."

"Well, that's lovely" Katie replied, a little overwhelmed by the double assault, "Do come in, it's lovely to meet you both."

"Oh thanks" they replied in unison, and stepped through the door presenting her with a bottle of wine for everyone and another present 'only for you' as Tamsin put it. It was a handmade carving in the shape of a love knot and polished so it was smooth and a pleasure to touch. "It was made by an ancient tribe in Africa, it brings good fortune to those who touch it - is that right Brad?" Tamsin referred to her husband

"Well, yes - actually it's a blessing it gives, but that's supposed to bring good fortune I suppose."

"It's absolutely beautiful and extremely kind of you" Katie answered, she was quite touched by the gesture from this bouncy couple who she had only just met. As she followed them back into the now fairly crowded kitchen she took her opportunity to have a proper look at the Dixons. She had formed an idea in her head from Mo's notes about vegetarians and good causes that they would be very earnest people in hand knitted sweaters and beards (well Bradley anyway!) but they were

67

very smartly dressed, Next more than Armani and clean shaven (Bradley again) and although they were obviously committed to their causes almost as much as to each other they didn't appear to be at all preachy. Although Tamsin did tell her later 'just tell me to shut up when I start banging on about something, I tend to get on my soapbox and don't get off until someone shoves me!'

It turned out that Cliona knew Tamsin quite well they had sat on some fair trade craft committees in recent years. Tamsin was an administration manager for a fair trade charity in Rawlinston and Bradley was a lawyer for a national children's charity's regional office. Katie was impressed and bemused at the same time that he had decided to earn a significantly smaller income working for a charity than he could have in business and before she could stop herself a question popped out,

"But Bradley surely if you worked in a law firm you could work for yourself and your charity and have more money to donate?" There was a small gap in the conversations around the kitchen. "I'm sorry" Katie realised she might have over stepped the mark, "I didn't mean to be rude, I was just wondering what motivates you."
Bradley didn't seem to have taken any offence, perhaps it was a

question he was used to being asked a lot. "It's easy really, I trained to be a lawyer so I could make a difference, and I tried working in a practice with the intention of doing work for charities who needed it on the side, but it was always a conflict and the paying customer won. It became so frustrating that when the opportunity arose to work full time for a charity I believed in, it was an easy decision to make. Plus, I knew it was right as the second day in the job I met Tamsin." he gave his wife a playful hug and the conversation fell back to more everyday topics.

Katie found it difficult to shake Bradley's reply out of her head. She had known so many lawyers and barristers in London, they would all happily cough up for tickets to charity balls that it was necessary to be seen at or bid for memorabilia in auction in aid of a good cause, but she couldn't think of one, not even Marcus, who would have given up their potential earnings to help one. Just as she was pondering this conundrum Poppy appeared back in the kitchen with Guy Chambers at her side.

"I just went up to get him - I knew he'd forget otherwise!" Poppy emphasised the word 'forget' as if to imply he had chosen to forget rather than actually forgotten. By the uncomfortable look on his face it was likely she was right.

"Well Guy, it's nice you could make it." Katie said in her best soothing hostess voice "let me get you a drink and something to eat."

Poppy rolled her eyes "I wouldn't worry about it Katie, he's like all techies, he exists on fresh air and plugs himself into the internet to keep going." Guy gave a stern look in Poppy's direction suggesting he wasn't amused and replied with gravity to Katie,
"Actually I'd like something to eat, it's just I get a bit carried away when I'm working, lose track of time." Guy followed Katie towards the table and started to help himself to a large plateful of food and then retreated to the farthest corner of the kitchen so that he didn't have to actually speak to anybody. Katie felt it was her duty as the host to help him overcome this obviously crippling social shyness.

"So Guy, what is it you're working on at the moment that keeps you so engrossed?"

"Well, I don't think you'd understand - not to be rude or anything." he replied being exactly that!

"Well, just give me the layman's version then. What will it do when it's finished?" Katie encouraged him.

"It's a way of storing data and systems differently so that it reduces the capacity needed and therefore reduces the amount of hard disk space required." Guy answered with little hope of being understood.

"Oh I see and what's the practical application for this?" Katie had slotted into her perfect PA role in no time and she tilted an enquiring and interested face to Guy, who it appeared, was no less susceptible to an interested audience than any other man Katie ever had met.
Guy launched into a speech full of jargon and probably made up words as he explained his brilliant idea. Katie held an interested look on her face as best she could whilst assessing what food and drinks needed replenishing until he had finished with a flourish and a couple more seven syllable words.

"So" she pondered "do you have anyone interested in this project?"

"Yes quite a few" Guy boasted "in fact, I've got meetings with a couple of big names in the next few weeks." Katie smiled warmly at Guy and reflected that actually he was quite a good-looking man in that pale and interesting way. He could be worth a bit of effort as he was obviously going places. Just goes to show, Katie thought, you really shouldn't judge people on first impressions. Just as she was reflecting on this Poppy shouted over

"What do you think Katie? Do you agree with this lot?" Poppy grabbed Katie's attention and she looked over to where Cliona, Declan and Ben were talking with Poppy.

"I'm sorry Poppy, what was that then?" Katie attempted to saunter over nonchalantly but ruined the impression by tripping over the table leg and spilling wine down herself.

Poppy explained she had been complaining about a guy at college, Miles, who was on her course and was always teasing her, shoving her, disagreeing with her opinion and generally been a pain in the backside. She thought he was out to sabotage her course as he obviously saw her as a threat. Cliona, Declan and Ben all agreed he fancied her.

"So" Poppy prompted "do you agree with them?"

"Oh absolutely Popps, it's a classic case I'm afraid." Katie laughed and winked at Cliona who took up her cue,

"It's like when you were at primary school Poppy, the boys had no idea what to do when they liked a girl, so just to get their attention they would trip them up or pull their pigtails. This Miles sounds just the same, he's just too scared to ask you out. I'm right aren't I Ben?"

Ben smiled ruefully "Unfortunately you are, my sex is an unimaginative lot and any attention is better than none."

Poppy seemed nonplussed by this new angle on her problem and retreated to the kitchen table to get another slice of coffee cake.

"I think she's reassessing her opinion of Miles at the moment" Katie whispered

"Hmmm," Ben replied "and are you reassessing your opinion of the IT geek. Does he have a fascinating line in small talk?" Declan looked up sharply at this, it was unlike his friend to be pointed and mean about someone, he was usually generous in his opinions until proven otherwise.

"Well, actually, if you must know, he's invented some technological advance that's going to change the face of the whole IT industry. He's meeting with some big names in London next week." Katie ad-libbed haughtily to Ben's barbed comment and was rewarded by seeing Ben's face fall.

"Oh right, well he must be a bright guy then." Ben replied a tad more graciously.

"Yes, Guy is a bright, erm, guy" Katie couldn't help laughing as she said it and Ben did too.

The get-together was in full swing and everyone chatted, drank and ate. At eight o'clock a breathless and very agitated Hermione appeared at the door.

"Oh my dear" Mary Clackett clucked, as she saw her on the threshold clutching her hands to her breast. "What on earth's the matter? Come and sit down. Ken, get Hermione a drink at once, no you silly man, not water, a glass of wine to calm her nerves." As Ken was dispatched and returned triumphant with a glass of Chardonnay, they all gathered round as Mary urged Hermione to tell them what the problem was.

"Well, it's probably a bit silly" Hermione started hesitantly with so many faces around her "but I just don't know what to do." As everyone still seemed interested Hermione decided to carry on "You see I'm the chair of the spring fair committee, as you know, Cliona" Cliona nodded as she was also on the committee representing the crafts people invited to attend "And" Hermione continued "we need to have our first full meeting in a fortnight and I've no idea where I'm going to find space for fifteen people."

"Well don't we usually use the function room at the back of the pub?" Cliona chipped in.

"Yes, yes" Hermione replied, nodding vigorously "and I'd booked it but Vera Latham, the landlady, has phoned to say they've found rot or worms or something in the beams and they've closed the room off. It might take three months before it's in use again. I've spent the last two hours trying to think of somewhere, but everywhere's too small or too far away." Hermione was almost wailing now.

"How about your flat?" Poppy interjected helpfully. Hermione shook her head

"I don't know where I'd put everyone. I did a plan and I could fit ten in at most, and then there's no room for plans or a flipchart - oh God I'm going to be a failure before I've even started." Hermione's big blue eyes welled with tears, this was clearly extremely important to her so that everyone in the flat wanted to help. They all pondered for a few minutes until Mary exclaimed,

"But of course, the answer's right in front of us all along. It'll be perfect." They all looked at her expectantly until Declan asked

"What'll be perfect Mary?"

"The old drawing room of course, across the hall, it's huge in there, it'll fit more than fifteen and as many flappy charts as you like."

Katie was somewhat taken aback at this turn of events and watched as the whole circle of people turned to look at her.

"Well, I don't know" she started tentatively, "I mean I don't mind, but the room hasn't been used for years. I've no idea what state it's in and it was always bloody freezing in there to be frank."

Ben jumped up from his stool "Well let's go take a look then."

Everyone, sensing an expedition, jumped up and followed Ben out of

Mo's flat and across the hall to the drawing room. As Ben opened the

door a blast of cold air hit them in the face and they all immediately

huddled together as they piled through the entrance and viewed the

potential meeting room.

"It's certainly big enough" Ben commented

"It's a little on the chilly side" Declan added a touch sarcastically.

"We could sort that out, a new radiator or two; check the pipe work -

maybe open up the fireplace." Ben added.

"It's a bit shabby though" Poppy said as she broke cover from the group

to view the wallpaper a bit more closely.

"A coat of paint" Ben answered, assuming the role of Project Manager.

"What about the sofa and chairs?" Declan asked "they've definitely

seen better days."

"Once we get some heat in here, the edge will go off them" Ben responded, refusing to find an insurmountable problem.

"Yes, and we could put a few throws on them, a cloth on the table if it doesn't polish up." Cliona added

"I could give you a few prints from college to stick on the walls if you wanted" Poppy said as they all began to get swept up in the idea. Katie looked at them all suddenly so excited by the project. She didn't want to pour cold water on it but reality had to be addressed

"Look everyone" she started quietly "it's a lovely idea but it sounds very expensive to do all that and I don't really." she tailed off not wanting to reveal she was stony broke.

"Honestly, it won't cost a lot" Ben answered "I'll call in a few favours for the plumbing and fireplace, could you stump up for the paint?"

"Well yes, I should think so" Katie was still feeling a bit railroaded.

"Great, that's settled then. Hermione, you now have a beautiful Victorian drawing room for the first meeting of the Spring Fayre committee." Ben grandly swept his arm across the room. As they all surveyed the rather lack lustre and freezing cold room they burst out laughing and quickly adjourned to Mo's kitchen with the heat from the range, and copious amounts of food and drink. They happily talked on about what they could do to help with the conversion of the drawing room. Bradley and Tamsin would bring some spare chairs and a flip chart from their office, Poppy would bring the prints and some scented candles. Cliona would organise throws and Declan said he would bring some old cups and saucers and plates so they could all have a cuppa at the same time. Hermione gasped

"Oh refreshments! I'd forgotten about them. I'll just have to do them upstairs and bring them down."

"Nonsense" Cliona answered robustly, "Katie can do them, she's obviously got the knack" as she spoke she pointed to the huge kitchen table as every scrap of food had been eaten.

"Oh would you? I'd be so grateful" As Hermione turned her big blue eyes towards her; Katie knew she was cornered, well and truly caught.

"Of course I will, I'd be delighted," she answered, whilst

simultaneously she slipped round the back of the chair giving Cliona a sly dink on the way.

The get-together began to peter out soon after, the Clacketts returning to their flat and the Dixons heading off to finish some work from the office. Poppy bounded out shortly after and Guy took his opportunity to leave then too. Katie walked him to the door and thanked him for coming. Ben watched and muttered to Declan,

"I don't know why she's being so nice to him; he's the only one who didn't offer to do anything - miserable sod."

"Well, to be fair, there wasn't much call for an IT expert" Declan offered.

"He could have offered to pick up a paint brush. What's Katie being all nice to him for?" Ben said, refusing to acknowledge Declan's point.

"He's a guest in her house - what do you want her to do? Shove him out and slam the door in his face." Declan laughed. Ben's face suggested that actually he might want her to do just that, but he settled for saying

"I just think she's going over the top, she irritates me when she's like that, she did when she was nine too. It makes me want to …."

"Pull her pigtails?" Declan cut in with as straight a face as he could manage. Ben put his drink down.

"I think I'll be going now Dec" he said as he left. Declan was still chuckling to himself ten minutes later when Cliona returned from the Clacketts and suggested they too made a move home.

CHAPTER 6

Ben arrived at work early the next day. It was one of those clear, dark, winter mornings. There was a heavy layer of white frost over everything, so thick it almost looked like snow. Ben opened up the office, flicked on the lights and the heaters straight away. He still got a frisson of excitement in his stomach when he entered his office, almost as strong as the first day he had opened it when he had properly started BW construction after four years being a self-employed builder. It had been a gamble almost six years ago, but now it was a successful small business with a good reputation and a plan to grow even more.

Ben loved Friday mornings, they always had a staff meeting to review the week's progress and discuss requirements for the following week. There were only four of them, as well as Ben, there was John, BW's site manager, Charlie, a carpenter and a friend of Ben's from building college and lastly Jean, the matronly lady who looked after all the office paperwork for the company and was an absolute godsend. She had come from another building firm that had gone bust so she knew all the rules and regulations of the game and was a stickler for seeing they were adhered to. This was why Ben had hired her; his business was to be strictly above board, no dodgy dealings on his patch, that and she frightened the life out of him so he wouldn't have dared not offer her the job. But, over the years he had found that actually, she was a softie at heart and loyal to a fault.

Ben put the coffee machine on and, as it started to hiss and gurgle, he got the mugs out of the cupboard. They took it in turns to bring breakfast in. Jean always brought freshly baked croissants and muffins, Ben picked up bacon butties from the 'Sarnie Shack' at the end of the road. John brought in French sticks or bloomers and they broke off slabs and slathered them with butter and jam, but today was Charlie's turn so it would be McDonalds McMuffins all round. Charlie thought you could never have too much fast food.

Ben had just finished pulling his notes together half an hour later when the door swung open to herald the arrival of another person.

"Bloody Hell, Ben, you didn't really cycle here did you? - its brass monkey weather out there." The lilting, teasing, Geordie tones belonged to John, BW's site manager for all the sites at present. Ben had hired John just over four years ago when he had taken on his first full conversion job of an old four bed-roomed house, when he also had the work at Declan's restaurant. He realised quickly it was too much for him to try and design and build and supervise the projects - and get it right! Besides managing other people was not Ben's strong point, he preferred to do things himself rather than order others to, a trait that would have cost him a lot of money had he not hired John. Ben was forever grateful that this deceptively benign, gentle Geordie had come through the door as the first applicant for the job. Although he had a quiet manner there was an edge of steel inside and the guys on the site who missed this soon found out when they tried to pull a fast one.

John rubbed his hands together and stood over the heater trying to defrost his nether regions.

"Of course I cycled," Ben replied "anyway you've worked outside all your life, a bit of frost shouldn't bother you."

"Are you kidding?" John laughed, "Days like this I always made sure I had a job inside - did you never notice?" John winked and walked over to the coffee machine just as the door swung open and Jean shuffled through it. At least they presumed it must be Jean underneath the layers of coats, scarves and the woolly hat pulled down nearly over her eyes.

"Morning Jean" they chorused and were rewarded with a grunt.

"I hate winter" she snapped when she had finally removed enough layers to be heard, but she still kept her hat, gloves and one scarf on, "I'm definitely retiring to Spain, sunshine, golden beaches, warmth, half naked Spanish men."

"Coffee Jean?" John said, not wanting to venture any further into Jean's fantasy.

"No, I'll have tea please" she broke off from her Spanish dream, "When can I retire Ben?"

"On the pension you get from here - about 2050 I should say."

"Fine, I'll only be about a hundred by then. Why the hell do I work for you?" she regarded Ben with an evil eye, but he could see the gleam behind it.

"Because you couldn't do without us Jean. You need at least half a dozen people to tell what to do or your day's been wasted - you'd die of boredom sitting by the pool all day."

"Mm, maybe, but I wouldn't mind giving it a go, especially on a day like this." She shuddered and finally dared to remove her hat causing her thick honey blond hair to stand on end, giving her the look of a slightly mad aunt. She sipped on the steaming tea and felt herself starting to thaw, just as the door opened again and let in an icy blast to blow right down her back.

"Shut that bloody door Charlie" she chastised.

Charlie bounded in with his hands full of MacDonald's bags. Ben thought he hadn't really changed in the thirteen years he had known him. He still entered every room like a small child at Christmas leaving chaos behind him, but no one could take offence with his disarming smile and clumsy but charming manner. Ben and Charlie had become friends as soon as they met on the first day of college and it was a friendship that had continued to this day. Charlie was a fine carpenter and worked on all Ben's jobs, but his real love was to make individually crafted pieces of furniture which he did in his spare time. Not that he had much of that Charlie had married his childhood sweetheart, Anna, five years before and they now had two boisterous 'under-fives' to keep them busy.

Charlie handed the MacDonald's' bags round, a separate one for each of them with their order in.

"Aah the glories of fast food" Charlie sighed as he bit into his muffin. "How civilised is it that I can now buy fast food twenty four hours a day."

"Well with yours and Anna's culinary skills I should say it's essential to your survival." Ben responded drily. He had suffered many aborted dinner parties at Charlie's when they had thrown the prospective dinner in the bin and phoned the local Indian takeaway instead.

"Now" Ben continued "shall we get started as I know John needs to get over to Cheadle House for ten." They all gathered round the table immediately clicking onto business mode. Jean reached for her pad in order to take notes and distributed the last meetings minutes.

"Right" said Ben "any action points from last week?" He scanned the notes. "No - OK let's move on to the current jobs review. Cheadle House, progress report John" John proceeded to give them an update on the work they were doing at the local retirement home. They had been contracted to build a huge extension onto the back of the converted house to give them a new dining room and activity area, in addition, they were extending at the side of the house for a new suite of offices so the current ones could be turned into more rooms. The project, John reported, was into its second month and so far was on schedule but there were problems with the architect who kept revising plans on the hoof.

"Who is the architect again?" Ben asked.

"Brian Galton" John answered.

"Brainless Brian, of course, what do the owners think?" Ben enquired

"Well, I think they're starting to lose confidence in him, ever since they realised he'd forgotten to put ramp access into the dining room. Fortunately we picked up on that so it's covered now but he's flapping around trying to regain favour. It's going to cause some problems later down the line, I know it." John had a nose for a potential problem long before it arrived. It was one of the reasons he was worth every penny BW paid him.

"What do we think?" Ben asked the table.

"You need to go see Bill Cheadle and work your charm." Jean was definite in her suggestion "plant the seed and drop Stewart's name into the pot." Stewart Jackson was another local architect with a better reputation than Brian Galton. BW Building had worked with him on a number of conversions and they had a good rapport going. John considered the idea,

"I think it's worth a shot anyway - like I said they think well of us at the minute so they might be guided."
"OK" said Ben, never one to linger too long making a decision, "I'll come up this morning and start the ball rolling."

Charlie then gave them an update on Burnside, a conversion of dilapidated cottages by the riverside coming into Laxley Heath. The conversion was nearly complete Charlie was overseeing the fitting of the new kitchens and final decorations.

"So" he concluded "the estate agent will be round on Friday to get them up for sale properly, although there are a couple of interested parties already, so they should go quickly. They definitely won't be another Hawthorns." They all groaned. Hawthorns had been their second development project and a salutary lesson to them all. It was a renovation of two rail side terraced houses but they had gone way over budget on the refurbishment and then taken over a year to sell either of them. They had cost the business a lot of money and Ben had nearly made the decision to give up after it, but they had got through it by taking on a lot of maintenance work and small jobs until they secured a bigger contract and sold Hawthorns, but they remained a cautionary tale.

They finished their discussions about all the existing jobs on BW's books and turned their attention to future prospects. It was a little less rosy here at present.

"So" Ben started slowly as no one really wanted to start the discussion, "apart from the renovations at Rippley due to start in six weeks and the extension build at the Stewarts in Copham, have we anything else secured?" There were shaking of heads and Jean pursed her lips, she'd seen a thin order book in her last job and that had not ended well. Ben needed to inject some optimism and motivation into the team as he could see the concern etched in the expressions on their faces.

"Right, let's get cracking then. What prospects do we currently have?" "Rawlinston Main Street, there is the opportunity for the retail and residential units in the old terraces at the far end." John returned "the local council is funding the job, so planning shouldn't be a problem and the conversion is right up our street."

"Excellent" Ben responded "so when are tenders due in?"

"February 2nd"

"Right, John, you and I will complete that this week and get it off. What other projects are we aware of?"

"I've not heard of any others at the moment." John shook his head.

"Me neither" Charlie added

"It's a bit of a lean time for development at the moment." John continued "local authorities are holding back for new budgets and other developers are taking their building work in house to keep hold of as much profit as possible." Ben pondered this for a while and then snapped his fingers and jumped to his feet, almost knocking the table over as he did so.

"Watch out mate" Charlie cried, as he rescued his mug of coffee as it hurtled to the edge of the table, "are you having a 'eureka' moment?"

"Actually, yes I am" Ben grinned "let's stop finding someone else who's developing and pitching for the job - let's find a site and do it ourselves, or find some land and build on it ourselves." They all looked at one another, a few seconds later Charlie and John grinned.

"We could do it; we know enough people and we've got the knowledge between us." Charlie was excited about the prospect.

"Yes but its riskier remember" John sounded a note of caution "everything rests on BW, if it goes wrong we get nothing."

"But it won't go wrong" Ben responded in earnest "we won't let it and yes it is riskier but that's how we get the rewards. In the long run it's better for everyone."

John, Charlie and Ben carried on the discussion, talking about possible sites, contacts they could use, if a new build or renovation was a better option, only Jean remained quiet. Eventually the conversation trailed off as they realised Jean hadn't spoken since Ben had first voiced his idea.

"Come on Jean, I can tell you're worried about it. Tell us what's bothering you." Ben asked.

"It's the money" she replied simply "where does it come from? How do we find enough to keep going? This is completely different cash flow for the business, it could take you down and I don't want to see that, not again." Jean was genuinely concerned "I'm not trying to scaremonger but you've got to consider how you'll fund it."

"OK, fair point Jean" Ben frowned as he thought "I don't want to get this wrong but we've got a fair amount in the business reserve, we'll have all the payments from Burnside shortly."

"Yes" agreed Jean "but it'll still be tight. Cash, or lack of it, takes a business down."

"I could put something in" John offered quietly from the corner, Ben turned to look at him. "I've got some policies maturing I'd love to put them into BW if you want other partners - no pressure."

"Me too" Charlie added "you know I've got that money dad left me, I think he'd like me to do something ambitious with it." Ben stared ahead of him, he was deeply touched by John and Charlie's desire to be a part of the business he'd created, it took no time at all to know he'd accept their offer, whether he needed the money or not. They were like the three musketeers Ben would trust them with his life, let alone his business.

"OK" he said aloud "let's do it - but we do it right. Jean, make an appointment with John Richmond at the solicitors and we'll get the paperwork sorted out." Charlie and John looked at each other and then at Ben, they all raised their mugs and cracked them together with glee.

"One for all and all for one" they chorused.

"God help me" Jean mumbled "now I've got three bosses!"

Ben left the office about an hour later; they had talked more about how it would work but agreed that all their roles stay should pretty much the same. Charlie and John would each buy 20% of the business leaving Ben as the majority shareholder still. Lastly they had drawn up a list of potential projects and contacts and divided it amongst them. They would work through the list and report back in a week. Ben felt exhilarated; he had not felt this good since he had decided to run his own business. They were taking a step up, it was a risk but he couldn't stand still. Planning, designing and building his own projects had always been Ben's ultimate dream; he was now many steps closer.

CHAPTER 7

Ben spent the rest of the day visiting Cheadle House and speaking with the owners, allaying their fears and getting them to agree, he hoped, to a change of architect. Then he phoned Stewart, the new architect and filled him in on the details. It was only 3.30pm but Ben decided to call it a day and returned back to his flat on the west side of Rawlinston in a busy, up and coming area that had been revived due to a lot of warehouse loft conversions and a number of lively bars and cafes that had sprung up around them. Ben's flat, on the corner of West Lyme Street and Lofthouse Road, was a first floor apartment; he passed through the shared entrance lobby at the front and ran up the steps two at a time. He hadn't felt this energised in ages, he couldn't wait to get in the flat and start working on the finances for the business and trawl the internet for other leads to possible projects. As soon as he opened the flat door the deafening music hit him full square in the ears, the latest R & B rhythms that Ben found incredibly repetitive. There was only one person who played this music, this loud, on his sound system.

"Lucy, Lucy" he yelled, heading into the living room, "turn that bloody thing down."

A blond haired, extremely pretty teenage girl jumped off the beige

leather couch and turned the sound down one notch, making virtually

no difference to the decibel level.

"Luce, NOW" Ben bellowed. She smiled a rebellious smile but turned

the music down to a dull thud in the background.

"Better?" She asked cheekily

"Much" Ben replied "So, Luce, what are you doing here? You're not

supposed to visiting for another couple of weeks - have you had a row

with Mum again?"

"No" Lucy replied with exaggerated affront, "Mum brought me over

here actually."

"She brought you here - I'm not you're babysitter I could have plans

tonight. I can't just drop everything cos she's got a new fella to go out

with." Ben paused "Has she got a new bloke?"

"No, she's still with 'Clever Trevor' actually - and she's not on a night out. I'm nearly fifteen you know. I can manage an evening on my own without any trouble" Lucy said belligerently.

"Actually, that's highly unlikely as you can scarcely manage five minutes without getting into trouble, but I'm not getting into that now. So why has Mum brought you all this way for the evening?" Ben waited expectantly but Lucy seemed reluctant to answer this direct question and merely let her gaze rest in the far corner of the room by the door Ben had just entered. Ben, with an impending sense of doom, followed Lucy's gaze to the rucksack and suitcase placed just so they wouldn't be seen when you first came through the door. Ben swung round instantly

"No, no way, absolutely not - get the bags I'm taking you back now."

"Too late, big brother, she's on the plane by now." Lucy took great relish delivering this news to her brother.

"She's on the what?" Ben boomed in disbelief "and where does she think she's going?"

"You know Mum; she said she needed a break, so she booked a week for her and Trev in Spain. She thought you'd be more than happy to look after your little sister while she recuperated."

"Recuperated from what?" Ben asked, momentarily distracted.

"Oh from the stresses of everyday life, you know Mum, it doesn't take much to set her nerves off." Ben knew this was true, ever since he had been a small child he had been conscious of his mother's nerves which always made an appearance when she either didn't want to do something or wanted an excuse to leave all her responsibilities behind for a while on some jaunt or other. When Ben was small he had spent many weeks at his grandparents, his father having left when he was still a baby. His mother had never really got over this slight and despite many other lovers, including Lucy's father and 'Clever Trevor' an estate agent from York; she had remained a martyr to her nerves. A role she played to perfection. Ben realised Lucy was looking at him expectantly waiting for him to provide an answer to her situation. Her big blue expressive eyes looked defiantly at him, but not quite masking the vulnerability behind them. Ben had, in fact, been the most stable factor in her life, and despite her propensity to get into many and varied scrapes he loved her to bits, even though she drove him mad, frequently!

"OK titch," he said, using his nickname for her, designed to annoy her, but it was also affectionate "looks like you're here for a week or so, so let's go through the ground rules."

"Oh God, not again" groaned Lucy, sliding back onto the sofa.

"Yes again," Ben replied sternly "so this time there can be no confusion."

Ben passed a relatively quiet weekend considering the addition of his unexpected guest, and apart from a small pan fire in the kitchen and a humungous row about going to a club on Saturday night, which he won by simply standing in front of the door for an hour until Lucy gave up and retreated to her room to play a variety of extremely loud dance music until she got bored of it and put on a 'Friends' DVD instead. This was all par for the course with Lucy, and Ben had many years' experience to call on. Lucy was, in fact, a good kid at heart but she had always had to compete for attention from her mother who was usually working or developing a new relationship, and from a father who had shown absolutely no interest in her from the moment she was conceived. Ben was probably the most stable and normal thing in her life, it was no wonder she kicked against the traces now and again, but deep down he thought she appreciated the rules and discipline he insisted on, it showed he was genuinely concerned for her welfare.

On Monday Ben spent the day catching up on the work he hadn't been able to do over the weekend. He worked on the figures for the investment in the company and the potential outlay for the types of projects he was interested in. It was a very tight equation but Ben felt the time had come to spread BW's wings. Just as he was completing his report for Cheadle House the phone rang, not recognising the tone at first he realised Lucy must have changed his ringtone to the 'Crazy Frog' when he wasn't looking, cursing her quietly again he picked it up.

"Hello, Ben Wilson" he answered in a businesslike manner.

"Hi Ben" Jean's motherly tones answered "how's the parenting going?"

"Don't ask Jean, she's the sister from hell. I can't see the 666 but I know it's there somewhere."

"Ah, don't say that, she's a good kid really - just high spirited." Jean remonstrated with him.

"Oh really" Ben grimaced "well shall I bring her round to stay with you for a few days" he challenged.

"Hmmm, I'm sure she wants to be with you" Jean side-stepped neatly, "Now look, about work," she continued matter of factly "I've arranged for Billy Naylor to pop round to that house and look at the plumbing at 4.30 this afternoon, I know its short notice but he said can you meet him there?" Ben struggled to recall which house until he remembered his promise to Katie about Tolpuddle House and the artic front room.

"Oh yes that's fine - have you let Katie know we're coming?"

"Yes, I just spoke to her and its fine with her. Also Stewart Jackson rang and said can you ring as he might have something for you."

"Sure Jean, thanks, anything else?" Ben enquired.

"No nothing that won't keep until the morning - you are in tomorrow?"

"Yeah, I'll see you then." Ben put the phone down. He quickly dialled Stewart's number. Stewart was a great architect with good contacts he might have an interesting lead.

"Hi Stew, it's Ben Wilson"

"Ben, thanks for getting back to me. I think I might have a lead on some developments you could control yourself."

"Yeah, the other works dried up a bit at the moment, and I'm finding it a real drag having to compromise. We all thought the best way was to do it ourselves."

"Well, look I might have an interesting opportunity for you. I'm just heading out to meet a client now, how are you fixed to meet up around seven?" Stewart asked.

"I'm fine, I've got an appointment at 4.30 in Laxley Heath, but I'm fine after that."

"Laxley Heath, excellent, how about the Rose & Crown in Laxley? You can get me that pint you owe me."

"Sure that's fine - see you later." Ben put the phone down feeling more optimistic by the minute. Stewart was a good honest guy, if he thought a deal was a good one then it really could be.

The door banged shut with a thuddering crash. Lucy was home! Ben shuddered there was no way he was leaving her to run riot on a school night.

"Get changed Luce; we're heading out in half an hour." He shouted into the hall way.

"Going out - cool" Lucy stuck her head round the door, her blond ponytail bobbing in anticipation, "where are we going?"

"I've got a meeting in Laxley Heath and you're coming with me" Ben answered.

"Laxley Heath and a poxy building meeting. That's hardly going out." Lucy sulked, "I'm not coming there!" She turned to leave in a huff.

"Oh yes you are Lucy Chapman" Ben's tones brooked no argument "one fire this week is enough for me. I'm not leaving you alone in the flat for at least another seven days!" He tugged her hair as he walked past, softening his tone with a half-smile. Lucy grimaced, she knew Ben's

tones and it wasn't worth arguing with him in that mood. She'd save

the fight for when she really wanted something.

CHAPTER 8

Half an hour later Ben and Lucy were sat in his van heading through the early rush hour traffic towards Laxley Heath. Lucy still had a face like a wet weekend. She had planned an evening of manicures, pedicures and loud music; this unexpected turn of events was not good at all.

"Cheer up Luce," Ben teased as they pulled up at Tolpuddle House "it's not the end of the world."

"No, but it's definitely in sight" she groaned, peering out of the window at the wilderness garden in front of the house, "How long will you be?"

"Not long - I've just got to see Billy and agree the work then we'll go get something to eat."

"Ok brother I'll wait here till you ..."

"Oh no" Ben interrupted "out of the car - you're no safer in there than in my kitchen." Lucy stared at him aggrieved.

"OUT" Ben bawled once more and Lucy got out, trying to convey a teenage nonchalance and give a very clear impression that she had decided to get out of her own accord and not because of Ben's instruction. They walked up the garden path and Ben rang the doorbell, a newer version, he noted, added since the previous week. Shortly after Katie pulled the door open and invited them in.

"Hey" Ben greeted her "is Billy here yet?"

"Oh yes" Katie replied with emphasis.

"And?" Ben asked

"And he's banging random pipes, shaking his head and talking in 'plumbspeak' which means nothing to me - you go in there and translate."

Ben laughed, "Ok, in just a minute"

"Er, no, now" Katie countered "if he hits many more bits something's going to come apart, pipes or him or possibly you!" Katie's face showed she might not, in fact, be joking so Ben shot off into the front room to talk plumbing with Billy. Lucy started to take more notice of Katie at this point. She hadn't seen many people able to make her stubborn brother jump into action. Katie was definitely an exception. Lucy came out of her ponderings as she realised Katie was speaking to her.

"I'm sorry" Katie said "Ben didn't introduce us before he disappeared. I'm Katie Collins; I'm looking after this house at the moment." Katie extended her hand which Lucy shook a little self-consciously as she didn't usually shake hands with new acquaintances.

"I'm Lucy, Ben's sister. I'm staying with him for a couple of weeks while my Mum's away."

"Well, it's nice to meet you. Do you fancy a drink while you're waiting?" Katie wanted to make the girl feel welcome. She had a rather mutinous set to her face but Katie could see the vulnerability in her bright blue eyes.

"Oh ok," Lucy answered "Do you have any hot chocolate?"

"I do" Katie smiled "and I have some oat cookies to go with it if you like."

"Oh cool" Lucy brightened immediately and followed Katie into her flat. Katie soon had the milk warming on the range and spooned chocolate into the mugs, mixing them into a froth as she added the milk.

"There you are" Katie handed one of Cliona's hand painted mugs to Lucy, "help yourself to cookies." Lucy was soon tucking into the homemade biscuits, happily munching the crunchy treats. To Katie she suddenly looked like a different person, not much more than a child despite her typical teenage attempts to look grown up.

"So, Lucy, where has your Mum gone?" Katie enquired.

"Oh, I'm not sure really. She's disappeared off with Clever Trevor on a holiday or something."

"Clever Trevor?" Katie questioned

"Yeah, he's her boyfriend - well her current boyfriend anyway." Lucy's attempt at cynicism was at odds with her blonde childish face Katie thought.

"You don't get on then?" Katie added

"With Trevor, not really, he's not as bad as some of them."

"What about your Mum?"

"She's ok; she's just in another world, really, not the same one as us, that's all." Lucy said sadly, "she's always got some flight of fancy to follow, this time it was a romantic holiday in the sun or something."

"So she arranged for you to stay at your brother's - that's ok isn't it?"

"Well, half-brother actually. Ben's ok, but she didn't arrange it, she just took me there and left. Ben was a bit pissed off at first, but its ok now."

"Oh" Katie didn't know what to say. Her parents had always been away, working on some project or other across the world so she knew what it felt like to be left behind but she'd always had Mo and Granddad to fall back on - and at least they were always expecting her, it seemed that Lucy wasn't so lucky.

"What about your Dad?" Katie asked

"Never met him, he was a very brief part in Mum's life" Lucy said matter-of-factly "it's ok really; I expect he was a bit of a waster anyway."

"Maybe" Katie smiled at Lucy's world weariness, "men are generally more trouble than they're worth." she added with feeling, "Do you want another biscuit?" Lucy nodded and grinned

"You're ok Katie - and these are gorgeous" she said biting into the golden biscuit "So how do you know Ben, he's never mentioned you before."

"Well, I knew him at school when I was nine and ten, he was a pain in the neck behind me in class, always kicking my chair and trying to be clever. But more recently I came back to look after my Gran's house as she had an accident and Ben came to fix the door for me."

"You missed the part about knocking me off my bike - you keep doing that" Ben had come into the kitchen with a stocky man in blue overalls

111

behind him.

"Actually I didn't knock you off" Katie bristled "you were unable to control your bike and drove yourself into a hedge as I recall."

"Okay, okay" conceded Ben, laughing, "We've had a good look around and Billy needs to go through the problems."

"Oh god" groaned Katie "would you like a coffee first?"

They both accepted and as Katie was boiling the kettle Poppy stuck her head round the door.

"Hi Katie, sorry to bother you, could you - oh" she paused as she saw Katie had company "sorry, oh hi Ben, how are you?"

"I'm fine, Poppy - you?"

"Yeah great, bit of a problem actually but nothing major. I'll catch you later Katie."

"No, no come in" Katie pulled Poppy back into the kitchen, thinking any distraction from the potentially expensive plumbing problems was welcome.

"This is Billy, the heating expert, and this is Lucy, Ben's sister"

"Hi" said Lucy "your earrings are really great - where did you get them?"

"I made them actually. I'm doing a design course at Rawlinston College" Poppy answered.

"Really, I love design at school. What else do you design?" In no time the two of them were happily chatting away on the sofa, discussing colours, materials and favourite designers. There was no putting off the plumbing discussion any longer for Katie.

"So" she said, pulling up the big wooden chair to the kitchen table, "tell me the worst."

"Well in short, the systems pretty sound but the radiators are nowhere near big enough to heat a room that size." Ben began.

"Yes, my dear" Billy continued in a fatherly fashion, "the pipes are old, but they're fine, not the old lead ones we have to replace, but you need some double radiators in there and there's a couple of lengths of piping to replace but it's pretty straightforward. I've run the water through them all and there doesn't seem to be any blockages, so we should be able to get you up and running quite quickly."

"Oh" Katie was a bit dumb struck, "so you don't need to take the house to pieces and start again?"

"No" Ben said, exasperated, "a couple of new radiators and a bit of pipe and you'll be as warm as toast in there."

"Well, okay, but how much is this going to cost? I don't really want to use Mo's money for this but I haven't got a great deal to play with." Katie said forlornly.

Billy looked at Ben slightly puzzled "But it's alright my dear, Ben here ..." Billy started but Ben cut in quickly

"Has some radiators and pipes from a house conversion we did recently and Billy can use them - so they won't cost anything." Billy was looking more puzzled by the minute; after all he had just negotiated a price for parts and labour with Ben in the front room.

"Oh, well that's great, thanks. What about the labour cost?" Katie continued "how much will that be?" Billy was stumped what to say as he knew the cost but for some reason Ben didn't seem to want Katie to know. Fortunately for Billy, Ben had now taken control of the conversation.

"Billy owes me a few hours for some work we did on his house a couple of months ago, so I'm calling it in. I'll come down and give him a hand, it'll only take an afternoon right?" Ben looked at Billy for confirmation, who nodded in a slightly befuddled manner.

"Well if you're sure, that'd be great" Katie was mightily relieved; she had been really quite worried about how she would afford the work. Ben and Billy were discussing the dates and settled on the following Thursday afternoon.

"That'll give you another week after, if you decide to give the room a lick of paint" Ben pointed out helpfully.

"Great" Katie thought and wondered how she had gotten into this at all, oh yes - Ben had suggested it!

Billy was making moves to leave so Ben offered to show him out; as they reached the front door Ben shook his hand.

"Thanks for that Billy, sorry I didn't explain but Katie's looking after the place for her Grandmother, Mo Collins, and she hasn't really got the money to pay for the whole thing. I'll give you a ring tomorrow and we'll agree the terms. Is that ok?"

"That's fine Ben" Billy had known Ben for a long time and always suspected he was a bit on the soft side, good job he had John on his books or he'd be falling for every sob story going. Although, Billy thought, this might have a lot more to do with the very attractive auburn haired Katie than Ben's altruistic motives! Chuckling to himself Billy shook Ben's hand and went off into the night.

Ben walked back into Katie's kitchen, Lucy was still talking eagerly with Poppy, and Katie was clearing away the pots they had used. Ben was suddenly struck by the cosy domestic nature of the scene and he was extremely comfortable to feel a part of it as Katie smiled at him as walked over to the range. Not really wanting to leave just yet but knowing he had no further reason to stay he reluctantly said to Lucy.

"Come on Luce, we'd better be going I'm meeting Stew at seven." Lucy's face fell.

"Ah but Ben, can't I stay, you're only going up the road to the Rose & Crown, you can collect me on the way back." Lucy put on her most pleading face.

"No, Luce, Katie will have things to do." Ben insisted

"But Poppy says I can help her sort out photographs and material for her next project. She doesn't mind - do you?" Lucy turned to Poppy, her blond head bobbing with enthusiasm.

"No, it's fine with me." Poppy said "in fact I could use the help. I'm rubbish at making a decision and I'll end up with too many photos to fit on the board." Lucy looked triumphantly at Ben as if to say 'so there'.

Ben was touched to see Lucy so enthusiastic about something other than loud music that he didn't have the heart to stand in her way and besides Poppy seemed a good kid; she was already having a positive effect on his wayward sister.

"Okay, if you're sure Poppy. I'll be back at about eight o'clock"

"Thanks Ben" Lucy was pleased her brother had decided to trust her after her 'accident' over the weekend and in this spirit of generosity she didn't want him to go to the Rose & Crown on his own.

"Why don't you take Katie with you" she announced, as if struck by an idea of great quality, "I'm sure she could use a drink after having all us traipsing in and out." Lucy looked to Katie for her assent.

"Well, I'm sure Ben doesn't want me tagging along to his business meetings." Katie was uncertain as to why she suddenly felt a bit shy.

"Why not?" Lucy answered belligerently, "he was going to take me" she added with incontrovertible logic. Ben decided to step in.

"Why don't you come? I'm not meeting Stew 'til seven and it won't take long. You can buy me a drink to say thanks for all my help." he added, tongue slightly in cheek.

In fact, the idea had some appeal for Katie, it was the first chance she'd had for an evening out of any sort since arriving in Laxley Heath, so she may as well grab the opportunity whilst it was on offer. "Okay then Ben" she agreed, "but I think you owe me the drink, as you started this whole pantomime." Ben laughed, "So what am I? Prince Charming"

"Ugly brother" said Lucy and Katie in unison.

Shortly after Ben and Katie were making their way up the main street in Laxley, the earlier rain had cleared and although it was still wet under foot there was a clear, crisp feel to the air that felt invigorating. Lucy had been installed in Poppy's flat for the next couple of hours with many and varied instructions from Ben about her behaviour, to which Lucy had listened to at least half!

As they walked through the familiar street they chatted about times past, how the main street had seemed like such an adventure when you were nine, how running past the shops, buying penny chews in the grocery store from old Mr. Beadle as you tried to hide another five pence worth in your pocket until you reached the green at the end. For Katie this had been a magical place, she revealed slightly embarrassed.

"Oh yes" Ben enquired "So what magical qualities did it possess?"

"Well, you see, the bridge" Katie pointed "at the far side was the magical land of 'far far away' - if you could get past the troll under the bridge. Over there," she pointed to the shelter in front of the little row of antique shops "is the castle where the princess grew up, but she had to cross the green with all its swamps and dragons and then cross the bridge to reach her Prince Charming." Katie felt herself blushing at her childhood fantasies.

"So was he there when you made it?" Ben asked gently

"Oh, not really - well not how I thought he'd be anyway" Katie sighed and Ben looked at her thoughtfully, wondering who had brought such a sad look into her expressive brown eyes.

"And what about you?" Katie asked, shaking herself out of her reverie, "what did it all look like for you?"

"Oh that's easy" Ben laughed, "this was the American Plains - Injuns lived over the bridge and we had to fight them. We weren't very PC at

nine!" he added. Katie laughed and they passed on into the Rose &
Crown at the side of the common. The pub was decorated like a typical
village hostelry, exposed wooden beams, gleaming brasses around the
central hearth, which even had a real fire merrily burning and popping
away. The slightly orange glow from the various lamps and wall lighters
added to the welcoming warm feeling as Ben and Katie entered. Ben
pointed to an empty table in one of the bay windows overlooking the
green and Katie sat down as Ben walked over to the bar. In no time a
cheery man appeared behind the bar as if he had been waiting there
for Ben to arrive, business looked a bit thin, so he probably had been
Ben reflected wryly.

"Hello Ben," the deep gravelly Yorkshire accent assailed Ben "how are
you, young man? I haven't seen you in here for a while. Is it a special
occasion?" he added with a wink and a knowing look across at Katie
making herself comfortable on the red velour window seat. Ben ignored
the innuendo and ordered a white wine for Katie and a coke for
himself. Andy, the landlord gave him another knowing smile as he gave
Ben his change,

"Have a nice evening!"
"Get lost Andy" Ben replied, finally rising to the bait. Andy disappeared

back into the black hole he had appeared out of, still chuckling to himself, getting under anyone's skin was an added bonus for him. Of course he never tried it when Lily, his wife, was about then he kept up the jovial landlord image, benignly looking after his flock of customers.

Ben returned to the window seat "So what did you say to him to have him roaring" Katie enquired.

"Well, actually I told him you weren't my girlfriend - he found that hugely entertaining" Ben told her

"Oh" Katie didn't know how to reply to that and they both sank into quiet reflection as they surveyed the common through the slightly flaky and slightly condensated bay window. Ben felt fidgety, why had he said that, it had only made them both uncomfortable - he decided not to examine why. And they had been having such a laugh before. He hated these silences, he never felt comfortable in them, he thrashed around in his head for an opening gambit, just as a drowning man thrashes around for anything to hold onto, but the more he sifted through his head the less he could think of to say, it either sounded contrived or rude, or worse - both! Just as he felt the waters closing over above his head he spied a life raft

"So why wasn't the prince so charming in the end?" he asked. Katie jumped out of her solitary thoughts with a start.

"Sorry?"

"You said, when you were the princess that the prince came to rescue you - but that it wasn't worth the bother or something like that."

"Oh you know" Katie tried to laugh it off "Prince Charming, all talk, no substance. Shiny hair, empty brain - never like the story."

"What happened? How did your prince become charmless?" Ben persisted and he watched as Katie fought with herself as to whether to share the story of her humiliation or to bat on with the faux humour and keep the conversation light

"It's not a pretty story" she answered eventually "I don't come out of it very well either."

"Hey - we've all made mistakes" Ben replied sympathetically,

"Oh and talking about them cleanses the soul, cleans the slate - helps me to 'move on'" Katie said, not a little sarcastically.

"Well possibly" Ben replied "but I was thinking it might just give me a good laugh" he paused, then smiled and Katie smiled back. So she told him, the whole sorry tale about Marcus and their unhappy demise.

"So" Katie concluded "did it give you a laugh"

"Well, it's not exactly a jaw breaker, no - but at least I understand why you're back in Laxley Heath. A bit of respite from a cruel world."

"Yes that, and the broken hip and mild concussion!"

"Well that was just- Ummm- 'convenient'" Ben plucked the word out carefully.

"I wouldn't let Mo hear you call it that" Katie laughed "she thinks it's anything but convenient."

"But she's still glad you're around - she missed you a lot." Katie was just about to enquire how Ben knew Mo missed her granddaughter when he stood up to greet someone who had just entered the pub.

"Stew, Stew mate over here" An extremely tall, almost lanky, and angular man strode over to them

"Ben, hi, how are you?" They shook hands and Ben introduced Stewart to Katie.

"My cue to leave I think. I know you have business to discuss." Katie stood up as she spoke.

"There's no need really" Ben answered, "it's nothing covert - is it?" he asked Stew, realising he didn't actually know what it was about.

"No, nothing covert - just a possible opportunity" Stew confirmed

"Well as intriguing as that may be, I've just seen Tamsin appear with her yoga class - so I'll make myself scarce and go learn a few chants or possibly a few new positions." Katie coloured immediately the words were out, double entendres and risqué talk were not her thing. She scuttled over to the bar where Tamsin's crowd soon welcomed her and to her relief were actually discussing last night's reality TV show to which she was able to add plenty to the conversation, having sat through every episode. Ben and Stewart both gamely resisted the urge to laugh at Katie's less than graceful exit and turned to the business in hand.

"So Stew - what's on the table?" Ben set the ball rolling.

"Well then" Stew continued "I might have the perfect job for you." Ben felt his stomach tighten, BW needed a break, maybe at last they were going to get one.

"Go on then" Ben prompted

"Well it's a renovation, but it's two rows of derelict terraced housing, going for a song because they're at the wrong end of the town, but I happen to know that a lot of the derelict commercial buildings around them are going to be pulled down and a new commercial and residential cosmopolitan precinct built with bars, cafes and apartments, which should make twenty newly renovated town houses in an up and coming area extremely desirable. But the plans for the precinct are going to be released at the end of next month so we've only got a window of about four weeks before everybody will see the potential and the price could double." Stew could barely contain his excitement.

"So you want to be a part of this?" Ben asked

"Yes, 10% plus design for free."

"Okay, tell me a bit more about it, I can't think of the area you mean in Rawlinston." Ben pondered.

"Ah well, that's the point. It's not in Rawlinston." Stew announced

"Where is it?" Ben took the bait.

"Southampton" Stew produced it like a magician pulling a rabbit out of a hat.

"Southampton" Ben repeated incredulously, "could it be any further away. We don't have anybody in Southampton." Ben could see the dream which had been so promising slipping through his fingers.

"But that's the beauty - you don't need to" Stew answered, "if you send down a few of your best workers who could live on the site during the week, pick up the rest from the pool down there and then supervise it yourself."

"Me!" Ben was incredulous.

"Yes - if you worked on it full time you could have it done in six months and the property's all sold within a year. Plus you'd keep full control of the project." Stew was very persuasive.

"And you think it's do-able?" Ben was starting to hope

"Look, absolutely it's do-able - if you want it. But like I said we've only got a short time frame."

Ben sat back and exhaled, in his stomach he could feel the butterflies of excitement starting to fly. This could be just the project they were looking for, but Southampton, it was a shame it had to be so far away.

"Stew, thanks, give me a couple of days to talk to John and Charlie and I'll get back to you."

"It's a great chance Ben. I wouldn't let it go if I were you. First step to your first million!" he joked.

Ben laughed "First step to my first thousand will do me - or even to paying off the overdraft." They shook hands with an arrangement for Stew to email Ben all the details so he could bring it to the BW team. Feeling the need for a small celebration he tried to catch Katie's eye to see if she wanted another drink. Tamsin's friend Rita nudged Katie as they sat talking about the lotus position; at least that was the last position they had been talking about when Katie had actually been listening, they had soon moved off reality TV and onto their shared love of yoga. It seemed to Katie that yoga was definitely a participation sport. Rita nudged her again

"Don't look now but I think someone wants your attention?" Rita giggled

Katie looked up to see Ben gesturing did she want a drink - Oh God, yes and a large one! Seeing her chance to escape any more talk about mantras she made her excuses and headed to the bar.

"Another one?" Ben asked

"Oh please, yes - remind me never to take up yoga, it is possibly the most boring conversation piece ever." Katie rolled her eyes and grabbed the large glass of Chardonnay that Andy had just plonked in front of her, taking a large slurp she smiled,

"Ah, now that's much better" she sighed

"So not to your taste then?" Ben raised an enquiring eyebrow as he nodded Tamsin's crowd.

"No, not really. I mean they seem very nice people - with all that meditating and communing with nature they really ought to be - but they take it so seriously! So how did your meeting go?"

"Actually I think it went very well. Stew had a good proposition for BW. It needs more looking into, but it could be a goer." Ben's eyes lit up as he talked about the project and the possibilities that it could open up for BW. It seemed that an extra light had been turned on inside and the shower of blue from his now quite remarkable eyes would have drawn ships into port if Ben had been taking a stroll along a cliff. For the first time Katie noticed that Ben was a man as well as the good mate he was turning out to be.

"Sorry" Ben interrupted her musings "you look a bit glazed - I get a bit carried away about work."

"No no" Katie protested "Actually I think it's two large glasses of Chardonnay on a basically empty stomach. I've hardly had a drink since I've been at Mo's house. I think my tolerance levels have dropped." Katie giggled. Ben looked across at her and for a moment he thought he was ten again, looking at Katie Collins from the next seat with a desire to get her attention no matter what. Okay, he thought, we're back to pulling pigtails, now just grow up and behave like an adult.

"So let's get you something to eat" he offered "I'm starving and Lucy's probably eating Poppy by now. Or worse she might have tried to cook something!"

"She can't be that bad surely?" Katie laughed. Ben told Katie about the 'kitchen' incident over the last weekend, "it was only a small fire - but definitely a fire." he finished. Katie picked up her bag, looking a little concerned

"Perhaps we should be getting back - we can call for something on the way. Do you know any numbers?" Laughing Ben followed Katie out of the pub and called up a number on his mobile.

"How does Indian sound? The Kaghan Valley delivers to Laxley too." Ben offered.

"Oh yes" Katie replied "I haven't had a good bhuna for ages." Ben rang the number and ordered a set meal for four to be delivered to Tolpuddle House, including a chicken bhuna. Snapping his phone shut he caught up to Katie who had hastened up the road now that a fine drizzle was hanging in the air and clinging to her coat and hair, defying it not to go frizzy. They arrived back at Tolpuddle House in half the time it had taken them to get to the pub. Just as Katie was opening the door into the flat Lucy came flying down the stairs screeching to Ben.

"Ben, Ben, we don't have to go just yet do we? I'm polishing up a stone and Poppy says she'll set it in a pendant for me. Honestly Ben it's beautiful, you can see about seven different colours in it depending which light it's in, it's called a quarter or something. What is it again?" she said to Poppy who had appeared behind her at the top of the stairs.

"Quartz" Poppy supplied

"Yes a quartz" Lucy repeated "so we don't have to go straight away do we?" Ben couldn't help but smile at Lucy's enthusiasm, he could hardly reconcile it with the sullen and moody teenager hanging around his flat only two days ago when he had banned an outing to the beauticians on the parade for a third ear piercing.

"Well, actually, titch, no we don't, we've ordered an Indian it'll be here in about twenty minutes, so you've got a bit longer. Why don't you join us?" he shouted up to Poppy "I've ordered plenty and it's the least I can do after you've been babysitting Luce." He threw a sidelong glance at Lucy and was gratified to see her rise to the bait. "Only joking sis - you're far too big to babysit - so what do you say Poppy?" Poppy accepted in double-quick time, after all she was a student and they never turned down the offer of a free meal unless there were serious strings attached. Half an hour later all four of them were happily ensconced around Katie's huge pine kitchen table with an assortment of foil containers, cardboard lids and polystyrene pots scattered between them. Lucy was still clutching her new pendant in one hand and kept running a finger over the smooth polished surface. Ben marvelled at the animation in her face as she told him about the process and all about Poppy's project, he realised he didn't see her

happy very often. In fact, he reflected ruefully, he didn't really see

Lucy enough full stop. He made a mental resolution that once she was

back at Mum's he would make more of an effort to see her (and Mum)

more regularly and invite her round more too. But he reflected she

would have to go back to Mum's shortly what with all the jobs at BW

and the investigation work required for the Southampton project and

the investment in the company he really didn't have a lot of time to

spend with Lucy now and he couldn't afford to lose out on the

opportunities, he'd ring Mum in the morning and sort out when she'd

be back to pick up Lucy. Looking at his watch he realised it was nearly

nine thirty and time to get Lucy back home for school in the morning,

although he himself was loathe to leave the cosy atmosphere. Ben had

to admit it had been a really enjoyable and relaxing evening, stretching

out like a cat awakening in front of the fire he gave a stifled yawn and

told Lucy to grab her stuff as they had to make a move. Ben and Lucy

thanked Katie and Poppy for the evening and reluctantly walked out

into the chilly damp night.

CHAPTER 9

The following morning after packing a still excited Lucy off to school still wearing her new pendant despite Ben's best efforts to tell her the teachers would probably confiscate it, Ben sat down at his desk at home and wrote himself a quick list of the tasks he needed to do in the day. He always liked to do this as he found it immensely satisfying to keep putting a line through items as he completed them. The list was relatively short;

1)   Ring Mum

2)   Ring solicitor (re: investments)

3)   Do a search on the Southampton project

4)   Tie up any other possible projects

5)   Put some budget figures together for Friday's meeting

Ben looked up - nothing too difficult on today's list but he needed to sort out item one to give him a chance at getting the rest done. Ben looked at his watch, it was a quarter to eight, there was no point phoning Mum yet, even if they were an hour in front in Spain it was still far too early to ring his mother who would not emerge from bed for at least another couple of hours. Ben decided to head for the office and ring her from there. After catching up with John and Charlie they had added another three possible projects for the business, including the Southampton one, and he now had the details he needed to put some budget figures together but first he had to tackle his mother. Picking up the phone he tapped in the number for his mother's mobile and waited, after about six rings someone answered with a very languid "Hello"

"Hi Mum, it's Ben"

"Oh Ben hi, why are you ringing?" not a promising start Ben thought as she sounded genuinely puzzled.

"I just need to know what time you'll be home on Friday so I can drop Lucy off. I've got a lot of work visits I need to do and I can't arrange them until Lucy's back home - and by the way you really could've rung me to ask about Lucy staying" Ben admonished

"Well" Trudy Chapman bristled "I didn't think having your sister to stay would be such a problem to you."

"It's not a problem Mum," Ben sighed "I could've done with some notice - just to arrange things. I love Lucy and most of the time she's good fun to have around."

"Yes you see dear. I knew you wouldn't mind really and what with my nerves playing up dreadfully I really had to get away. I needed peace and tranquility to rediscover my inner core."

"Oh God" Ben groaned inwardly, she'd obviously discovered another guru to follow and Trudy continued right on cue

"As I was reading Professor Deschanel's 'Your inner core and how to stop it peeling' I realised this was me. I'm being stripped of my emotional layers, exposing my core to the elements which cause me deep psychological and physical pain."

"Yes I'm sure" Ben replied wryly, he was used to his mother's reliance on fairly dubious self-help books into which she flung herself until she found another book more to her liking, generally ones that blamed everyone around her rather than herself, "but" he continued "now that you've had chance to recuperate, what time is your flight in so I can bring Lucy home."

"My flight darling?" Trudy replied dreamily "what do you mean?" Ben's stomach started to sink, this wasn't going very well.

"I mean your flight home Mum, you went last Friday so you must be catching your flight back this Friday."

"Oh no, Ben darling, I'm not coming back until I'm fully healed. We're staying at Nick and Helen's villa and I only got one way tickets. We'll book the returns when the re-layering process is complete." Ben sat back in stunned silence; Jean looked over concerned as Ben dropped the phone onto the desk.

"Is everything alright Ben?" she enquired, concerned. Ben nodded in an automatic fashion. Ben could hear Trudy on the other end

"Ben dear, are you there, you've gone very faint. I can't hear you."
Ben picked up the phone and spoke very carefully,

"So what you're saying Mum, is, you're not coming home on Friday and you can't say exactly when you will be, except it's when you've been re-layered." Ben almost choked on the final word.

"Yes that's right, and Lucy's with you - you said it was nice to see her." Trudy confirmed, almost reproachfully.

"Yes, but Mum, staying with me for a week is a bit different to staying with me indefinitely. I've got a business to run; I can't run around after Luce."

"Oh Ben, what's more important than your family?" Trudy replied, without a hint of irony "Lucy's no trouble, you'll hardly know she's there." Ben knew it was a lost cause, his mother had always had the knack of being able to ignore anything that didn't fit in with her plans and no amount of coaxing, arguing or plain shouting would change that.

"Okay Mum, speak to you soon. Phone me as soon as you're getting back." Ben put the phone down and ran his hand through his sandy hair. Jean looked at him and could she could see the concern in his eyes, her motherly nature took over, she couldn't bear to see any of her 'boys' fretting.

"What is it Ben? Is your Mum okay?"

"Oh she's okay" he replied bitterly "except for finding her inner core and re-layering herself, which may take some time to achieve and she's not coming home until she has." he laughed, but with no humour. Jean raised her eyebrows, she knew Trudy of old and had laughed with Ben on many occasions about her latest fad, but she couldn't understand a mother who could just abandon her child without barely a backward glance.

"So Lucy's staying with you for a bit longer then?" she asked. Ben nodded

"She'll have to, poor kid, but I don't know how I'm going to cope with it. I've got loads of visits I need to do and she's not the sort of teenager you'd leave on her own - generally havoc ensues."

"Well that's no surprise" Jean clucked "with a mother like that, sorry Ben, but it's got to be said, it's no wonder she does some things to get attention, maybe a bit of discipline and time from you is just what she needs. And don't worry if you need to go away for a night she can always come and stop with me. She won't get away with anything with my lot." she added. Ben looked gratefully at Jean. He had no choice but to look after Lucy and if that was the case he should try to do it to the best of his ability, but he still wasn't sure how Lucy was going to take the news of her extended stay.

Ben spent the rest of the day researching the Southampton project and it looked like Stewart was right. The potential to turn these houses into new desirable accommodation was certainly within BW's capabilities and, if his first figures were correct it was within their banking abilities too. Ben's only concern was the distance, would he really want to spend six months in Southampton, or would John or Charlie with their family commitments? Ben pondered on this as he walked down the street into Rawlinston to grab a coffee and a sandwich. Ben was weighing up the pros and cons of a cheese and ham baguette or a cheese and onion pasty when he heard a tapping at the window he was passing, looking up he saw Declan's grinning face beckoning him into the restaurant. Ben had done the whole refurbishment on Declan's restaurant over four years ago and they had become firm friends as the project progressed.

"Hi there" Declan boomed as Ben came through the door "what had you so deep in thought – or should that be who?" Declan's throaty laugh made Ben shift uneasily.

"I'm thinking about a project actually" he answered defensively "it could really make things happen for us."

"Okay" Declan smiled, deciding not to tease his friend anymore "do you want a coffee? And you can fill me in about it?"

"Yeah, black please – oh and throw a sandwich together – I'm bloody starving!"

Just over an hour later Ben had filled Declan in, not only on the Southampton project but also about his missing parent and his new house guest. He was actually feeling much better now, Declan's calm manner and refusal to get wound up by almost anything was having a soothing effect on Ben. He started to see that with some help from his friends he could actually cope with Lucy and work.

"Cheers Dec, and not just for the sarnie. I needed a bit of clear Irish thinking"

"No problem mate, I needed to speak to you anyway. Cliona's having another of her dinner parties four weeks on Friday and as I need someone who lives on this planet to talk to I thought you might like to make up the numbers." Declan saw Ben hesitate and decided to press home his advantage before Ben wriggled out of it, "and, of course, as you owe me a favour now, after my sage advice on your present predicament ….."

Ben groaned

"Okay, okay, I'll come – but only cos you'll be cooking. Cliona's artistic friends can be a bit hard on the digestion." Declan said nothing but a flash of recognition flew across his face

"I'll ring you next week and give you the time" was all he said with a wink.

Later that evening, as he poured himself a well-deserved cold beer, Ben congratulated himself on handling the situation with Lucy much better than expected. She had taken the news about staying with Ben for an indefinite period in a relatively calm, and possibly even adult, manner. In fact there had only been a small skirmish when he had set out some of the rules, in particular about having at least two days' notice when she was going to be out for the evening, so he could check out the facts followed by a particularly heated debate about Ben checking Lucy's homework. However he had come out on top for both by using the age old elder brother trick of shouting louder, sitting on her and tickling her until she conceded. All in all he was pleased with his evening's work. Now all he had to do was sit down and work out the detailed costing for the Southampton project and he could call it a

night!

CHAPTER 10

By Thursday morning Ben was shattered, he had now spent two nights into the wee small hours trying to get his costing right and he was still a fair way from making it affordable. He was glad Thursday had arrived and he had some physical work to do, checking the progress at Cheadle House and then fixing the plumbing at Tolpuddle House later that afternoon. Ben couldn't wait to get to Katie's and get his hands dirty doing some real work (and that was the only reason he was looking forward to it he told himself). By three o'clock Ben was ready to work off some pent up frustration by hard graft. The assessment at Cheadle House had not gone as well as he had hoped and he had to get rid of a couple guys on the site - something he never enjoyed, so as he waited outside Rawlinston Girl's College to pick Lucy up he was ready for an afternoon of uncomplicated plumbing.

Three hours later this noble object seemed a long way away. 'Uncomplicated' was the last thing this plumbing was. Billy and Ben had uncovered numerous quirks to Tolpuddle House' plumbing that had caused a lot of scratching of heads, rubbing of chins and muffled curses. Billy was a determined man and had never let a plumbing problem defeat him yet, so he was sorting out each challenge as it arose. Ben had been pretty much reduced to labourer and assistant with responsibility for wrench holding. Still this had given him plenty of opportunity to speak to Katie who, when they had arrived had opened the door in oversized overalls and streaks of magnolia paint down each cheek. Katie had started to paint the walls in the front room to give it a lift before the meeting the following week. As she painted and he unattached and re-attached radiators under Billy's watchful eye Katie asked how Lucy was getting on. Lucy, herself, had disappeared into Katie's kitchen with homework, cocoa and a slab of marble cake to keep her going.

"She seems a bit quieter than usual" Katie continued

"It's Mum," Ben sighed "she's done a runner on us again."

"A runner? What - left her?" Katie gasped

"Well, she says it's a holiday to find the 'centre of her core' – or was it the 'core of her centre' – either way it involves staying indefinitely in another country, so Lucy's got to stay with me. I'm not sure she's entirely happy with all my ground rules." He smiled ruefully.

"Well, I never liked being told what to do when I was a teenager" Katie grinned

"Or before that as I recall – you probably don't like it much now either as far as I can tell" Ben teased and ducked as Katie flicked a splodge of magnolia 'one coat' at him.

"Oh and I bet you're a stickler for the rules Ben Wilson – especially ones you get to make up yourself. I'm beginning to see Lucy's problem" Katie retaliated

"Everyone needs a bit of discipline to keep them on the straight and narrow – and, believe me, with our mother, Lucy's had precious little of that at home" Ben retorted indignantly. Katie turned and looked at Ben with a serious expression.

"Is it really that bad then?" she asked carefully. Ben groaned

"Oh, that's only half of it. She's an absolute nightmare. Don't get me wrong, she's not cruel or abusive, just completely self-involved, always rushing from one guru to the next in some desperate bid to find herself. All the time missing all the things that are going on right in front of her nose."

"Was she always like that?"

"No, it started after my Dad left when I was twelve. She never came to terms with it. I think she thought it was her fault."

"And was it?" Katie asked gently

"No - not really, Dad found a junior model. Cliché of all clichés - his secretary" Ben said bitterly. Katie didn't respond immediately, as some emotion he couldn't quite distinguish ran across her face. It almost looked like guilt, but it couldn't be, it wasn't her fault after all.

"So Lucy misses her?" she finally asked

"Well I don't know if she misses her - but she certainly misses having a stable parental role model. Mum and her trail of boyfriends have never given her a settled home. Actually it's a wonder she's not a worse handful than she is. I think underneath all that bravado she's a sensible kid really - just lacks a bit of direction." Ben paused.

"And now she's got her big brother to provide it for her" Katie joked to ease the tension a little.

"I guess so" Ben replied a little uncertainly

"Hey, don't knock it" Katie added "I was an only child. I'd have given anything for a brother who cared about me enough to yell at me now and again. Lucy's lucky to have you – and she probably knows that deep down." Katie turned back to her painting and Ben felt better than he had since that conversation with his mother. He was doing his best and maybe Lucy would appreciate that.

He soon had more pressing plumbing matters to attend to, as an unexpected leak appeared out of a radiator he had just attached and as he worked on that they both sunk into their own thoughts until Poppy stuck her head round the door.

"Wow, look at the three of you deep in concentration. It was so quiet I thought you'd sloped off to the pub or something." She joked.

"Hey, this is difficult work I'll have you know" Ben answered, "not just anyone could do it and it takes a skilled craftsman to get it right." As he spoke he turned and very carefully turned the water tap at the junction of the pipe and water came rushing out of the joint at the end of the radiator spraying Ben straight in the face.

"See what I mean" he said, without a flicker "expertise like this can't be bought." As Katie and Poppy creased up with laughter Ben returned to his problematic joint.

"Lucy's in the kitchen if you want to say Hi" Katie shouted across to Poppy

"I know – that's why I'm here. I went in to beg a few of those oatmeal cookies off you, and she'd drawn this. What d'you reckon? For a border I mean." Katie stepped down from the step ladder and looked at the card Poppy was holding out. On it was a flowing Celtic design with crosses and rings delicately shaded in bronze and gold tones that would lift the magnolia walls of the room. Katie gasped,

"It's beautiful, it would look beautiful, but wouldn't it take a long time to do?"

"Not if I give her hand" Poppy replied "shall I tell her she's got the commission?" Just as she spoke Lucy popped her head round the corner and was greeted by Poppy's broad grin.

"C'mon then Pablo, you'd better get started if we want the whole room done by this time next week."

Lucy responded with a grin even broader

"Really? Do you like it?" she asked, still a little uncertainly

"I think it's beautiful" Katie confirmed "and if you're really happy to do it I'd be very grateful – although I have to admit now that I can only pay you for the paint." She added a touch sheepishly.

"Oh I don't want paying" Lucy answered "It'll be great just to do something I've designed. I didn't really think I could."

In no time Poppy and Lucy had set to work, measuring the length and depths required on the walls that Katie had finished painting and were busily stencilling the design on the wall in no time. Before any of them knew it was eight o'clock. Billy had just left after finally locating and fixing (with Ben's expert help of course) all the leaks and pipes, and there was a warmth beginning to radiate around the front room as the boiler heated the water now circulating in the system.

"Jeez, I'm starving" groaned Poppy, and although this was nothing unusual the others had to agree that they too were, in fact, pretty hungry.

"Actually some of that gurgling before might have been me rather than the pipes" Ben joked "We'd better get off Luce, and get some dinner inside you."

"Why don't you stay?" Katie asked "I threw a stew in the oven hours ago as I wasn't sure what would be happening and there's plenty to go round - if you'd like? It's the least I can do really, after all your help."

Poppy was already heading for Katie's kitchen as Lucy looked to Ben

"Well sure, if that's okay - is that okay with you Luce?" Ben said to the back of Lucy's blond bobbing ponytail as she too disappeared into Katie's flat. For a moment Ben felt a bit shy and awkward as he and Katie were left alone.

"Well, I think that's a yes - if it's okay?" he added quietly.

"Absolutely" Katie replied, playing with a strand of her hair and covering it liberally in magnolia. "Oh poo!" she said as she squinted at it, "I'm going to have two tone hair for days now!"

"Two tone skin too!" Ben teased as he dipped a finger in the paint and flicked it down her cheek – making a quick exit into the hallway before Katie could respond.

Katie caught up with him just as they entered the flat and tried desperately to rub her paint covered fingers through his hair as Ben ducked and dived to escape. It was a few minutes later when they became aware of the two open mouths staring at them in disbelief and they came to a standstill looking sheepishly about them.

"God, when I'm marvelling at the immaturity – you've got to be worried" Lucy said haughtily – to which they all started laughing.

Ben dropped Lucy off at Katie's the following two evenings so she could finish her border in Katie's front room, but, despite a desire to go in and join her, he had too much work to complete and had to settle for a quick conversation on the doorstep as he picked up Lucy. It was strange, he reflected, how quickly somewhere could become familiar and comfortable to you. Maybe it was partly to do with the scary big things happening at the business, which meant he needed space away from there to escape – or maybe it was the company! Ben had had two very important meetings in the last day. Firstly he had met with John Richmond at the solicitors and drawn up paperwork for John and

Charlie's investment into BW. They were going to complete the formal signing on Friday at the weekly meeting and were following it up with a celebratory lunch at Declan's restaurant. And now that the money would be in place, Ben was keen to move on the Southampton project straightaway. To that end he had met with Stewart Jackson earlier and gone through his first draft of the costing. They had agreed that it was definitely possible and Stewart was setting up a meeting with the local council the following Thursday, they currently owned the land and buildings and could tell them what planning permission was required for the redevelopment. They would combine this with a visit to the site so that Ben could get a proper look at the scale of the job. Ben was excited and mildly terrified by the idea, but he'd come this far and he was going to make sure he left no stone unturned in his pursuit of the opportunity.

CHAPTER 11

The following Wednesday, the day before the most important meeting of his business life so far, Ben awoke to a dull, grey overcast sky. The leaden outlook of damp drizzly rain made him want to head immediately back under the covers, but this was a day when he had much to prepare for. He had completed the figures on the development and, with John and Stewart's help they had prepared a presentation for the local council about BW and their vision. Ben just had to review all this, see his accountants to check the financial figures were correct and then bind the copies they needed. He then planned an easy evening and an early night to give him the best possible start on Thursday. Sleep had been a bit lacking over recent weeks, working on the figures, dropping off and collecting Lucy from Katie's, and frequently staying longer than he intended to as there was always some tempting food on offer. (Ben ignored any implication that there was anything else tempting at Tolpuddle House that could have been keeping them there longer than planned!). Katie was becoming a friend and it was great to have somewhere where Lucy was happy to go, without giggling schoolgirls who were solely interested in clothes, music and boys, and not usually in that order. Thinking of Lucy made

Ben shake himself, with one last glance of longing back to his bed he headed into the hallway and banged loudly on Lucy's door.

"Luce, its 7.30 – GET UP" he shouted into the wooden panels.

He could hear movement, but not nearly enough to make him think Lucy was actually up, so he kept on banging. This had become something of a ritual in the flat. Like most teenagers, Lucy was notoriously bad at getting up, mainly due to the fact that she was equally bad at going to bed at a reasonable hour! Ben had taken to knocking and shouting constantly until Lucy put in an appearance. Just as he was about to resort to singing, (his renditions of various rock classics had never failed yet) Lucy's blonde head, hair ruffled and face scrunched from her night's sleep appeared around the door.

"Jesus Ben, I'm up okay – do you have to make such a noise – don't you think the neighbours will complain? It's a wonder they don't get you thrown out" she grumbled as she pushed past him and headed through to the kitchen.

"Well, actually sis, all my neighbours, like me, are working people and are actually up themselves so a bit of knocking won't worry them. However if you wandered out into the corridor by mistake, that might do the trick" he teased, messing up her, already very tousled, hair.

"Ha ha ha bruv – and you're a picture first thing aren't you?"

"I have my moments" Ben conceded, "now come on, get a shift on; I need to get you off to school. I've got a busy day ahead of tomorrow so I want to get on" Ben started shooing her towards the bathroom as he spooned coffee into the filter machine.

"Oh yes" Lucy turned as she reached the door, suddenly looking much brighter, "I thought you'd want me out of your hair this evening and Saffy's having all the girls around tonight. I can go over and keep out of your way." Lucy tried to look innocent as she asked but Ben knew Saffy of old. Anything she was organising was likely to be out of control within the space of an hour. He didn't have time for worrying about Lucy tonight.

"Sorry Luce, but I know Saffron Wilding and there's no way you're going there tonight. One, it's a school night, and two, I've no intention of having to spend the latter part of the evening bailing you out of whatever scrape you've got into!"

"But Ben, it won't be like that" Lucy whined "it'll be …"

"No Luce" Ben answered sharply "You're not going - okay? Deal with it!"

Lucy's bottom lip stuck out as she turned and stalked to the bathroom muttering under her breath what Ben could only assume were many and varied curses on him. It was the last thing he heard her say that morning as she stopped speaking to him and sat, shoulders hunched, looking resolutely out of the passenger window as he took her to school. Ben didn't worry about this, he had been the target of Lucy's silent treatment on many occasions over the years and they never lasted long. Lucy, despite her teenage tantrums, had a sunny nature and couldn't stay mad at anyone for long. She was also very pragmatic and knew that if it wasn't working she may as well try a different tack.

At 4.30 that afternoon when Ben got home, after a frustrating couple of hours with the accountant who had pointed out a number of errors in the figures and left Ben with more work to do that evening than he had anticipated, it was clear that Lucy had decided to change tack as she presented him with a coffee and digestive as he passed the kitchen. He responded with a raised eyebrow. Lucy chose to ignore this.

"So did you have a good day?" she asked.

"Not really no, and I've got twice as much work to do this evening as I thought I would, so you'll have to keep the noise down," he answered with seriousness, and a tone that brooked no argument. Unfortunately Lucy chose to ignore this too.

"So really," she started brightly, with a sharp look from under her eyelashes, "it really would be better if I was out of the way. I could go to ….."

"No Lucy" Ben snapped "you are not going to Saffy's and spending the evening doing God knows what - I've told you you're staying here where I know exactly what you're up to."

"But I wasn't …" Lucy started.

"I don't care, Luce" Ben shouted now "you're not going, okay! Get over it!" He glared at her as she stomped off to her bedroom and slammed the door. Ben stalked off to the living room and flicked the computer on and pushed a disc into the hi-fi, in no time he was engrossed in his spread-sheets and projections.

It was nearly three hours later when Ben ran a weary hand through his hair and realised how much time had passed. The noisy rumblings in his stomach reminded him that he had not eaten since breakfast and was in dire need of re-fuelling. Realising Lucy wouldn't have had anything either he pushed himself up from the chair and wandered into the hall grabbing a couple of takeaway menus from the shelf as he passed. He was too exhausted to think about cooking and he didn't really have the time either, knocking on Lucy's door, he shouted

"Hey Luce, Chinese or pizza? – you choose, I'll pay" he said jokingly. There was no response from Lucy's room. Obviously still sulking, Ben thought.

"C'mon Luce, I'm sorry for shouting earlier but it's a really important day tomorrow and I guess I'm stressing about it a bit. Let's get some food in and declare a truce eh!" he tapped gently on the door but there was still no reply. Leaning closer to the door he realised something wasn't right, there was no dull thud in the background that accompanied the music Lucy always had on. With some trepidation Ben pushed open the door, still really expecting Lucy to be asleep on the bed, but the room was empty. Quickly he ran into the bathroom and then the kitchen but Lucy was in neither, with a sinking feeling and growing anxiety he realised Lucy was not in the flat at all. She must have sneaked out when he was engrossed in his work.

"Bloody Saffron bloody Wilding" he raged, under his breath. Lucy had obviously decided to ignore Ben's instructions and take herself off to the party anyway. He grabbed the phone and dialled Lucy's mobile number, it went straight to voicemail.

"Lucy, where the hell are you?" he bellowed into the mouthpiece, "ring me as soon as you get this message. I'm on my way to pick you up. I'll be there in twenty minutes." With that he grabbed his jacket and keys and launched himself out of the flat and down the two flights of stairs into the van parked outside.

Fortunately Ben knew where Saffy Wilding lived having collected Lucy from there on a number of occasions. Her parents were successful consultants; one medical, one public relations and they lived in a huge house on the far side of Rawlinston, one big enough to a have a driveway in and another one out. The house was painted perfectly and the gardens immaculately maintained, not that Ben was in any mood to appreciate that as the van sped over the gravel drive, spraying out stones behind it as he skidded to a halt outside the front door.

Jumping out of the van Ben ran up to the door and held his finger on the bell. He could hear its incessant ring resounding down the hallway and echoing in the atrium. Not long after, the door was pulled open by a sulky looking girl with jet black, poker straight hair and a scowl stretching from one side of her face to the other. She also managed to look down her nose at this impatient person on her doorstep at the same time. Saffron Wilding herself Ben noted.

"Yes?" she said, in an exaggerated plumy tone, gained in her days at some minor ladies college in the south.

"Lucy Chapman – Where is she? Tell her, her brother Ben's here and it's time to go." Ben replied in his broadest northern tones before he could help himself.

"Lucy's not here." Saffron replied shortly and started to close the door. Ben put his hand out and stopped her.

"Look, I know she's here. She wanted to come and I said no, so she's snuck off anyway, but the games up and it's time to go." Ben added what he hoped was a winning brotherly smile to this, to encourage Saffron over to his side. He thought it might be working as she smiled back but it soon became apparent it was a smile of derision not camaraderie.

"Look, I told you she's not here and guess what? She's - not - here. She never came, she told me at school she couldn't come as her saddo brother was being a pain and wouldn't let her."

For the first time it crossed Ben's mind briefly that Lucy might not be here, but where else could she be? No, she was definitely here and this little trust fund princess was just trying to throw him off.

"Nice try" Ben said "I nearly believed you then, tell Lucy you did your best and get her out here."

Saffron sighed, it seemed she was bored of this conversation now; she took a deep breath and then bellowed,

"MUM!" very shortly after an immaculately made up Mrs Wilding dressed head to toe in Chanel tottered into the hallway.

"Saffron darling, there's really no need to shout in such an unladylike manner. Now what's the problem?" she raised a perfectly tweezed eyebrow as she asked.

"Mrs Wilding, I'm Ben Wilson, Lucy's brother. She's staying with me at the moment. I've come to collect her. Unfortunately she came out tonight although I'd told her she couldn't and I need to take her home now." Ben answered.

"Oh I see" Mrs Wilding replied, slightly puzzled "but Lucy's not here tonight. Saffron's got a few friends over but Lucy couldn't make it tonight could she sweetheart?" Mrs Wilding turned to Saffron for confirmation.

"I've already told him that" Saffron replied dismissively, "but he's having trouble understanding."

Ben went cold from head to foot. It was one thing for Saffron to deny Lucy being there to cover for her, but there was no way Mrs Wilding would. Lucy wasn't here and if she wasn't here – where the hell was she? Quickly, making his apologies, Ben made his exit and jumped back into the van, trying Lucy's mobile again. It was still on voicemail, leaving another garbled message; he set off out of the drive. Next he rang his flat to see if anyone answered. The answerphone clicked in after seven rings.

"Luce, if you're there – pick up. I just want to know you're okay." Ben hung on for a couple of minutes but no one answered. Setting the phone on hands free Ben rang some of Lucy's friends as he headed towards his Mum's house. He thought maybe Lucy had bolted back home in her effort to teach him a lesson.

Twenty minutes later Ben pulled up outside the terrace house that had been his home for the first eighteen years of his life. None of Lucy's friends' parents had seen her that evening so Ben was now praying that Lucy would be here. The house was in darkness but he hadn't expected anything else. Lucy wouldn't give the game away that easily. Ben let himself through the front door pushing the post back that accumulated on the doormat to one side so he could open the door properly. Not a good sign. The house was silent, enveloped in that thick darkness of emptiness, nothing seemed to stir. Ben's optimism was fading fast, leaving the pit of his stomach as fast as the leaden fear was entering it.

"Lucy, Lucy – it's Ben" he shouted up the stairs, "Look I'm sorry if I upset you, I'm not mad I just want to know you're okay." There was no response – no breath stirring the heavy atmosphere except his own. Taking the steps two at a time Ben then checked all the rooms upstairs and then downstairs once more. No one was here and it didn't seem that anyone had been here for quite a number of days. Ben finally had to accept that Lucy wasn't here and now he had absolutely no idea where she might be. He had exhausted all the contacts and he couldn't

think of any other friends Lucy might have sloped off to. Ben turned

cold, what if she had set off to one of those friends and not got there.

On these winter evenings darkness fell early and Lucy could have been

attacked and was now laying injured waiting for him to find her. Trying

to dispel his own rising hysteria Ben tried to think straight. What was

most likely? Most likely was that Lucy was back at the apartment having

a good laugh at the wild goose chase she had managed to send him on.

Keeping this positive image in his head he rang home again, still no

answer. Ben tried to think of who else he could try when Poppy popped

into his head. She might know some of Lucy's friends that he didn't.

Lucy would have talked to her about an unsuitable boy or a dodgy

friend that she might have kept concealed from her big brother.

Finding his hopes rising Ben jumped into the van, he was only twenty

minutes from Laxley Heath, he could drive round there now and pick

Poppy's brains.

In much less time than the twenty minutes it should have taken, Ben

pulled up outside Tolpuddle House. It was quite possible Ben had

gained enough points to lose his licence on the drive there if he had

been unlucky enough to encounter a policeman at every set of traffic

lights he'd jumped or speed limits he broke. Running up the path Ben knocked impatiently on the door, completely forgetting the doorbell at the side. Just as he was about to hammer again the door opened and Katie, with her hair pinned high in a ponytail looked out enquiringly. On spying Ben she broke into a smile.

"Oh Ben, at last, we were starting to get a bit worried about you. You're usually here by eight for Lucy, it's already eight thirty. Well come in" Katie held back the door as Ben entered.

"What do you mean you were getting worried about me?" he asked.

"Just that, Lucy's been here hours now. I thought maybe you'd forgotten about her - what with your big project." Katie smiled to indicate she was teasing as she realised Ben's face was growing darker, like a thundercloud was immediately overhead.

"Are you telling me Lucy's here?" he asked through clenched teeth.

"Erm, yes - and you're here to pick her up" Katie said slowly, a little uncertain as to why Ben was acting so strangely. She didn't have long to find out.

"LUCY" Ben bellowed "get yourself down here - NOW!"

In a few seconds a very pale faced Lucy appeared in the doorway of Katie's flat.

"Ben, I was just ...." she started.

"I know what you just - I have been half way round the country looking for you, at Saffron's, and Mum's. Do you have any idea how worried I was?" Ben was shaking, both with rage and relief in equal measure.

"I just wanted to get out of your way and Katie said I could come round whenever I wanted I just thought.."

"Stop Lucy, I don't want to hear it - Okay. Just get in the van we're going."

Katie, who had just realised why Ben had been acting so strangely, and that she had been somewhat duped by Lucy herself, felt she should still try to defend Lucy a little.

"Look, I'm sure she didn't mean to scare you, she just thought she was getting out of your way. Don't be too hard on her." Katie looked pleadingly at Ben. By now the relief that Ben felt was turning into a white hot anger that he had been put through the ordeal of the last few hours. The red mist setting around his flashing blue eyes was clouding his view and he wasn't fully in control of what he was saying.

"I'll deal with my sister how I see fit, thank you" Ben said, in clipped tones, "You want to concentrate on behaving as a responsible adult, not some over aged student trying to hang out with kids. When a child turns up on your doorstep in the future I suggest the first thing you do is to contact their guardian – not set them up with milk and cookies." With that Ben turned on his heel and exited Tolpuddle House slamming the door so hard it echoed through the stonework. Katie's stood open mouthed in disbelief. Her response dying on her lips as she drew breath to make it.

CHAPTER 12

The following morning started as dull and grey as the previous. As Katie struggled to awake, she wandered through the kitchen fixing herself a strong black coffee, she thought the damp, overcast weather was creating that damp overcast feeling in her, but as she gradually unfogged the sleep from her head she started to recall why she had such a knot in her stomach and a quiet rage in her head. Ben 'bloody' Wilson! How dare he go off at her about his sister? He wanted to look at himself before he started throwing accusations about. What was he doing that a fourteen year old girl could leave the flat and travel easily ten miles and then not even to miss her for the best part of three hours! Then he had the cheek to suggest that she was irresponsible. Katie was back to full level fuming by now. Her brown eyes flashing with flecks of amber as she wrestled with the injustice of it, and what was worse, she never got the chance to answer him back! He had slammed the door and left by the time she had drawn breath. Katie wasn't sure that this hadn't got her madder than the unfair insults thrown at her. Katie liked the opportunity to have her say (something she'd inherited from Mo) and she felt the weight of unfinished business in her mind as she ran through the many and varied – and creative ripostes she could have fired back at Ben.

After a hearty breakfast of porridge with a huge dollop of honey, followed by a bracing shower Katie was still twitching with unspent energy created by her unfinished argument.

"Well, Katie Collins" Katie said bracingly to her reflection in the bathroom mirror, "there is no point fuming impotently here – you may as well put all this excess energy to good use." With that she put on her oldest clothes and grabbed an old pair of gloves and headed out to the front garden.

Ever since Katie had been back at Tolpuddle House the overgrown state of the garden had been tearing at her, calling her to uncover the beauty she remembered from her days there as a child. She may as well use this new found energy to see if she could restore some part of it.

An hour later and Katie had started to make some real progress in the garden. Having cut away and cleared the overgrown clematis that had been overhanging the fence and obscuring a quarter of the bay window, Katie was now uncovering the path and a small patio area that had been hidden under many years of neglect. Katie let out a little cry of delight as she uncovered the stone bird bath she had loved as a child. It was shaped like a large sea shell and had a small frog sat on a lily pad on one side. She had loved this as a little girl and spent much time cleaning it and filling it with water. With renewed energy from her happy find Katie set too, digging up the weeds that were choking the beautiful plants in the beds around the patio. At least she hoped it was the weeds she was digging up, she smiled grimly, she was not exactly a knowledgeable gardener or even an enthusiastic amateur. In fact she had generally gravelled, flagged or decked any green areas she had previously owned and the fact that her penthouse in London only had a balcony had been a source of great relief to her. But, Katie reasoned, as she continued pulling and cutting, anything had to be better than the wilderness the garden had become. Coming across a particularly stubborn root formation Katie let fly with the spade, attacking it from angles.

"And exactly whose head are you imagining that to be" Katie swung round and smiled at Cliona's laughing face, "Could it be Marcus?" she teased.

"Actually, no" Katie answered, a little surprised herself, "it was mainly Ben Wilson - and the jobs not finished yet" she continued ominously aiming a few more swishes at the root.

"Ok, ok" Cliona cut in, "it's most definitely time for a break. Come on, kettle on and you can tell me what on earth Ben has done to get you into such a rage. Ooh and you can try these throws out in the living room too." She added suddenly remembering why she had come round in the first place.

Shortly afterwards Katie and Cliona were ensconced in the kitchen, tucked up in the big sofas munching chocolate biscuits, sipping steaming hot coffee. Katie had also told Cliona the full story about Ben's behaviour the previous day. Cliona, however, could only see the funny side of it at present.

"Oh God, Lucy - she's a right a handful, always has been. I can't believe Ben fell for it again." She giggled as she wiped her eyes.

"You mean she's done this before?" Katie asked, interested in spite of her indignation.

"Oh yes" Cliona replied emphatically, "She was always disappearing off a couple of years ago. I think it was when the mother's latest beau came on the scene. Lucy kept being sent to stay with Ben - just to get her out of the way really and she just kept disappearing, turning up at home or at a friends. But, to be fair, she's been okay recently. I wonder what made her do it this time?" Cliona pondered.

"She probably wanted to get away from that bad tempered bloke. I wouldn't want to hang around with him glaring at me all evening." Katie grumbled.

"Come on, be fair Katie" Cliona remonstrated with her friend, "I know he was out of order, but he was worried sick. His fourteen year old sister was missing and he didn't have a clue what had happened. He was probably ringing the police in his head and assuming all sorts of terrible possibilities that he would feel responsible for."

"I suppose" Katie allowed grudgingly "but he could have let me get a word in edgeways!" she added.

"Ah, so that's the problem is it?" Cliona said knowingly, "He disappeared before you got to answer him back. Nevermind, you can give him a piece of your mind next time you see him" she teased.

"I most certainly will not." Katie replied indignantly "I won't speak to him until I've had a full and proper apology." Katie stuck out her chin in a determined fashion that Cliona was starting to recognise, it meant she had dug her heels in.

"Okay, Okay," Cliona held her hands up in mock surrender, "I'm not getting in the middle of someone else's fight. You can sort it out with Ben – or not as the case may be." Cliona shot Katie a sly look before changing the subject. She thought it was extremely interesting that they had both had such a strong reaction to the same situation, but she knew better than to voice this comment at the moment. Instead, keeping her thoughts strictly to herself, with a post script to share them with Declan later, Cliona dragged Katie into the living room to try out the throws.

Katie had to admit the throws worked really well in the living room as she surveyed the finished room at six o'clock that evening. When she had first seen the assortment of brightly coloured fabrics Cliona had brought she thought they would be a bit much in the Victorian room, but actually the splashes of colour against the magnolia walls picked out the more muted colours of Lucy's border and added a warmth to the room that had already been much increased by the new radiators. Ben had certainly got those right she had to admit, even if he had got everything since wrong. The room was laid out with chairs, flipcharts

175

and crockery, delivered as promised, by her new village friends and the food was all ready in the kitchen to be brought through at seven thirty when the meeting had been in session for an hour. Katie took one last look at the room and wandered back into the kitchen, deciding how to fill the next hour. As it turned out she needn't have worried, the next hour flew past as she opened the door and greeted committee members and calmed Hermione down, who was doing a fine impression of a headless chicken under pressure. Once most of the committee had arrived Katie slipped back into the kitchen and put a huge pot of water to boil on the range and filled the kettle, flicking the switch on and taking a good sized slurp of Chardonnay at the same time. Lastly she put a bottle of water and a jug of orange juice on a tray and returned the wine to the fridge, she had suggested having some wine to Hermione but she had nearly fainted at the idea.

"No, no, oh absolutely not, this is a working meeting. We want focus and ideas. It's not a social occasion" she had said, horrified. Personally Katie thought the ideas might be somewhat more interesting if they did pass round the Pinot Grigio and Merlot, but it wasn't to be.

Slipping into the back of the living room from the second door further down the hallway, which Katie had managed to unblock from clutter on both sides, Katie placed the drinks on the table which she had previously covered in one of Mo's beautiful cream lace cloths. Then, carefully, she brought through the food she had spent the afternoon preparing. They had settled on a selection of sandwiches, cakes and biscuits but Katie had added a large tureen of hot tomato and basil soup when the temperature had plummeted during the afternoon. She was still a bit worried about the room being cold and she hoped a big mug of soup would go some way to maintaining an acceptable body temperature for all the committee members. Lastly she had made a chocolate cake and a lemon cake, both light and fluffy, cut into pieces just large enough to feel indulgent without seeming greedy. Katie slipped back out again giving Cliona a wink as Hermione started to open the meeting and Cliona rolled her eyes back. There were many items on the agenda and Cliona knew only too well Hermione's tendency to go off at a tangent until they had all forgotten where they had started. Katie was booked to replenish drinks in an hour and a half, and Cliona was planning to have Hermy through at least ¾ of the agenda by then. Sighing as she thought enviously of Katie heading back to her big old sofa and Emmerdale, Cliona turned her attentions back to the meeting.

Katie was indeed ensconced on the sofa after helping herself to a bowl of soup and a large chunk of crusty bread as a tapping sounded at the back door. Knowing this could only be one person Katie dragged herself out of the sofa and let Mary in the door. Katie had realised soon after moving in that Mary, who was a genuinely lovely and caring soul, if a little bossy, especially to Ken, was also capable of talking at great length on any subject whether she actually had any knowledge about it at all. So Katie's heart sank slightly as Mary made herself comfortable in the armchair, this wasn't going to be a fleeting visit then!

"So Mary, how are you and Ken?" Katie enquired politely as she brewed a strong cup of tea for Mary and a slightly less scary one for herself. "Actually" Mary started "Ken's not so well at the moment, he's worn out and a bit off colour. I came round here to give him a bit of peace and quiet – sometimes I can go on a bit you know" Mary said without a hint of irony. Katie smiled to herself at such a marvellous piece of understatement.

"Has he seen the doctor?" Katie asked

"Oh no, not Ken, he doesn't hold with modern medicine. Plenty of rest, good food and some fresh air he thinks will cure anything. I suppose he's right really. Most of those medicines the doctors give you are just to make you think they're doing something aren't they? He'll be fine in a few days" Mary looked at Katie for reassurance. It seemed that perhaps Mary wasn't quite as convinced by Ken's cure as she was saying.

"Well, I'm sure seeing the doctor won't do any harm, but sometimes we all just need a bit of a rest and some TLC." Katie tried to be reassuring and Mary's anxious look passed as quickly as it had arrived.

"Of course, I don't know why I'm fussing. It's not like he's ever been ill in his life, so it must have worked so far. Anyway I came round because I wanted to give you these. Mo asked for them last time I popped in to see her" Mary waved a cluster of pamphlets that Katie took and quickly glanced through. They were an assortment of glossy brochures for various retirement homes around the area.

The Hawthorns - Residential Home for the elderly

Cheadle House - Independence with security and peace of mind

And the unfortunately named

Gilly Rock Bottom - First class care in a first class home

Katie was slightly thrown by this development, although Mo had mentioned some convalescence care after she was able to leave hospital, this seemed to suggest she was thinking about something more permanent. Katie couldn't really reconcile the lively and mischievous Mo with living in one of these places. To be fair they all looked more like four star hotels but they also all seem like the final stop on the bus route. Mary must have picked up the look of slight horror on Katie's face.

"I'm sure she's just having a look at what's available. Mo's got many years ahead of her yet."

"Oh yes I know, it just took me back for a minute. Maybe this accident has affected her a bit more than she's letting on" Katie said thoughtfully. But just as the mood was about to get melancholy Mary jumped to her feet, clapping her hands, causing Katie to drop all the glossy pamphlets on the hearth rug.

"Goodness me!" Mary exclaimed, "Is that the time? It's Eastenders in five minutes. I must be off. See you later dear." Mary was out of the door before she'd even finished the sentence. It was only the pamphlets scattered all over the floor that left any sign she had been there at all. Katie sighed and was just about to start picking them up when she realised it was nearly time for the second raft of refreshments.

"Shit" she said under her breath as she burnt her finger on the kettle as she rushed to prepare fresh pots of tea and coffee for the Spring Fayre Committee. Sneaking in the back Katie tried to be invisible as she placed the pots on the table. It seemed the meeting had been going quite well. Hermione was summing up;

"So we've covered all the points, we've agreed the number of stalls and each person running them. Lily's going to arrange the licence for the temporary bar through her own licence." Hermy smiled at a rotund lady in the corner. Presumably the landlord's wife, Katie thought. "And we've agreed on the entertainment for Friday and Saturday evening. Evelyn is kindly going to book them. We are going to ask the vicar and his wife to be the judges for the baking competition and the children's fancy dress. I think that covers everything – Yes?" Hermy looked around the group with enquiring eyes.

"Oh actually, there is one thing" Lily sprung forward from her seat, remarkably sprightly for a lady of her size, "we need someone to run the refreshments and we need somewhere to put them. We've always used our back room but, as you know, it's out of action."

"Oh my, how could I have forgotten" Hermione was horrified, whether it was more at her forgetting or the lack of sustenance for spring fayre visitors it wasn't clear. "Is there anybody interested in doing refreshments?" Hermy passed hopeful eyes across the group.

"I think we've all got our hands full Hermy" Cliona replied.

"Oh yes of course, do we know anyone? They need to be organised, available and a dab hand at catering." Hermione looked expectantly, as if awaiting an answer from on high.

"Well, I might" Cliona answered, with a huge grin on her face, "Why don't we ask Katie to do it?" Cliona turned and looked straight at Katie as she tried to back out of the room unobtrusively, clattering into the door handle with a startled yelp as Cliona looked at her. Feeling like a deer caught in the headlights, Katie thrashed about for a polite way to say no.

"Oh I don't know, I mean I've no experience of this sort of thing. I wouldn't want to make a mess of it."

"Nonsense" Cliona replied briskly, "hasn't she done a wonderful job tonight Hermy? - and the other week for the party?"

"Oh absolutely" Hermy agreed readily, "it's been wonderful. Would you do it Katie?" The whole group turned to look at Katie, pinning her to the wall with the varying degrees of pleading in their eyes.

"Probably to get themselves off the hook", Katie thought, and even as she was forming a polite but firm way to decline, Cliona, who was fast becoming her nemesis, jumped in.

"Of course she'll do it, you were only saying this morning you wanted something to focus on" Cliona looked the picture of innocence as she looked at Katie, then at the committee. They all started to murmur their assent and gratitude and Katie could see all her roads of escape disappearing swiftly. With a resigned sigh Katie said,

"Well, if you're sure you want me I'll give it a go." She managed to pull a face at Cliona as the others returned to their original positions now that the catering problem was solved. Cliona simply smiled and winked. Katie was just about to leave as Hermy said

"Well Katie, welcome to the Spring Fayre Committee, take a seat and we'll fill you in on the details." Katie knew she was beaten but as she sat down she gave Cliona a huge pinch on the arm causing her to jump into Evelyn who was sat next to her.

CHAPTER 13

The following day Katie recounted the full story much to Mo's amusement as she visited her in hospital. Mo let out a deep throated chuckle.

"Good for Cliona – it's about time you got involved in something. Take your mind off ….."

"Take my mind off what?" Katie countered defensively.

"Oh this and that, wallowing round the flat won't help – getting involved is just what you need, besides Katie K, you love baking and you love organising things. So you'll love it" Mo wasn't one to tactfully beat around a subject.

"Okay" Katie conceded "and it might help take my mind off these too!" Katie dumped the pamphlets Mary had given her the night before on Mo's bed. Setting them down like a gauntlet thrown. Katie raised her chin and waited for an answer.

"Oo great" Mo rubbed her hands together, "I wanted to get a look at these." Mo picked up the first glossy brochure and flicked through the pictures oh-ing and ahh-ing as she spotted dining rooms, cultivated gardens and other dazzling amenities. Katie was flabbergasted!

"You're actually interested in going to one of these places" she gasped "I can't believe you're looking at these seriously." Katie was actually quite upset at the thought now that it was a real possibility. Mo was her tower of strength, invincible, fearless, the thought that she was getting older and frailer was a scary proposition. Mo, sensing the unquiet in Katie, patted her hand gently and said

"Now don't look so worried, I'm not putting myself out to pasture just yet – although there's plenty who think I'm a bit of a cow." She added under her breath, making a slight nod towards a rather prim looking lady in the end bed. Katie smiled and relaxed a little just as Mo had intended and then continued

"I need somewhere to convalesce for the next month or two; my hip isn't going to be up to running up and down the stairs at Tolpuddle House or to tripping up the road to get what I want."

"But I'll look after you Mo. I can do whatever you want" Katie cut in.

"I know you would sweetheart" Mo answered, "but I don't want to have you running round after me like I'm some sort of invalid. Look at these places, they're like hotels. Bert says his home is like five stars, and it's not all institutionalised – you get your own space and freedom. Bert says I should take a look round his home, he says I'd love it."

"Hmmm, it seems like Bert says quite a lot" Katie said wryly, stealing a sly glance at Mo's animated face, "so which establishment is this paragon of luxury?"

"Cheadle House" Mo answered, waving the brochure in Katie's face, "and I need you to go and take a look at it for me" she added.

"Me" Katie said, taken aback, "why do you want me to look at it?"

"Oh you know just make sure it looks alright, make sure it's clean, no bodies in the basement, that sort of thing."

"Mo you want me to go snooping basically" Katie sighed

"Absolutely, I mean you wouldn't want your old gran ending up in some dodgy establishment now would you?" Mo pointed out very reasonably.

"Mo, I don't want you 'ending up' in any establishment, dodgy or otherwise" Katie countered with spirit, "but if you're determined to go through with this, then I guess I'd better go and take a look, see if they're up to looking after you. Although to be fair," she added, "I'm more worried for them than for you!"

Mo grinned,

"Oh yes, I'll keep them on their toes alright, isn't that right Bert?" she asked as Bert wandered up behind Katie.

"They won't know what's hit them, Maureen; you'll knock them off their feet - just like you did me." He said and winked conspiratorially at Mo. Katie was amused and a little taken aback to see a slight flush fill Mo's face as she smiled back at Bert. Mo had been alone for a lot of years now. Maybe a bit of companionship was just what she needed. As Katie pondered this, Mo signalled Bert to pull up a chair.

"Anyway that's enough about me - now tell me, apart from signing up for the spring fayre what else have you been up to? Have you seen anymore of Ben?" Mo poked, in a none too subtle way. Katie groaned and rolled her big brown eyes to the ceiling.

"Oh yes I've seen Mr Wilson, but hopefully I won't be seeing him for some time to come" she added.

Mo, knowing there was a story to come asked Bert to pass her a drink of orange, pretended to make herself more comfortable and then looked expectantly at Katie.

"Okay, okay" Katie conceded and proceeded to tell Mo and Bert about her recent confrontation with Ben and her indignation at not being able to get her own back. Mo listened and Katie could soon see her shoulders heaving as she tried, pretty unsuccessfully, to stop herself from laughing. As she wiped her eyes surreptitiously Katie stopped and demanded to know why everyone thought that this was so funny.

"Ben Wilson was totally out of order, unreasonable, unfair and rude – and I think you should all be on my side." Katie was aware she sounded like a seven year old again but she was getting fed up of no one rising to her defence.

"Oh Katie love, I'm always on your side, you know that." Mo sympathised, "but this isn't a proper argument. Poor old Ben had been run ragged by that precocious little sister of his and you got on the wrong end of it. I'm sure he didn't mean it."

Katie wasn't convinced, if that was case why hadn't he apologised. He obviously thought he was right she pointed out fairly reasonably.

"He probably feels a bit foolish" Bert chipped in "blokes don't like admitting we're in the wrong you know. He probably needs a bit of time to stop feeling so stupid."

"Yes and after all," Mo added "making up's no fun at all if you do it too quickly - it takes all the drama out of it. And let's face it making up's the best bit of an argument. Isn't that right Bert?" Bert took Mo's hand and brushed it with a light kiss.
"Of course my dear, I could have an argument with you just for the making up" he ribbed. Katie decided it was probably time to make a move, she was starting to feel decidedly green and hairy and she had never fitted into the 'gooseberry' role very well.

"Well, we'll see" she said as she rose to go, "but it's not really the same, Ben and I were just friends. It's not like there was anything going on between us." She added as she kissed Mo goodbye.

Under her breath Mo whispered "Oh I wouldn't say that" and as Katie looked back she could see Mo and Bert laughing at some private joke as she waved from the end of the ward.

CHAPTER 14

The weather continued fine and dry the next few days so Katie donned her gardening gear ready to do a few more hours in the fast disappearing wilderness at the front of the house. She had spent an hour every day since that initial burst after her argument with Ben and she had to admit she was starting to get a bit of order in the area. She had even started to plan how she might like it look when it was finished. Heading out of the front door Katie gulped as she took that first freezing cold breath into her lungs in the crisp winter morning. January had proved to be the best of the winter months so far, with plenty of very cold days, but they were bright with sunshine, filtering golden rays through the bare branches of the undressed trees. There had not been too many of the drizzle filled gloomy overcast ones that sunk your spirits to your boots. Katie only had one corner left to clear of weeds and brambles and after the first back breaking hour she had completed this with a fine array of scratches for her trouble. She had uncovered a beautiful paved area with sandstone paviers, which, if divested of the weeds and moss that were fighting an all-out war for supremacy over them, would look even better when offset by some terracotta pots with plants of unpronounceable names. Here Katie had to admit she was beaten, she certainly didn't have green fingers, not even a hint of a green fingernail and her knowledge of plants was woefully small. In addition she had a long-cultivated skill of killing almost every plant that had ever been given to her. In short, Katie was the sort of person who plastic plants were invented for. But with her new found determination, and a severe shortage of anything to do but cleaning, Katie decided to venture to the local garden centre and see if she could find someone who would take pity on her ignorance without making her feel like a complete idiot.

The Downdale Garden Centre was on the main route to Rawlinston and was one of the new style centres that, whilst continuing to sell plants, they had been relegated down the scale and replaced by a café/restaurant, an unusual gifts section, conservatory furniture and numerous toys and rides to try and encourage visiting kids to play with them instead of the petrol powered chain saw or amusing themselves by knocking the heads off garden ornaments. Katie pulled up in her car and for the first time realised her two-seater sports car with a shoe box for a boot might not be the most practical mode of transport for this particular outing. She parked up between a transit van that had seen much better (and more exciting) days and a designer pickup truck (i.e. not designed to do any actual work.) Smiling to herself, Katie noticed her car was actually invisible from every angle except when standing right behind it. Katie spied the outdoor plants area through the glass at the far end of the centre but it was far less easy to actually get there. After a number of aborted attempts that saw her appear unexpectedly in the aquatic section and then startle a couple trying out garden furniture as she appeared in the middle of the display apparently out of nowhere, Katie was about to give in and suffer the humiliation of asking one of the scruffy, spotty assistants who were clearly about ten years younger than her, where and indeed how she could get to the outdoor plants section when she suddenly spotted a familiar face examining what looked like some piece of medieval torture equipment masquerading as a garden implement. Katie almost ran towards him

"Mr Clackett," she cried "I can't tell you how happy I am to see you. Can you tell me how I actually get to the plants in this garden centre?" she added without any hint of sarcasm. After his initial surprise at being accosted by a pretty young woman whilst assessing the various pros and cons of secateurs Mr Clackett regained his composure and took pity on Katie's dilemma.

"Of course I can tell you my dear, but first you must call me Ken" he insisted and Katie smiled her agreement

"Absolutely - Ken" she laughed "now point me in the right direction and I'll get out of your hair."

"Oh I'll do one better than that, I'll take you there myself. It'll make a pleasant change to have someone who's interested in gardening. I'm afraid Mary finds it all a bit boring. She's not really happy unless there are plenty of people to gossip with. She finds the plants a bit short of stories." He winked at Katie as he spoke and she couldn't help sharing the joke with him. She knew only too well how Mary liked to talk! With no false starts Ken guided Katie out to the plant area and looked at her expectantly

"So where do you want to start, begonia semperflorens or some liniodendrumtulipifera?" Katie realised she hadn't fully thought this plan through as she had absolutely no idea what she wanted. Deciding that a full confession was the only alternative Katie threw herself on Ken's mercy.

"Well, Ken, I actually haven't got a clue what I want, I know absolutely nothing about plants or flowers - except how to order them from Interflora. So I might need your help for just a bit longer. How does that sound?" she asked with a winning smile.

"Ooh, excellent – now what are we buying for." Ken rubbed his hands together with glee. A project was just what he enjoyed. Katie explained how she wanted to transform the front garden at Tolpuddle House now that she had cleared it of the weeds, brambles and the assorted rubbish accumulated over the last five years. Ken didn't need any more information, he soon had them charging round the centre with one of the carts that went in every direction except the one he wanted and soon had it filled with pots, compost and plants with some wonderfully exotic and even slightly risqué names, even made Katie blush slightly. After forty five minutes of horticultural exploration Katie was all gardened out.

"Ken, can we have a break now – lets go grab a coffee before we try to purchase all these things" she flung her arm in the general direction of the cart overhanging with greenery "let me get you a bun or something it's the least I can do." Katie knew Ken had something of a sweet tooth and would find it difficult to resist and so it proved. In fact Ken had already removed his tweed cap and was heading towards the Victorian themed tea room. After purchasing the required drinks and a sticky fruit bun as promised Katie sat down and sipped the milky sweet latte and let herself relax after her morning's exertions. Ken chuckled to himself,

"You look just like you're Granddad used to when he took his first sip of Tetley's you know." Katie sat up and asked

"Did you know Gramps well?"

" Oh aye, we used to wander up to the Rose & Crown quite a lot, leave the women to gossip. We used to enjoy a pint and game of dominoes." Ken reminisced. "Alfie was a competitive old git when he got going, but a good mate, always on hand when you needed a bit of help."

Katie smiled as she recalled "Yes he was a bit competitive wasn't he - he always said I had to learn to lose, I don't think I ever learnt how to win! He even beat me at my Miss World game!"

Ken chuckled "Oh yes, Alfie liked to win alright. I remember him trying to take out half the pub when we lost the regional final of the Mid Yorkshire Walcott Cup. I had to escort him off the premises for his own safety. Still I think he would have lost to you with good grace." Ken added "You were the apple of his eye. He used to tell anyone who would listen, and a few who wouldn't, all about his wonderful grand-daughter, 'heart of a lion', 'brave as a soldier', 'bright as a button' and 'more beautiful than a princess' that was his little Katie. Now dear don't upset yourself." Ken patted her hand as he noticed the tears welled up in Katie's eyes, glistening in the harsh lighting of the café.

Katie gulped and tried to swallow the sizable lump that had formed in her throat as Ken talked on about the old days. After a while Katie felt herself lulled by Ken's deep Yorkshire burr and allowed his stories to slip past her as she drifted back to her childhood playing games with her Grandfather and them both being gently scolded by Mo. Raising from her reveries Katie checked her watch and realised they had been there reminiscing for over an hour, the stewed tea and congealed butter confirming this only too well.

"Oh Ken, I'm sorry, look at the time, I didn't mean to keep you so long." Katie started clearing up crockery and tried to balance it precariously on the faux wooden tray, noting to herself that no matter how easily things fitted on the tray when you bought them, the crockery and left-overs seemed to take on new and awkward proportions when you tried to put them back on to it. Breaking into her thoughts Ken said,

"Don't worry about me, dear. It's not like I've got a crucial meeting to get back for," he chuckled, "unless you count Mary's daily discussion on what to have for dinner - and even then I'm fairly surplus to requirements!" Katie smiled; the undisguised affection underlying Ken's words was clear and caused her a pang, like a snapping elastic band in her chest. Would she ever have a man who felt like that, and for that long about her? From Katie's experience men disappeared when the going got tough, look at Marcus! Even Ben hadn't been in touch since his appalling over reaction the other night.

"Don't worry" she whispered "I'll come in with you and take the heat." She heard Ken's chortle as he headed towards the exit. "Alfie always said you were a brave girl" he laughed.

Collecting their trolley, overloaded with pots, compost, plants, small shrubs, possibly even a small wild animal hiding in the undergrowth, they moved towards the checkouts. Katie suddenly came to an abrupt halt in the middle of the garden implements aisle, sending a rather portly lady behind her cannoning into her back and narrowly avoiding a fairly serious injury from the garden hoe she was examining. Tutting loudly and commenting on the inconsideration of young people these days the lady moved on, Katie didn't hear a word. A thought had just occurred to her that really should have registered before.

"Oh Ken," she wailed, "where am I going to put all this - my car fits two people and a shoebox in the boot. This isn't going to fit in. I can't believe I didn't realise before." Katie looked at Ken with a stricken face, Ken chuckled. Katie realised this was fast becoming Ken's trademark reaction, there didn't seem to be a problem, comment or situation that didn't make Ken chuckle, with a deep throaty laugh that suggested there really wasn't a problem at all. On this occasion, as it turned out, there wasn't.

"Look" he said "pointing to one of the bright orange signs hanging over the customer service desk in foot high letters

[FREE HOME DELIVERY FOR GOODS OVER £100]
(Within a five mile radius or a £10 charge) in much smaller possibly 2inch letters.

Twenty minutes later Katie had paid for her goods and arranged for them to be delivered the following day, (for the small additional charge of £10, due to Tolpuddle House being 5.2 miles from the store) and had seen Ken off in his 1991 Ford Fiesta which looked every bit as good as when it had been delivered. This made Katie feel slightly ashamed of her mud spattered, bird muck covered car that was precisely six months old. I really must call into a car wash, Katie reflected, although she hadn't seen one of those hand wash places that seemed to have sprung up all over the city. Katie preferred these to the petrol station car washes, not least as you got a free air freshener every time. Still there was no time for that now; Katie had another mission to fulfil just as she had promised Mo she would. Katie was on her way to visit Cheadle House, the residential and convalescence home Mo had selected from all the glossy brochures provided by Mary Clackett. It was not a trip Katie was looking forward too. Whilst being away in London Katie had quite successfully managed to forget about Mo's age or the fact that she wasn't as sprightly as she used to be. Now she was back here, there was absolutely no escaping the fact Katie was finding it hard to come to terms with. It's a harsh fact about growing up and older that those people who seemed invincible and indestructible get older too, and the roles of carer and 'cared for' gradually reverse. Katie still felt like a child in so many ways she wasn't sure she was ready to start looking after Mo just yet. Katie gave herself a mental shake as she turned the corner into Bluebell Lane searching for the entrance into Cheadle House. It wasn't difficult to spot. A low newly white washed wall with a huge laurel hedge above, immaculately cut with geometric proportions and leaves so bright and shiny it looked like each one had been personally polished with 'Pledge' and a duster. In front of the perfect hedge was a huge sign proclaiming 'Cheadle House, Retirement Complex and Care Home'. Turning sharply into the driveway Katie was reluctantly impressed with the surroundings. On her right was a semi-circle of about ten or twelve bungalows each slightly different from the next by a clever use of bay windows, roof lintels and door placements, to make each one seem individual. In front of them was an immaculately kept lawn, looking like a lush green carpet, and small garden pots which probably bloom into life in the spring. It was quite an idyllic setting Katie reflected. Even in winter there was still a tranquillity off-setting the bare branches of the surrounding trees and the dullness from the low clouds above.

Continuing up the drive Katie got the chance to see the main house that had previously been obscured by the bend in the drive and the planting of a row of beech trees. Gasping as she saw it, Katie realised this was nothing like the type of home she had been expecting. In her head she had pictured some Victorian style house, all dark soot stained stone, with dark heavy curtains and an unwelcoming air. Instead there was a beautiful Georgian mansion painted ivory and looking like it had been dropped there straight out of a Jane Austen novel. Katie could almost hear the horse and carriage crunching over the gravel and fully expected a bobbing maid in a floppy mop cap to open the door as she pulled the bell as indicated by a polite notice next to it. In fact a very smartly dressed lady in a tweed skirt and pale yellow twinset opened the door and, disappointingly, she showed no sign that she was likely to bob a curtsey at any time, but she did greet Katie with a smile that reached her pale grey eyes and illuminated her face and softened the edges of her angular jawline.

"Good morning, how can I help you?" she enquired in a deep velvet voice. Katie paused, she hadn't thought through how to introduce herself and suddenly thought, rather belatedly she had to admit, that maybe you didn't just tip up on the doorstep of a place like this, you probably had to make an appointment.

"Erm, well, I was wondering if I might be able to, erm, visit, to take a look at your home. My gran is in hospital and looking for a place to convalesce and she was particularly taken with Cheadle House, so I promised I'd come and take a look. But, of course, I should have made an appointment. It seems obvious now, but I was passing, if you could give me your number I'll ring you and ...." Katie babbled.
The smartly dressed, and now highly amused, lady held up her hand to break up Katie's stream of chatter.

"Of course you're welcome to come and take a look round. We have an open door policy for visits here. I'm Violet McCarthy, I'm the manager of Cheadle House – do come in" she added as she ushered Katie off the doorstep into the hallway.

"Now if you'd like to give me a few details about your grandmother and her requirements, I'll give you a tour round our little place and you can see if you think it would suit her." As Violet spoke Katie followed her through the hallway corridor painted in a beautiful pale primrose, almost an exact match for the twinset Violet was wearing. It gave the place a light and calm feeling, again very similar to Violet herself. As they walked, Katie filled Violet in on Mo's history and why she was looking for a place to stay.

"Obviously she'll be back at home once she's recovered" Katie continued, "but we just need to make sure she doesn't take on more than she can manage – not that that ever stopped her before." Violet smiled and replied in her deep soothing tones

"Well, of course, these sorts of accidents can be very frightening for all of us, especially when they make us realise we're not as young as we used to be." Katie nodded but added

"Oh Mo's as strong as an ox and she'll be back up and running in no time. I'm just looking after her place for her until she's back on her feet." Violet raised a quizzical, perfectly shaped eyebrow and just said

"Absolutely" in a non-committal tone.

"Here we are" she added "this is one of our convalescence bedrooms, as you can see it should have everything you, or should I say Mo, would need." Katie stood open mouthed , indeed it had everything a five star hotel room would have, large bed covered in a sumptuous duvet, TV, telephone – was that a network point?. As Violet showed Katie round the rest of the home it was clear it was all up to the same standard. Spotless kitchens with shining stainless steel units, TV lounges, activity rooms and from every window a different view of the wonderful gardens, hedges trimmed to perfection, gravel walks under vine strewn pergolas and even a small fountain in the centre of a circular patio, it could have been designed by 'Capability Brown' himself. Katie thought she could just imagine herself bumping into Mr Darcy with a fluttering in her breast.

"And this" Violet announced, breaking into Katie's thoughts, "is the dining room – as you can see we're having some work done at the moment to add a conservatory style extension onto the back so we have a bit more room. We're thinking about having tea dances once it's finished." She added. Katie looked across the room and it certainly looked big enough to host a fully blown ball let alone a tea dance. She was just imagining herself in the middle of a cotillion when a familiar face popped up beside her.

"Katie, how nice to see you."

"Bert" Katie answered warmly, "How are you? I didn't realise you were out of the hospital."

"Oh I'm fit as a fiddle now, but I'm missing Mo – things seem a bit dull without her around if you know what I mean," He winked mischievously at Katie. She smiled nervously at Violet McCarthy, she really didn't want Mo's reputation to precede her, they might not let Mo stay here and Katie wanted Mo's recuperation to be as painless and as quick as possible.

"Bert and Mo got on rather well in hospital, kept each other entertained" Katie explained as vaguely as possible. Bert guffawed at this understatement and Violet answered, her eyes sparkling with amusement.

"Ah, so your grandmother's Bert's Mo is she? Well, I've heard all about her, Bert's spoken about nothing else since his return. Poker tournaments, practical jokes and even a protest organised about the food wasn't there?" she asked Bert.

"Oh aye" he answered, smiling at the memory. Katie's heart sank; trust Mo to be branded a troublemaker before she'd even set foot in the place. Katie thought she ought to try and minimise the damage if there was to be any chance of Mo staying here.

"Oh it was just high spirits really. Mo didn't like being confined to a bed; once she's up and about she'll be as good as gold." Katie assured Violet, ignoring Bert as he rolled his eyes in a manner that suggested he didn't fully agree with Katie's assessment.

"Oh I do hope not" Violet replied

"Erm, sorry" Katie answered, assuming she had misheard

"I said, I do hope not – it's about time we had someone to liven things up a bit. I am really looking forward to meeting Mo. We like to have people here with a bit of life about them," Violet grinned, "after all this is a place where people come to live – not wait to die!" she added emphatically.

207

"Oh my goodness is that the time? I'm terribly sorry I have to place the fresh food order. Please feel free to look around the gardens. You can get there through here" Violet pointed to a new door in the conservatory and with a quick shake of the hand and an assurance there was a room for Mo if she wanted it, Violet disappeared, clicking quickly over the laminated floor in her stylish black shoes. Katie said her goodbyes to Bert who was disappearing to watch a poker tournament on the internet and decided she may as well walk back through the garden. The heavy grey clouds of earlier had started to lift a little and a few piercing shafts of sunlight were striking through, giving the garden a look of a photograph negative with bright points dazzling and darker areas almost invisible.

Passing through the door to the garden Katie noticed the van of the builders who were busily working at the far side of the conservatory. 'BW Building' it proclaimed along its side. "Oh no" Katie thought, she really didn't want to bump into Ben again and have round two of the fight, when she didn't really know why they were fighting, but her curiosity got the better of her and as she couldn't hear any workmanlike sounds of rustling newspapers, burping or scratching emanating from the van, she decided to take a closer look at the plans she could see strewn on the front passenger seat. Poking her head through the open window Katie squinted at the plans as she tried to make sense of what they depicted, realising that they could well be upside down for all she knew Katie was about to remove her head from the van when she became aware of another head that popped in from the driver's side window.

"Hello" it said "Can I help?"

"Oh my God" Katie tried to stand up straight, forgetting her head was through the window of a Ford van and promptly banged her head on the roof of it. "Ow – oh bugger, sorry, ow!" she cried as she did it again as she finally managed to extricate her head, generally in one piece, from the window.

"Um, hello, "she started "I was just taking a look at the plans for this place. My grandmother is coming here shortly and I wanted to make sure the development was suitable." She added in a haughty tone, somewhat offset by the wild sprig of hair stuck out from the top of her head from her tussle to get out of the window.

"I see" said the man, who had also removed himself from the driver's window and was staring at Katie over the cab with much amusement in his eyes, "and were they satisfactory?" he added in lilting Geordie tones and the hint of a smile.

"Oh, absolutely," Katie said "it looks like a very sound development. I'm sure it will add great value to the house." She finished with her best efforts to sound knowledgeable.

"Aye pet, you might be right, but I don't think they'll be much call for a bar area and nightclub here – although they are a lively bunch so you never know." He added calmly, looking her directly in the eye.

"Oh" Katie said as she couldn't think of anything else to say, and then laughing added "Busted – I was just being nosy, those plans could've been in double Dutch for all I know. In fact they probably are aren't they?"

"Not quite, but they're not for here. I'm costing up another job in my breaks as we've got a tight deadline. I'm John Buddle, by the way, the site manager and I can tell you this is a good home. I'm sure your grandmother will be okay here – and our work will be first rate!"

"Katie Collins" Katie said offering her hand to John over the top of the van, "actually I know someone who works for your company, Ben Wilson, do you know him?" she added, still a little worried that he might appear at any moment and start randomly shouting at her again.

"Oh yes" grinned John "I work with Ben quite a lot, it's not such a big firm at the moment but we aim to be. He's not on this job at the moment though."

"Oh" Katie responded, partly relieved and, strangely, partly disappointed too, though she couldn't really decide why. "Well I won't keep you, sorry for being nosy, but as Mo, my grandmother, always said I couldn't leave a box unopened even when it quite clearly said what was in it. I guess I haven't grown out of it!" John smiled and gave a quick wave and a wink as she set off round the gardens and back to her car. Really, she thought to herself, why had she babbled on like that? He must think she was a complete nutter.

CHAPTER 15

Katie asked Cliona much the same question the following evening when she went round, ostensibly to discuss the plan for the refreshments tent for the spring fayre. However so far they had drunk a large glass of chardonnay each and Katie had regaled Cliona with her adventures of the previous couple of days and they had as yet failed to even touch on the fayre.

"So you haven't heard from Ben yet? Cliona asked

"No, I don't expect I will" Katie snorted, "and even if I do, I won't be speaking to him" she added huffily.

"Well, maybe it's just as well, I mean, if you're pilfering blue prints for jobs, he'll probably accuse you of being a spy. I think its best you keep out of each other's way." Cliona said, keeping half an eye on Katie as she did so. Katie's face fell slightly and then she put on a nonchalant air.

"Yes, well, it won't make any difference to me either way. I don't care what Ben Wilson gets up to."

Cliona kept her own counsel!

"So let's get down to planning these refreshments then" Cliona said, changing the subject, "now I think we should break it down into morning, lunch, afternoon teas and evening. If we do menus for each day and then we can work out the staffing rota and the equipment hire. How does that sound?" Cliona asked, "Katie, are you okay?" she added in concern as she saw the horror in Katie's mahogany eyes.

"What is it Katie?" Cliona asked again

"Morning, lunch, tea and evening - for THREE days!" Katie spoke very slowly.

"Yes" Cliona confirmed "plus drinks and snacks all day. Why?"

"How am I supposed to do all that? I thought I was throwing a few sandwiches together and slopping tea and coffee in cups. I didn't know I was expected to be a one woman catering business" Katie replied indignantly, "I can't do all that."

"Of course you can" Cliona responded bracingly "it's all in the planning - just make things as simple as possible. You know, like quiche and salads for lunch, you can plate up, keep some frozen and cut smaller slices and put more lettuce on if you start running out. Come on Katie, I've seen you in action, you can do this - with a little help from your friends."

Katie looked at Cliona, somewhat sceptically but somehow her optimistic view was starting to rub off and she found she was actually starting to find the idea quite exciting. She grabbed the pad and pencil in front of her and soon she and Cliona were throwing ideas around. After an hour, and a bottle and a half of Chardonnay, they had agreed the menus for each day and had a list of all the equipment they would have to get into the marquee on the green. Katie looked at the list and groaned dramatically,

"How am I going to do all this?" she asked "if this is a disaster I'm blaming you entirely" she added, wagging a finger at Cliona.

"You'll be fine" Cliona responded, pushing her increasingly wild hair out of her face, "you can make most of that before the fayre anyway. Dec will let you use his kitchen and there's a spare freezer there for you to put it all in. That'll be fine won't it darling?" she asked as Declan came into the dining room and placed a pile of sandwiches and crisps in front of Cliona and Katie, who pounced on them as if she hadn't eaten for days.

"What'll be fine?" he asked as he grabbed a prawn sandwich for himself before they all disappeared.

"Katie can use our spare freezer to keep the fayre food in after she's cooked it in your kitchen - at the restaurant." Cliona said, through a mouthful of York ham and mustard, smiling winningly at him.

"Absolutely fine, my tipsy love" he said, ruffling her hair as he spoke in a fond gesture. Katie sighed loudly as she watched.

"I wish someone wanted to ruffle my hair" she said with longing, "the men that I like want to ruffle their wives hair - not mine" she added forlornly, biting into her third sandwich, "I think men don't want girls like me!" Cliona and Declan looked at Katie with her mane of wavy auburn hair, her expressive amber flecked eyes and pouting mouth, and then looked at each other and burst out laughing.

215

"Oh yes, go on, laugh at me. Not only am I unattractive to men. I'm a source of amusement to my friends." Katie moaned.

"Friends are exactly what you need at the moment." Cliona announced, "What does a girl need a man for when she has her friends" she added whilst giving Declan a reassuring pat on the knee in case he felt threatened by this statement. Generally he merely seemed amused by his partner's and friend's rambling.

"Who needs a man" Cliona shouted again, "not you" she added quickly when Katie looked like she might well answer in the positive, "I know how to cheer you up – we're having a dinner party next Friday with some of our friends, you should come. It'll be good fun!"

"Will they all be couples?" Katie asked ominously

"No, no, they'll be a mixture, some of my friends, some of Declan's" Cliona answered

"Yes" Declan interjected "you'll know some of them and of course B......"

"Bob and Marge will be there too" Cliona cut in, shrugging her shoulders as Declan mouthed 'Bob and Marge' questioningly at her. Katie seemed satisfied with this and accepted the invitation but as her eyelids were starting to droop she decided it might be time to start making a move home and unsteadily got to her feet and set off in search of her coat.

"I hope you know what you're doing" Declan said to Cliona "you know Ben's coming and if they're still not speaking to each other I don't think it'll add to the evening."

"Oh no, it'll be fine. They just need their heads banging together ever so slightly." Cliona said breezily.

"And I'm guessing you're the woman to do it." Declan answered with amusement "well, don't blame me if more of the dinner lands on the walls than on the plates."

"Don't I always know best?" Cliona whispered and dropped a kiss on Declan's head, "now" she added more loudly "Dec, be a love and walk Katie home as I think she may end up in the gutter without assistance." Declan turned to see Katie sprawled head first over the arm of the chair she had just walked into, giggling gently to herself. Declan decided Cliona might be right, Katie was just the sort of friend Ben needed to drag him out of himself but he still had some reservations about effecting a peace accord in their dining room. Rising to his feet he headed towards the front door hoisting Katie up on the way, it was certainly true, he reflected, life with Cliona had never been boring!

CHAPTER 16

The following Friday as Katie was getting ready for Cliona's dinner party, she was beginning to wonder why she had agreed to attend such an evening. She had always had a phobia about such events; it came of not being part of an (acknowledged) couple. Katie found she spent most of these evenings avoiding a wet looking eager bloke that her hosts had somehow (possibly out of desperation or a sick sense of humour) picked out as an ideal partner for her. A fact they had usually shared with the rest of the group; which meant that Katie was, for the rest of the evening, feeling like the main participant in some social experiment as the others kept notes behind raised palms. Or if no suitable 'sad and lonely' could be found, then Katie spent the evening as the object of everyone's pity, being given pithy but inspirational words of wisdom from around the table. Like a condemned woman Katie trudged up the road at eight fifteen as instructed, clutching her bottle of Pinot Grigio like a drowning man to a rope. Only two hours to survive before she could make her escape, and there would be some wonderful food to eat in that time. Declan was a masterful cook without a shadow of a doubt. With this thought cheering her up slightly Katie knocked on Cliona's door with more bravura than she would have thought possible half an hour ago.

Cliona swung open the door, in a rainbow of materials that on anyone else would have looked ridiculous but on Cliona simply looked wild and interesting,

"Hello Katie, come in, we were wondering if you were going to show." She said in an overly loud voice to the adjoining room.

"You told me to come at eight fifteen" Katie said indignantly. Cliona smiled conspiratorially, "I know I did" she whispered, "I wanted you to make an entrance." Cliona grabbed Katie's arm as she tried to make a bolt for the front door.

"Everybody, Katie's here" she announced in a theatrical voice, dragging Katie into the living room, so that all the conversation stopped as everybody turned to examine the new guest, " Katie has been looking after Tolpuddle House for Mo, whilst she's been in hospital, she's single and between jobs at the moment" Cliona added. Katie looked for the hole that was due to open up now so she could jump in before she died of embarrassment. No such luck arrived for her, and as Katie looked around there was still at least eight pairs of eyes turned her way. Katie smiled, pinching Cliona's arm making her jump, "Hello, it's so nice to be here and ….." Katie tailed off as her eyes rested on Ben in the corner and then snapped back to Cliona, whom she grabbed by the sleeve and dragged back to the doorway.

"Cliona" Katie hissed "you never told me Ben was coming – I wouldn't have come if I'd known" Katie felt the colour rise from her neck and flood her face. Ben had turned away and was whispering something to Declan – probably along similar lines to what she had just said to Cliona, which at least made Katie feel marginally better to think that Ben was as uncomfortable as she was.

"I did – I'm sure I did" Cliona answered breezily, "Declan asked him weeks ago" she added for good measure.

"You most certainly did not or I wouldn't have agreed to come" Katie answered out of the side of her mouth, "and I may not be staying now!"

"Oh come on, don't be so dramatic" said Cliona, with a touch of the kettle calling the pot very dark indeed, "There are loads of people here – you won't even have to speak to him if you don't want to." Katie accepted defeat gracefully, after all she was not going to make a show of herself by turning round and walking out – nor would she give Ben Wilson the satisfaction of thinking he'd won. Although judging by the way Declan was covering the back exit it was entirely possible Ben was having exactly the same idea as her.

Putting on her brightest PA smile, Katie moved to the first group of people and was soon introduced to Jenny & Mike and Lulu & Simon and spent the half hour before dinner chatting politely about Mike's farm and Lulu's handmade card business, all the time conscious of Ben talking animatedly to the other couple she later found out were called John & Sue, Sue was Declan's front of house manager who was currently on maternity leave.

When Cliona called them all to the table Katie soon realised Cliona's earlier declaration that she wouldn't have to speak to Ben was not strictly true as Cliona had seated them next to each other, and, as she had cleverly manoeuvred everyone else to their seats first there was no alternative but to sit down next to each other with an attempt at good grace. Katie glowered at Cliona as she placed the bread baskets on the table and Cliona smiled sweetly back, safe in the knowledge that Katie wouldn't really hurl the bowl of butternut squash soup at her - despite the huge appeal of the idea!

Katie studiously broke up her seeded wholemeal bread roll and proceeded to spread butter on it with military precision, consciously avoiding any glances to her left where Ben was involved in a similar process.

"So, Katie" a voice boomed next to her, causing her to drop the piece of bread she had so meticulously buttered, "Not married yet, and how old are you? Over 30?" Simon's voice carried right round the table. Katie jumped as she hadn't really heard him speak until now.

"Oh, no, not married at the moment" she confirmed. Simon waited expectantly; he had asked another question after all! Katie ate a spoonful of soup and a crust of the roll but Simon was still eyeing her and now Lulu joined in.

"I'm 29" Katie mumbled, waiting for the conversation to move on, but she wasn't to be that lucky.

"So not quite 30 yet, but the clock's ticking eh? Got your sights set on anyone? After all you don't want to get left on the shelf do you?" Simon laughed heartily at his own joke. Katie smiled politely wondering what time machine Simon had found to enable him to make his appearance from the 1950's.

"Well obviously it would be lovely to get married to the right man, but better single than with the wrong one" Katie managed to reply.

"Hmmm, yes I see" Simon pondered this information, "So no-one's asked you yet then – Nevermind, someone's bound to eventually!" With this he returned to slurping his soup as Katie felt the colour rise through her cheeks, forgetting who she was sat next to, she quickly turned away from Simon so that she didn't have to talk about children and her ticking clock too. She found herself looking directly into the clear blue eyes of Ben, who was doing a poor job at repressing a smile.

"You had better not be laughing at me" she informed him in the haughtiest voice she could muster. Ben shook his head, not trusting himself to reply at first.

"No, no" he finally said "I'm sure you've been asked to get married lots of times" he added with a dead pan face. Katie took a deep breath intending to be very offended but the absurdity of the whole conversation struck her and she burst out laughing instead.

"Well actually for your information, no, I've never been asked, unless you count Jeremy Pitman when I was seven" she giggled, Ben laughed with her

"If he was serious I don't see why you shouldn't count it?" Ben's cleared his throat and he became more serious "Katie, I'm so sorry about before - behaving like a total prat. I know it wasn't your fault that Lucy was at Tolpuddle and I didn't know she was. I was just terrified by the time I got to you. I had no idea where she was. I wanted to ball her out but I was convinced she'd disappear again so I balled you out instead. I'm so sorry."

Katie thought for a moment, "Lucy was fine with me you know. I'd never let her do anything stupid."

"I know, I know, I'm an idiot. I knew it the next day but I'm not great at apologising" he added ruefully.

"Show me a bloke who is" Katie said, "But to be fair, you did ok there. Let's forget about it, if for no other reason than to stop me having to have another conversation with Victorian Simon here on my right." She added in a whisper. Ben was only too happy to agree and soon they were chatting and laughing as they always had. Cliona allowed herself a triumphant wink and dig in the ribs to Declan who grinned back. The evening passed without further event, even Victorian Simon relaxed a little enough to loosen the top of his tie. Katie giggled as she stage whispered the news to Ben. They had demolished about 3 bottles of Declan's superb Merlot between the two of them and despite a couple of espresso's Katie knew she was certainly two sheets to the wind if not quite three and decided that as the other guests were starting to drift off that it was time for her to take her leave too. As she wobbled towards the door Ben jumped up and offered to walk her back home, Katie made a half-hearted attempt to decline but she actually welcomed the company on the way home, she was going to need someone to lean on and Ben fitted the bill perfectly.

Katie and Ben set off down the road in a rather haphazard manner. Declan and Cliona watched them to the bend and heard Katie's giggle as she slipped off the kerb into the road dragging Ben with her, who was doing a rather ineffectual job at steadying her. By the time they reached Tolpuddle House they were both in the throes of uncontrollable laughter, Katie due to the large amount of Chardonnay she had consumed, Ben due to Katie's drunken antics, and a soaring of his spirits that came from being with her.

After successfully opening the door on the third attempt Katie turned and saw Ben standing on the doorstep, looking uncertain. He wasn't sure if the reconstructed friendship of the evening extended to actually coming into her house and clearly didn't want to presume anything. Katie's heart went out to him; he really was a sweetie when it came down to it.

"Aren't you coming in for a coffee? I know I've maybe had a glass of wine too many but I think I'm capable of boiling a kettle" she asked. Ben smiled and raised an eyebrow replying

"Well, I'd love a coffee but I think you might need a bit of supervision to make sure you put coffee in the cup and not the gravy granules." He winked as he walked past her into the hallway. Katie maintained a dignified silence and then caught Ben off guard with a good natured pat to the cheek instead. For a second their eyes met and it seemed to Katie that a tiny spark passed from one to the other but as Ben turned into the flat Katie thought she must have imagined it – another effect of the 'one glass too many'.

Katie's suspicion was confirmed as she followed Ben into the kitchen and he took up a seat at the kitchen table, surely if he'd had designs on her he'd have opted for the sagging sofa, whose over-worked springs would surely have brought them together. Feeling vaguely disappointed, though she couldn't understand why, Katie threw her coat and keys on the armchair and set about making the promised coffee, all the time chastising herself for inappropriate romantic inclinations simply because Ben had been nice to her. After all he really wasn't her type, she preferred the dark, handsome, thrusting successful man, not the sandy haired boy next door with a twinkle in his china blue eyes. Realising she hadn't spoken in a while and fearing Ben may have nodded off with his head on the table Katie turned round saying brightly

"So how is Lucy? Have you forgiven her yet or is she locked up in a tower somewhere until she turns eighteen?" she teased. Ben started, clearly he had been on the way to falling asleep she mused, and her question had startled him out of it.

"Oh, if I locked her in a tower it'd be until she was at least 35 and even then I'd only let her out for an hour at a time - unfortunately the namby-pamby laws of this country won't let me. So she's still grounded until Monday but she is talking to me again - although that's not always a good thing!" he added, grinning.

"Well bring her round when she's a free girl again. I know Poppy would like to see her - and me too. You know, if you don't mind, if that's okay?" Katie spoke hesitantly; remembering last time Lucy had been round and not wanting to trample all over their newly formed peace.

"Of course I will" Ben replied, pulling his hand through his hair in agitation, "Katie, I meant it when I said I was sorry. I was a total idiot; I don't know what came over me. I know Lucy's fine when she's round here - honestly" a worried crease lined his brow as he strived to persuade her so that Katie found her hand was itching to smooth it away. Choosing to ignore this impulse she quickly turned and started banging cups onto the counter, opening and shutting cupboards as she made the coffee. Handing a mug over to Ben she asked
"I don't suppose you want a biscuit after all that food at Cliona's?"
Ben looked at her sheepishly,

"I could manage one if there's one on offer" he said, Katie rolled her eyes at him.

"Why is it blokes can eat as much as they want whenever they want and girls put on half a stone just looking at a chocolate digestive" she moaned

"Well I'm a fit active man who needs plenty of fuel to keep going - I burn off all those calories in no time - maybe you should take up a sport or something?" he teased, as Katie absent-mindedly picked up and nibbled one of the digestive biscuits.

"A moment on the lips - a lifetime on the hips" he added for good measure with a twinkle in his eyes. Katie decided not to let that one pass and picking up the tea towel from the range she aimed a perfect flick on Ben's left arm.

"Ouch" he screeched, rubbing his arm where the offending towel had caught him, "you're gonna pay for that you know" he threatened, rising purposefully to his feet. Katie sought refuge round the other side of the table and aimed another flick at Ben's right arm.

"You see" she goaded; "we're all good at different things" Ben was already half way round the table as Katie tried to escape.

"Not so fast, Katie Crabsticks!" he shouted, as he caught Katie by the arms and swung her against the wall by the door, so she had no means of escape.
"You see" he continued "if you'd taken up sports sooner you might have got away – now where's that towel?" he growled in an attempt to be menacing. Katie giggled.

"I don't know why you're laughing" he said indignantly, "you're about to pay the price for your foolishness." He started to sound like the villain from a bad Victorian melodrama. This just made Katie giggle even more as she held the towel behind back and Ben tried to wrestle it free. Suddenly the absurdity of the situation hit Ben too, so that he and Katie were collapsed in fits of giggles against each other, tears running down Katie's face as she tried to catch her breath. Without stopping to think, Ben gently wiped the tears away from her cheek with his thumb. The desire to laugh left Katie abruptly and she caught her breath as a slow fluttering started in her stomach. She could still feel Ben's touch on her face even though his fingers were now gently twisting a strand of her curled auburn hair, studying it with an intense fascination. The silence, heavy with anticipation, filled the room only broken by the loud thuds of the clock on the mantelpiece. At least Katie thought it was the clock, it could have been her heart thumping in her chest. Raising her eyes she could see Ben had stopped examining her hair and was searching her face with his honest, earnest blue eyes, as if for a sign. She could see the desire and the uncertainty etched in his expression. She slowly raised her face to his and smiled. Ben needed no further encouragement and wound his fingers into her hair and tilted her face to his, kissing her with a force, and an expertise, she hadn't anticipated. Katie stopped thinking altogether then.

Several blissful seconds later there was an enormous bang as someone came into the house and shut the door with superhero strength. Ben and Katie jumped apart guiltily, the moment broken. Feeling awkward and uncertain as to what to do next Katie turned to the table and grabbed the coffee she had made earlier, trying to drink it in a nonchalant manner, hoping that Ben would follow her to the sagging sofa. Ben, however, seemed rooted the spot and appeared to be wrestling with some thought or other in his head, trying to help it escape by vigorously ruffling his hair distractedly with his hand.

"Sooo.." he breathed out eventually, "I guess it's getting late you were probably wanting to get to bed an hour ago." He continued, adding quickly "on your own, I mean, not with me or anyone – just you." He added for emphasis.

Katie decided dignity was her only option at this point, that, and to get Ben out of the flat as quickly as humanly possibly so she could die of embarrassment in solitude.

Effecting a yawn she said, "Actually I am rather tired, heavy day tomorrow, gardening, shopping, that sort of thing. It was good of you to walk me home." She added formally, holding open the door as she spoke. Ben needed no further sign and left, shuffling out like a guilty teenager.

Katie shut the door behind and leaned against it allowing the shame and humiliation to wash over her. How could she have behaved like a fifteen year old after their first bottle of cider, flicking towels, play fighting and snogging? No wonder Ben couldn't get out of here fast enough, first she tells him what a wanton harlot she was having an affair with a married man and then she practically jumps on him the first time she's alone with him. No this wouldn't do Katie told herself sternly, it was about time she decided to live her life on her own terms and not on those of the men around her. Starting tomorrow she would be a man free zone (romantically at least!) She would show Ben that he didn't have to worry about being pounced on by the local man-eater, she would turn into the friend/mate that he clearly thought she was.

CHAPTER 17

Ben woke the next morning with a groggy, vaguely pounding head and a nagging sense of disappointment in the pit of his stomach that he couldn't quite put his finger on. Rubbing his eyes to try and clear the fog in them and his brain, he padded into the kitchen and starting filling the coffee machine with the uber strength ground beans.

"You look like shit" Lucy's clear tone startled him into spilling half the coffee onto the counter.

"Shit" Ben growled "Where did you come from? You shouldn't spring out on people first thing in the morning? And you don't swear either – it's bad, very bad."

"I didn't spring out of nowhere, I was sitting here having my Cheerio's" Lucy replied indignantly, "and you swore too." She added for good measure.

"I'm allowed – I'm a grown up." Ben argued, in a reasoned manner, "now go away and let me wake up in peace." He started to shoo her away through the doorway.

"Jeez, bad mood much!" Lucy grumbled, "Who put you in such a strop?"

Ben's stomach lurched and that nagging sense of disappointment solidified into a ball of shame. Katie! He had been thrown out by Katie after way overstepping the mark. What had he been thinking of? The poor girl was three sheets to the wind, and they had only just started speaking again and he had decided the best way to move forward was to jump on her at the first opportunity. No wonder the poor girl had run to the sofa for safety. Ben groaned inwardly as he remembered – what a git he'd been. Katie needed a friend, she'd told him as much and he'd taken that as an invitation to pounce. Well, he'd learnt his lesson, from now on he was going to be exactly that, a friend, he'd make sure that Katie knew she could trust him and rely on him. Having taken this decision Ben pushed to the back of his mind how much he had enjoyed kissing her and resolved to focus on friendship – and work. There was much to be done now they had secured the Southampton site. Stewart had rung with the news earlier in the week to say the council had decided to let BW buy the site and redevelop as planned. Suddenly the dream had become a reality and Ben was going to leave no stone unturned to make it a success.

Ben slurped his freshly brewed coffee, wincing as he burnt the top of his mouth in his hurry to get the caffeine into his body. On mornings like this it really should be done intravenously he pondered grimly, and set about buttering a piece of toast to try and settle the churnings in his stomach. As the sleep receded further, clearing the fog on his brain, Ben realised the cement mixer effect wasn't only due to the copious amounts of wine he had drunk the night before. Today was a momentous date in the history of BW Building. Today Charlie and John joined forces with him to become part of the business and they signed the contract for the Southampton project. It was all going to become reality. Ben was monumentally pumped up and terrified at the same time. He could feel the tingling of anticipation running up and down his arms. Deciding that both his hangover and his first steps to multi-millionairedom required a fairly vigorous shower to blast the last of the sleep out of his system Ben sauntered into the bathroom, casually throwing Lucy out as he got there. She was not pleased.

Two hours later Ben was, as his grandmother would have said, 'scrubbed up, dressed up and thumbs up!' and feeling on top of the world, or at least much closer to the summit than previously. He spent the whole of his bike ride to the office planning the first Bentley he would buy, the swanky resorts he'd visit and designing the penthouse suite he would soon be moving into, fortunately, it being a Saturday meant the roads were a lot clearer than during the week so his slightly erratic progress didn't end up in an accident. Not even Jean's disapproving stare as he slapped her fairly ample backside could dampen his spirits, although he still had the presence of mind to duck as her right hand snaked out to catch him a small cuff on the side of his head.

"Jean, you are, as I have always said, a beautiful, ample bosomed, fine figure of a woman – would you like a cup of our finest coffee?" he winked at her, and turned away laughing as Jean harrumphed loudly.

The door clattered open and Charlie and John rolled in wearing three piece suits and carrying the largest cigars Ben had ever seen, they were more like small cucumbers in fact.
"We are now men of substance, business owners – we have left the working classes!" Charlie drawled in his interpretation of a high powered entrepreneur.
"Ha, it's more likely you've just joined the hardest working class" Ben responded with a smile, "Let's face it, if we buy the Southampton site we'll all be on twelve hour days!"

Charlie groaned, "Ben, let me have my moment, mate - my dad said I'd never amount to much, let me enjoy being a tycoon for at least 10 minutes."

"Sorry mate, but first rule of tycoondom is realism, and your dad never said such a thing!" Ben answered, "But seriously this is a big day and I can't think of two people I'd rather share it with more." He raised his big mug of coffee "to BW Building and its first million!"

They all responded, even Jean allowed herself a small indulgent smile, as proud as any mother would have been.

As Ben got home in the evening he was still as excited as he had been that morning. The day had passed in a whirlwind, they had signed the partnership agreement at the solicitors and then all three of them had signed the documents for their first project, the Southampton site. It had been a scary and simultaneously exhilarating moment, now they had about eight weeks for it all to complete before they could get on site properly but that wouldn't stop them getting things underway. Stewart had already been down to the site and started on his designs.

"You're looking pleased with yourself. What's happened?" Lucy had appeared out of her room, blowing on her fingernails which had been painted half pink and half green.

"I am pleased with myself" Ben shouted, lifting Lucy up and swinging her round, "I've had a great day –come on put you're glad rags on and let's go celebrate"

"You're a nutter" Lucy squealed, but she didn't need asking twice. It wasn't often Ben was offering to take her out! In less than twenty minutes she was dressed and ready to go. This had to be something of a world record for Lucy but she hadn't wanted to risk Ben changing his mind and going without her.

"Ready, titch" Ben asked, "come on then, I thought we'd go via Laxley Health and see if Poppy and Katie want to join us – what d'ya think?"

Lucy nodded, but added "I thought you and Katie weren't speaking after I, after, er, after, you know" she stuttered.

"No we've sorted that out now and we're all friends again" Ben reassured her, however he did feel a bit disappointed they weren't going to be more than that, but after last night's deeply embarrassing overstepping of the mark he had decided it was best to face Katie sooner rather than later and show what a great mate he was going to be – and nothing more. And anyway he couldn't think of anyone he'd rather celebrate with than his infuriating sister and the equally infuriating Katie Crabsticks!

CHAPTER 18

Katie had just put the phone down from talking to Mo when Ben and Lucy arrived with their invitation and she was in need of something to take her mind off the call. Mo had just told her she would be leaving hospital the following Wednesday and she was going straight to Cheadle House to start her convalescence, and although Katie had known for some time she was going to do this – the reality was still disturbing. She wanted nothing but the best for Mo and she knew that Cheadle House was exactly that but the little girl inside her just wanted Mo to come home and didn't want to be reminded that Mo was getting older. So an invitation to the pub for a meal and celebratory drink was just what she needed, so much so that Katie completely forgot to feel awkward about the last time she had seen Ben and when she did remember as they passed Cliona's house on the way to the Rose & Crown, Ben was being like his old self, excited and talking ten to the dozen about his new project, there didn't seem any reason to be awkward.

"You're quiet Katie" Ben's voice cut into her thoughts, "Is everything ok? It wasn't bad news on the phone was it?"

"Oh no, not really, good, really I suppose – Mo's coming out of hospital this week and going into Cheadle House" unconsciously Katie sighed as she said it.

"And you're wishing she was coming to Tolpuddle instead" Ben answered perceptively

"Yes, I know she needs to convalesce and Cheadle House will look after her really well but Tolpuddle isn't the same without her clattering about and ticking me off" Katie smiled.

"I'll second that" said Poppy, "not that you're not a good replacement, Katie, and to be honest your oat cookies are slightly better than Mo's – but don't ever tell her I said that - and if you do, I'll totally deny it." She added for good measure.

"She wouldn't believe me anyway" Katie laughed, "I don't know why I'm bothered she's going to lead them a merry dance over there, her and Bert. In fact she's asked me to take the karaoke machine amongst all the paraphernalia she wants – don't ask" she added as Ben raised an eyebrow, as if he had misheard her as they entered the warm and bustling atmosphere of the Rose & Crown.

"Oh bugger" Katie yelped as she took her place on one of the seats in the pub.

"What is it?" Lucy jumped up, "Is it something on the seat?" She looked accusingly at the burgundy velour below her.

"No, no" Katie reassured her, "I've just realised I'll have to hire a van – I can't fit all the things Mo wants in my car. I can't even fit a quarter of it in; I'll have to do about five trips otherwise."

"Why don't I help?" Ben offered, "I could bring the van from work, we'll fit it all in there."

"Oh I couldn't ask you to do that - anyway won't your bosses mind you using the van for personal use?"

"Uh, hardly" Lucy snorted, "He is the boss isn't he?"

"Oh" Katie said, feeling slightly silly, it had never crossed her mind that Ben owned the company. BW Building, Ben Wilson, of course, that would explain why he was so excited about this job, she thought he was an enthusiastic employee!

"Well, technically I'm not the only boss now Charlie and John are on board too, but I don't think they'll mind me borrowing the van " Ben grinned, "I can come round about four o'clock if that's okay?" he asked.

"Actually that would be brilliant" Katie breathed a sigh of relief, it was one less thing to think about - she already had her hands full as she was due to start all the baking for the spring fayre this week. She had spent the last few days up to her neck in recipes and moving Mo to Cheadle House was going to leave her little time to finish it all.

"Could I come too?" Lucy chipped in, "I haven't seen Mo since I was really young."

"Absolutely titch," Ben answered, "Anyway I'd rather know where you are anyway" he added for good measure. Lucy decided to let that one pass, after all he had said yes and he was just about to buy her steak

and chips, followed by a treacle sponge and custard, best to quit while

she was ahead!

CHAPTER 19

The next morning as Katie pulled her wellies on to attack the next bit of the garden, she reflected that maybe she shouldn't have had the treacle sponge. She was feeling pretty flabby as she bent over and saw a small muffin top appear over her jeans. She had always kept herself at a very precise size 10 in London, visiting the gym every day and eating hardly any carbs – but since she had been back in Laxley she had been baking constantly and therefore eating constantly too. Well, at least the gardening would give her some much needed exercise she reflected grimly.

Katie, with a lot of help from Ken Clackett, had effected quite a transformation in the garden over the last few weeks, uncovering a large patio area in front of the enormous bay window. They had dug out all the flower beds and added ornamental terracotta edges around them to keep the precise definition of the layout. Katie had restored the bird bath to pride of place on a stone column in the centre of one of the beds. They had also removed a large amount of ivy climber from the walls and fences, which had left the fence panels looking rather tatty, so today's job was to apply a fresh coat of stain to the panels to give them a lift, then she was going to scrub all the pots and planters they had uncovered so that they'd be ready once Ken told she could fill them with a dazzling array of plants now residing in Ken's greenhouse. Just as she was finishing the first panel, Ken himself appeared with a spade in hand.

"Morning lass" he greeted her, "I saw you out her so I thought I'd come and make a start at digging out the vegetable patch - if we get things ready I've started chitting some potatoes we can plant when the weather warms up a bit" he added, looking to the skies. Katie smiled "Excellent, if you're sure? I don't mind doing the digging if you want?" Katie didn't want to mention Ken's age but she knew he was the wrong side of 75 now.

"Nay, I'm alright for a bit of digging" he reassured her, "I've dug patches four times this size you know" he added for good measure.

"Okay Ken, but let me know if you need a hand."

They worked on in companiable silence for the next hour, Katie carefully covering every inch of the fence panels with stain and Ken turning over soil and pulling out stones and weeds as he went. Katie was just thinking it must be time for a cup of tea and a biscuit when she heard a thud behind her, turning quickly she saw Ken, sat on the deep brown soil he had been so carefully turning, rubbing his forehead a little dazedly.

"Ken, Ken, are you alright?" Katie rushed over, full of concern.

"I'm alright, just went a little bit dizzy for a minute but I'm fine now" he insisted, but a little shakily none the less.

"Oh Ken, I'm sorry, I shouldn't have let you do all that digging" Katie was distraught that she had allowed this to happen, "Come on, let's get inside and get you sat down." Katie scooped him up and led him into her flat and sat him down at the big pine table. Ken was certainly looking pretty peaky and the fact that he hadn't put up any resistance to being helped inside by a 'mere slip of a lass' confirmed to Katie that he must be feeling quite poorly.

Moving round the kitchen Katie put the kettle on to boil and made Ken a mug of strong, sweet Yorkshire tea. She didn't say anything else until he had taken a few sips and nibbled a digestive from the packet she had placed next to him and gradually his colour was starting to return to his craggy cheeks.

"Ken, has this happened before?" she asked gently, something told her it wasn't the first time but she wanted Ken to confirm it.

"Well maybe, once or twice, but I'm right as rain in a couple of minutes – look!" Ken held up his hand which certainly had fewer tremors than when he had first picked it up, "Steady as a rock" he added for good measure. Katie wasn't to be reassured so easily.

"Well, you must get yourself to the doctor and tell him all about them, get yourself properly checked over." Katie responded.

"Huh! I don't hold with that doctor at the surgery now, he's nowt but a lad and telling me how to live my life. He can come back when he's dry behind the ears - and that's a good few years off yet!" Ken growled.

"Ken, you have to go" Katie scolded him in her best teacher's voice, "and I'll be telling Mary exactly the same!"

"Now now," Ken jumped out of his chair, "there's no need to be telling Mary about this - she'll just go on fretting and worrying and nagging me more than she does now." Ken looked at Katie pleadingly, "You won't, will you?" Katie could see the fear in his eyes and she felt it had a lot less to do with Mary finding out and a lot more to do with his own worries about his health.

"On one condition" Katie said, in tone that she hoped brooked no argument, "I ring the doctor now and we make an appointment and I'll come with you." Ken looked like a man cornered so Katie ruthlessly went in for the kill, "it's up to you - the doctors with me or I tell Mary, in which case you'll have to go to the doctors anyway plus all the nagging!"

Ken looked defeated and nodded "You're Mo's granddaughter alright" he muttered, "talk about Hobson's Choice," Katie smiled "She taught me well, that's for sure - but look it's better we get things checked out now and if nothing's wrong then Mary need never know."

Katie got up from the table and left Ken to finish another digestive or two whilst she rang the doctor's surgery and fixed up an appointment for Thursday morning. Katie was taking Mo's things over to Cheadle House on Wednesday but she would be free to frogmarch Ken to see the doctor on Thursday however long it took. And looking at the expression on Ken's face as he left with two large slices of banana loaf for his lunch, it looked like frogmarching might well be necessary!

CHAPTER 20

Wednesday came as one of those mild early March days, with a gentle watery sun giving a little warmth to the atmosphere, encouraging the tulips and daffodils to open their flowers. Katie took her morning mug of coffee outside and sat at the small garden table she had placed in the newly uncovered patio in front of Tolpuddle House. Although the house was by the main road in Laxley it was hardly a busy one. Laxley Heath rush hour was three cars and a tractor! As Katie sipped her coffee and soaked up the spring sunshine she noticed a procession of people wandering past the house towards the village green, they were all fairly cheery and one or two offered a hearty "Good Morning" if they saw her sitting there. Katie was just wondering what brought all these people to Laxley Heath when she noticed Cliona fighting her way through them the other way.

"God! I'd forgotten they all started again today" she said with a groan as she sat down.

"What's all started again?" Katie asked intrigued.

"The coach trips! Burton Hall opens on 1st March to the end of December and all the coaches always have a stop off in Laxley - the coach park in the new car park is just down the road there" Cliona explained, pointing to where the visitors were appearing from, " and they all troop up the high street! It's why I set up my little hallway shop – I pick up quite a bit of business as the grey army marches past!"

"Cliona!" Katie gasped, "They might hear you"

Cliona shrugged, "I've nothing against them – in fact I intend to be marching at the front of them eventually! I wish I could have a bigger shop really, if they could mooch round a bit more I'm sure I'd sell a bit more, but once a couple of people are in my hallway the rest keep walking on. I wanted to use the living room but Declan drew the line at that" she grumbled.

"I'm not surprised – you'd have probably ended up inviting them all in for lunch too!" Katie laughed

"Well, maybe" Cliona conceded, "but it's still a good idea, in fact ..." she added standing up and surveying the house, " Tolpuddle would be ideal, look at the big window there" she pointed to the window that looked out from Mo's bedroom, which was currently Katie's room. "If you had a really good display in there and a sign above they'd soon be all walking up the path for a look – especially as you can now actually get up the path!" she added thoughtfully. Katie smiled at her friend who was already laying it out in her head and so decided to wind her up a bit more.

"Mmmm, yes, and I could serve tea, coffee and cakes in the front room as everyone sits looking out of the bay window!" she suggested

"Oooo!" squealed Cliona, "What a great idea, Tolpuddle Tea Rooms, Tolpuddle Coffee House – it'd go down a storm" Cliona clapped her hands with excitement.

"I was only joking" Katie cut in, "I can't open a café in Tolpuddle"

"Why not?" demanded Cliona

"For a start it's not my house, secondly, where would I live if I have tearooms in the front room and shops in the flat, and lastly, I'd have to be staying here permanently to run it, which I won't be" Katie finished decisively.

"Oh right" Cliona sounded a bit deflated, "I'd forgotten all that – still it's not a bad idea" she added a bit loath to let it go straight away.

"No it's not a bad idea at all" Katie said graciously, feeling a little guilty for taking the wind out of her friends sails quite so definitely.

"Hmm, oh well" Cliona let it go, "but aren't you staying around? I thought you'd settled in well here. Are you thinking of going back to London? And to Marcus?" Cliona prodded gently.

"Not Marcus, no. It's been two months since you know what – and I've not had a peep out of him, not even a lousy text!" Katie replied indignantly, "In fact I think I'm off men for the moment, I'm always so wrong about them, I mean I even got it wrong with Bbb … blokes before Marcus" she finished lamely. She had very nearly said Ben and Katie wasn't ready to discuss that with Cliona yet, "but I suppose I just assumed I'll go back to London once Mo's back up and running," Katie said to steer the conversation back to safer waters, " and the best jobs are in London."

"I guess so, but we do alright around here and I'm a mean matchmaker - if you let me!" answered Cliona, with a glint in her eye, "but I wouldn't count on Mo coming back here any time soon - I think she's looking forward to a bit of fun at Cheadle House with Bert!"

Katie had time to reflect on the truth of that statement later that same day as she got all the things together that Mo had asked her to take to Cheadle House. As well as the karaoke machine, she wanted playing cards, DVD's and a popcorn maker that Katie hadn't even realised existed. Katie added a few of the more mundane things such as clothes, toiletries, books and a few of Mo's favourite baking implements, once Mo was fully up and about she would be sure to make a beeline for the kitchen to whip up some biscuits or a fruitcake and she'd want her measures, spatulas and tins to do that. These were things that became very special to you in cooking, almost superstitiously, if you made a great cake with something then you always wanted to use that one - until it failed you!

Katie was just surveying the cases and boxes that were nearly blocking

the hallway when the bell rang and the door opened simultaneously as

Lucy bowled in mid-sentence, "no she won't Ben, we come all the time

now we don't need to wait for someone to answer the door" she

argued, without noticing Katie or the boxes in the hallway and

promptly fell over them.

"Oh bugger" she said as she stood up, rubbing her backside, "I didn't

see those" she added, stating the obvious.

"No?" Ben raised an eyebrow, "well that's why you wait for someone to

open the door so they can guide you through any obstacles waiting on

the other side" he chided.

Lucy seemed unimpressed with this advice but nearly fell back into the

boxes as she turned round and walked into Katie.

"Oh – what are you doing there?" she asked, somewhat indignantly

"Waiting for someone to ring the bell" Katie answered sardonically,

sharing a smile with Ben as she did.

"Ha ha – funny much?" Lucy drawled, "You're nearly as bad as him" she

added, flicking her ponytail in the general direction of her brother,

"I'm going upstairs to see Poppy – and I won't have to ring the bell!"

Katie and Ben managed to keep a straight face until Lucy had

disappeared round the top of the stairs when they both gave in to their mirth. Fourteen year old sisters were hugely entertaining! When they'd recovered and exchanged the usual pleasantries Ben surveyed the offending boxes and cases.

"I'm guessing this is all the stuff to take to Mo's then?" he asked, a tad unnecessarily.

"Yes, just as well you could come! I think this would be about eight trips in my car!" Katie laughed.

"And the rest" Ben added, "but it should all go in the back of Conan"

"Conan?" Katie had to ask

"The warrior – I bought that instead of the Kangoo, all this stuff should fit in the back and there's enough seats for all of us, so you don't need to take the car at all" he explained

To be honest, Katie was relieved; she hadn't felt like driving over to Mo's. She didn't like to admit it but she was feeling a bit depressed about Mo's move, at least with Ben and Lucy talking and bickering all the way, it should keep her mind occupied. Katie and Ben set to clearing the hall of all the boxes and cases and soon they were all stowed in the enormous back of Conan without incident, apart from Ben's slight double take at the popcorn maker.

Just as the last box had been stowed in the boot and the door was shut Lucy appeared, with immaculate timing, ready to go, and with Poppy in tow

"It's okay if Pops comes too isn't it? She'd really like to see Mo" Lucy asked

Ben looked to Katie who had no doubt, "Of course it is - Mo will love to see you" she said, "She can check if I'm feeding you enough - again!"

They all hopped into the wagon and in thirty minutes were pulling up outside Cheadle House with plenty of oh-ing and ah-ing from Poppy and Lucy who hadn't seen it before. Before they were all out of the van the big front door opened and Mo and Bert appeared at the threshold to greet their visitors.

"Katie, Katie, come and see the room they've given me, next to Bert's. It's like a hotel, TV, digital radio, automatic lights and a minibar!"

"What" Katie said, in disbelief, "a minibar, that can't be right, I mean, I know you can have a drink if you want one but a bar in your room, that's outrageous! I'll speak to Violet about that - how much will they charge? They cost the earth in hotels. I can't believe it!" Katie was in full swing now, full of outraged decency and ready for battle - so much so that she didn't immediately notice everyone repressing a smile but she then spotted Mo mid-wink to Bert.

"Oh I see" she laughed, "so you're feeling much better then?"

"I'm feeling fine, my dear" Mo said, "but still getting used to this bloody stick! Come over here and help me back to the room, Ben, you and Poppy, oh and Lucy can bring the boxes. That's alright isn't it?" she asked as she looked at Ben.

"That's what we're here for" he said, doffing an imaginary cap, as Mo linked Katie's arm and they set off down the corridor.

The room was, indeed, fabulous. Spotlessly clean with a deep, luxurious, cream carpet that almost ate your feet as you walked on it, there were heavy brocade curtains in a deep plum and a perfectly co-ordinated double bed. Katie looked at the bed and then at Mo, raising a questioning eyebrow.

"Well, you never know" Mo laughed, "I'm not quite past it yet!"

"No, you're probably not – I think I am though" she added under her breath. Mo appeared not to hear and soon everyone else appeared, ferrying boxes and cases and exclaiming over the room.

"Really, it's not old fogeyish at all" Lucy said magnanimously, "I could even stay in here - with a few changes" she added.

"Thank you, Lucy!" Mo said, "And exactly what changes would you make?"

Lucy pondered this for a moment, wrinkling her forehead in thought, " Well I'd have to have my iPod and docking station over there and the curtains should be black, to add a bit of drama, maybe paint a mural on that wall over there" she continued, warming to her theme

"Yes, well it's not Mo's room to change" Katie cut in before Mo got too interested in any of Lucy's more outlandish ideas as she already seemed to surveying the far wall a bit too carefully. "What time is it? I'm starving!" Katie said suddenly, realising there was a fairly loud rumbling beginning in her stomach.

"God, yes, look its 7.15 – we've missed dinner. I was going to treat everyone." Mo exclaimed, "I know, who's for fish and chips?"

Everyone, it seemed, was up for fish and chips so Ben and Bert were dispatched to 'The Happy Haddock' in the wagon to pick up six times fish and chips as Mo, Katie, Poppy and Lucy finished unpacking the boxes and stowing it all away.

In half an hour they were all sat round on the bed and in the deep comfy armchairs contentedly munching crispy, battered haddock and fat, golden chips out of the paper. There's something deeply comforting about food eaten with your fingers, still in their wrappers and everyone had gotten so comfortable they were loath to make a move when they had finished. The combination of the warm, comfy surroundings, full bellies and the cold March night outside made the thought of going out there very unappetising, but it was already 8.30pm and Ben knew he had to get Katie and Poppy home to Laxley

Heath and then on to Rawlinston at a reasonable hour so that Lucy wouldn't be yawning her way through school the next day. Reluctantly they said their goodbyes and promised to be back soon. They all drifted off into quiet reveries as they made their way back to Tolpuddle House, quietly contented. As Ben pulled up outside the house, Katie invited everyone in for a cup of tea and as Ben was feeling a little drowsy, or so he told himself, he decided to take her up on her offer before finishing his journey back to Rawlinston.

CHAPTER 21

Katie opened the front door, giving a silent word of thanks again for Ben's handiwork that meant she no longer ended up on her backside every time she came in, and they all trooped in behind her. Katie had barely had time to fill the kettle when there was an insistent knocking on the side door. Katie swore Mary could hear the kettle going on from a full mile away! Opening the door Katie was about to invite Mary in when she saw she was drip white and distraught.

"Help, Katie, help – Ken's collapsed. I don't think he's breathing, I don't know what to do, I can't lose him." Big tears welled in her eyes and were falling fast down her cheeks. Putting a protective arm around Mary, Katie started to lead her back to the flat as she left she looked over at Ben meaningfully, who, reading the signal, jumped up with a quick instruction to Poppy to call for an ambulance, and then followed Katie and Mary round to the Clackett's flat.

Ken was lying in the middle of the living room floor and looked terrifyingly still. Ben rushed straight over to him, checking his breathing and looking for any signs of life. Katie watched in a daze as he checked Ken's airways and began compressions on his chest, 30 compressions, 2 breaths, 30 compressions, 2 breaths, 30 compressions, 2 breaths. Katie shook herself. She needed to be more use and realising

Mary was becoming increasingly hysterical and didn't know what to do, Katie took her into the kitchen and sat her down with Poppy who had come round to say the ambulance was on its way.

"Mary, stay here with Poppy and look out for the ambulance so they know where to come as soon as they get here" she instructed Mary, giving her something to do. Quietly she told Poppy to keep Mary in the kitchen, Poppy nodded, instinctively understanding the need to keep her occupied and away from the living room.

Katie ran back into the other room.

"The ambulance should be eight to ten minutes – is there any response?" she added.

"I don't know, I know what to do but I've no idea if I'm helping." Ben answered desperately.

"Of course you're helping" Katie reassured him, "he would have no chance if you weren't here – if he comes through this it'll all be because of you."

Ben shot her a grateful smile and carried on for four or five minutes, though it felt like hours.

"Where is the ambulance?" Ben gasped, sweat pouring off him.

"It should be here any time now – let me do that for a bit, you're shattered" Katie offered, she gripped one hand with other as Ben was doing and took over the compressions, Ben did the first couple with her so she knew what pressure to apply.

"Count to 30 then stop and I'll do the breaths," he instructed. They worked on in perfect unison until finally the ambulance crew arrived and took over. Katie and Ben moved out to the kitchen and waited with Mary, Poppy and Lucy, all of them white and drawn and silently praying.

After what seemed like an age, Tom, according to his name badge, one of the paramedics came into the kitchen and told them that Ken was breathing now and showing some signs of recovery but they needed to get to hospital as quickly as possible now.

"Thank the Lord!" Mary collapsed onto a chair, crossing herself.

"You want to thank this pair here" the paramedic said, pointing to Ben and Katie, "without their intervention I don't think we'd have been so lucky."

Gently the paramedics, Tom and Jenny, lifted Ken onto a stretcher and pushed him out to the waiting ambulance. His face was as grey as a battleship and his chest rose and fell in short, sharp breaths, but at least he was breathing. Soon Ken was in the ambulance, with Mary holding his hand, blue lights flashing and off down the road to Rawlinston General. Mary had begged Katie and Ben to follow them.

They knew there was no way they could leave Mary on own at the hospital as Ken wasn't out of the woods yet, but Ben still had Lucy to sort out – there wasn't really time to get her across to Jean's on the other side of Rawlinston and she couldn't stay on her own. Ben was just deciding Lucy would have to come with them when Poppy piped up as she could see his dilemma, "I've got a put-me-up bed in the flat. Lucy can bed down at mine tonight and I'll take her in to Rawlinston on the bus in the morning – if that's okay? Then you don't have to worry or come trailing back over here" she offered, "if you're happy for her to stay with me?"

Ben simply hugged Poppy, "Thanks Pops – that's perfect" he added and with Lucy sorted out Katie and Ben were soon on their way to the hospital, both nervous about what they might find when they got there.

The hospital was quiet when they arrived, in that 'everything's going on behind closed doors' way that hospitals have. Katie and Ben entered the building and looked for anyone to help them. A efficient, but kindly, receptionist pointed them along the orange line on the floor to find the emergency room, as they drew closer a few more people appeared, in and out of doors along the corridor, pushing trolleys, carrying clipboards and the noise level increased as wheels squeaked, machines beeped and intercoms buzzed. In the midst of it all they saw

Mary, sat in her own stillness, gently weeping into her cotton handkerchief. Katie's heart lurched as she saw her and she instinctively gripped Ben's hand. What if Ken was dead? What if he'd gone?

Ben gave her hand a reassuring squeeze and led her towards Mary.

"Mary" he said gently, "what's happening? Have you heard anything?"

"No, they took Ken in there" she said, pointing to a door on the far side of the waiting area, "and I haven't spoken to anyone since. I don't know what to do" she added helplessly.

Ben took control immediately, "Katie, stay here with Mary and I'll go and see what I can find out," he ordered and disappeared towards the nurse's station they had passed back in the corridor. He was gone only five minutes but to Katie it felt ten times as long as she sat with Mary waiting, Mary twisting her handkerchief endlessly between her fingers. Ben returned stern faced,

"The nurse is getting someone to update us on what's happening," he told them, and true to their word a doctor in blue scrubs appeared from the emergency room and came over to speak to them. Katie realised she was holding her breath as the doctor got closer and her grip on Mary's hand tightened.

"Mrs Clackett?" the doctor enquired, in a gentle voice. Mary nodded.

"Well, the good news is we've got Mr Clackett stabilised, but he is quite poorly, he's had a very big heart attack I'm afraid"

"Will he be alright? Will he get better?" Mary stammered uncertainly.

"He's got a long way to go and he may have to have a little operation but there's no reason he shouldn't make a good recovery. He'll have to take things carefully from now on though." The doctor told her.

Mary jumped up and hugged the doctor, "Thank you, thank you so much, I thought I'd lost him but now .... Can I see him soon?"

The doctor said she could see him for five minutes now and led Mary across the waiting area and into the room where Ken was, leaving Katie and Ben to reflect on everything that had happened.

"Well that's good then isn't it?" Ben started, turning to Katie as he spoke and he saw the tears streaming down her face as she rocked backwards and forwards.

"Hey, hey" he soothed, enveloping her in a big hug, "he's going to be okay, I'm sure of it."

"But it's all my fault" Katie sobbed, "if only I'd made him go to the doctor's sooner – he was poorly on Monday morning but he wouldn't let me tell Mary and I made him promise to go to the doctors with me tomorrow but I didn't tell Mary – if I had ...." her voice trailed off as she thought of what might have been prevented.

"If you had" Ben cut in, "exactly the same thing would have happened. Except that he probably wouldn't have said he'd go to the doctor's at all if Mary had tried to make him! He's a stubborn bugger when he wants to be. It's not your fault Katie, these things just happen."

"Really?" Katie looked up at him with huge luminous eyes, brimming with tears.

"Really" Ben said, "it wasn't anyone's fault. Stop beating yourself up" he added giving her another comforting hug.

Katie smiled weakly and leant against Ben enjoying the reassurance of his embrace. Ben held Katie as she relaxed and thought, although he never wanted to see Katie upset, he knew he could quite happily hold her like this forever.

CHAPTER 22

The next few weeks disappeared in a whirl for Katie. She spent her mornings at Declan's restaurant preparing all the food for the fayre, then in the afternoons she was either visiting Mo or Ken, who, she was very pleased to see, were both recovering with remarkable speed. Then after her visits she was back to Tolpuddle House with a full programme of works, cleaning, painting, gardening and lots of other odd jobs she had listed to try and restore Tolpuddle back to its best. She had already transformed the front of the house, the creeping ivy gone and the pointing restored, she had sanded down and repainted the window frames and was currently toying with commissioning Cliona to make a hand painted name plate for the house. By the time Katie fell into bed each night she was exhausted but, surprisingly, content.

She hadn't seen Ben since the night at the hospital and she had heard from Lucy that he was working away quite a lot on a project down south and he was busy trying to put it all together, the details were a bit sketchy as Lucy clearly had virtually no interest in whatever her brother was doing other than how it affected her and Katie didn't like to ask too many questions in case Lucy misinterpreted her interest as something more than friendship.

It was now early April, with the shoots of spring visible all around the village, as trees budded, blossom bloomed and a parade of ducklings criss-crossed the green following their mother as if on an invisible thread. On a sunny Tuesday morning, Katie was in the garden preparing some ceramic pots for the potting plants she was going to display around the patio and filling the hanging baskets to hang either side of the front door that she had ambitiously decided to have a go at herself rather than buying the finished article. Katie smiled as she worked, who'd have thought she was an Alan Titchmarsh in the making! It was a beautiful spring day, one of the first of the year, when the sun had some real warmth in it. Katie had given herself the day off from any cooking, most of the food for the fayre was now prepared. Declan's freezer was bursting at the seams with twenty quiches, pies of apple, cherry, peach and plum, batches of fruit scones, cherry scones and cheese scones, sponges of many flavours, sausage plaits, Cornish pasties and much more. Katie only had cheesecakes and the fresh food to prepare on the day now. She would be able to report that all was well and under control to Sergeant Hermione when she saw her for the final planning meeting that evening, but firstly Katie was going to visit Mo that afternoon. Katie had been visiting Mo regularly since she had been installed at Cheadle House and she was delighted with how well Mo was doing. Katie thought she'd be able to move home soon, of course, that might mean Katie having to move out but that was always going to happen at some point she reasoned. Katie thought she might stay on for a few weeks once Mo was home just to make sure everything was alright. Mo had rung Katie the afternoon before and asked her to call in on her own, usually Poppy, Mary or Tamsin came along with her as they all loved to see Mo but not today Mo had asked, she had said she had something she needed to discuss with Katie in private. Katie was intrigued but thought it was most likely about Mo coming home – Mo always liked to make things as dramatic as possible! Just telling Katie on the phone would have been far too pedestrian for her.

Katie arrived at Cheadle House at three o'clock that afternoon, the sun was still shining through the clouds and had still enough warmth in it to let Katie leave her jacket in the car, she scrunched over the gravel and opened the huge front door and turned down the corridor towards Mo's room. Mo was definitely about as Katie could hear her mischievous laughter echoing down the corridor, interspersed with Bert's deeper guffaw. That was no surprise to Katie either as, these days, where one of them was the other was never far behind.

"And what are you two up too?" Katie affected a stern voice as she appeared around the corner of Mo's bedroom. Mo and Bert sprang apart guiltily like two teenagers caught by their parents, Katie couldn't be sure but she thought they were holding hands and just for a minute she was lost for words, feeling like she had intruded on something private. With forced bravado she carried on, "up to no good. I'll bet, so spill the beans"

Mo had recovered her equilibrium quickly and told Bert to push off so she could talk to Katie, Bert was a little hesitant until Mo gave him a swift slap on the bum and pointed him to the door. "It's all fine" she added cryptically, "I'll give you a shout when we're done" Bert gave her a reassuring pat on the arm and smiled, almost apologetically, as he passed Katie.

"Well, Katie, my love, how are you? Are you eating?" Mo started with her usual interrogation but Katie decided not to play along today, she could tell by the way Mo was fiddling with the fringe of her cardigan that something was amiss and she wasn't about to be fobbed off on pleasantries instead. "I'm fine and I had a tuna sandwich for lunch. Spill the beans Mo, something's up and I'm not leaving until I know what it is. Are you ill? Is there something else wrong with you?" she questioned, rather harshly, as she was worried and didn't want to show it. Mo burst out laughing, which, although somewhat reassuring , was also a little irritating, " Oh Katie K, don't look so worried , there's nothing wrong at all – in fact quite the opposite, I've got some news for you." Mo stopped and seemed to be searching for the right words, taking a deep breath she continued, " you know how much I loved your Granddad don't you Katie," Katie nodded, wondering where this was going but seeing Mo needed some reassurance she held Mo's hand and waited for her continue. "When he passed away a bit of me went with him, I thought that life would never be fun again. But you have to keep going – he told me I had to keep going and then all my guests, they had to be looked after too. So time passed on and gradually you start living again, but I always expected to be on my own – oh I know I'll have you" she added as she saw Katie start, "I mean as a woman, I thought that was all behind me now. Until I fell down those pesky stairs, I thought it was the beginning of the end for me, not been able to cope at Tolpuddle anymore, shuffling about like an old person in case I fell over again. But then a miracle happened, Katie, instead of being the beginning of the end it turned out to be the beginning of the beginning. I met Bert. We clicked from day one like we'd known each other for ages and we laugh together, I can't tell you how special that is Katie" "You don't have to Mo, I know how good Bert is to you and what great friends you've become." Katie interrupted. Mo smiled and continued "Well, that's the thing Katie, he's become more than a friend, he's come to mean a great deal to me and amazingly he feels the same way about me and he's asked me to marry him and I said yes" Mo finished in a rush and looked up at Katie, holding her breath as she waited for a

271

reaction, but nothing came. Katie's face looked like a slightly more lifelike waxwork from Madam Tussauds. "He'll never take the place of your Granddad, Katie, you know that, he was the love of my life but I care about him, love him in a different way and I ...." Katie held up her hand to stop Mo, she could hear the distress in her voice. "Mo, stop, I'm thrilled for you, of course I am – how could I be anything else?" Katie's grin spread across her face to show the truth of her words, "I'm just a bit gob-smacked too" Katie enveloped Mo in a hug and as she let go asked

"So, Mo, when's the big day then?" Katie began her interrogation but Mo cut her off, clearly dying to tell Katie all the details without further prompting.

"Well, pretty soon we thought – Spring Bank Holiday perhaps and well, it's so beautiful here, we thought we'd get married in the gardens here at Cheadle" Mo gathered pace, they had clearly talked this all through in detail.

"Spring Bank" Katie exclaimed, "That's only six or seven weeks away, it's only a month after the Spring Fayre!"

"I know, sweetie" Mo reassured her, "but really, it's not going to be a big thing, just close friends and family, all informal, that's what we both want."

Katie took a deep breath and then exhaled slowly, "It'll be lovely Mo, and I'll do whatever you want me to – you know that don't you?" she squeezed Mo's arm and then enveloped her in another bear hug until Mo had to extricate herself to breathe.

"I'm so happy for you Mo" Katie sighed, wiping a surreptitious tear away, "So will you and Bert move back into Tolpuddle straight after the wedding?" she asked, thinking it would be a whirlwind for her what with the fayre and then the wedding to organise and now in-between all that a new job and a new home to find, but she couldn't stay at Tolpuddle – Mo and Bert needed to start married life without her hanging about. As these thoughts raced through Katie's mind, she missed Mo's slightly furrowed brow.

"Ah well, funny you should say that Katie" Mo started, "the thing is, Bert and I are going to stay here, one of the bungalows is available and we can move in there straight away. It'll be our own little place but with plenty of friends and help on hand when we need it. I'm not getting any younger – and I realise that now, so this way we get the best of all worlds" Mo came to a hurried end and waited for Katie's reaction.

Katie realised she was holding her breath again and felt she was stuck in some sort of slow motion film as she slowly exhaled.

"You're not coming back to Tolpuddle?" Katie realised she was opening and closing her mouth like a goldfish. She shook her head to clear her thoughts and started again.

"So you're not going back to Tolpuddle" she stated the fact this time, "So what are you going to do with the house? Sell it or get a housekeeper in, or something like that?" she asked.

"Well, that's what I needed to speak to you about specifically" Mo started mysteriously, she patted the seat next to her for Katie to sit down, which she duly did. Five minutes later Katie was extremely glad she had sat down before Mo had got started, as she almost certainly would have fallen down without a seat to support her! Mo had just explained that she wanted to sign over Tolpuddle House to Katie, so she could stay there and do whatever she wanted with it. It turned out that Mo and Grandpa had made a lot of wise investments in the past and so Mo had a comfortable income that would more than cover her requirements, and, as Mo put it, Tolpuddle was always going to be Katie's one day so it may as well be now.

"And if I keep going for another seven years you won't have to pay any tax on it either" Mo chuckled, with that mischievous glint in her eye again.

Katie couldn't respond though, she was absolutely floored. She had never seriously thought about staying at Tolpuddle, she had always assumed she would eventually go back to London and pick up in another job where she had left off when she had come running back to Laxley Heath, but now there was another option – and much to her surprise Katie didn't dismiss the idea out of hand. In fact, she could see a lot of appeal about it. Since she had been back in Laxley Heath she had slotted into life here and felt more content than she had for some time if she was honest. But was it the sort of contentment that would last for years or was it just a safe haven after her troubled recent past? This was the dilemma she was discussing with Cliona over a glass of Pinot Grigio at Tolpuddle's kitchen table at the emergency summit, as Cliona called it, which she had called for as soon as she had left Cheadle House that afternoon, only stopping to give her sincere congratulations to Bert and Mo and to share a celebratory glass of champagne with them.

Cliona was currently finding the whole thing highly amusing, mainly due to Katie's stunned confusion about it.

"Come on Katie," she giggled, "it's not a bad thing – Mo's giving you a house, in fact a small mansion really, with recently restored gardens too! You're going to be a woman of substance!" she added mischievously.

Katie smiled, she realised she was coming over as ungrateful and she really wasn't at all, but it had come so suddenly, so out of the blue, she knew she needed time to digest it all.

"I know it's a wonderful gesture but I just don't know what to do. If I'm back in London I'll have to employ someone to look after the house and all the 'guests' or I'll be tripping up and down the M1 every time Poppy has a new idea or Guy hasn't surfaced for a week! Oh I know! You could look after it for me." Katie exclaimed.

"Oh no," Cliona shook her head vigorously until all her curls had taken on a life of their own, "I'm bad enough at looking after one little terraced cottage - ask Declan! I'm not looking after anything else! Anyway there is another solution …." She added cryptically.

"I know, I can sell it" Katie suggested, but she really didn't want to do that. She didn't want to break her bond with Tolpuddle and Laxley just yet and she knew it would break Mo's heart, she'd never say so, but it would all the same.

"I don't mean sell it" Cliona cut into Katie's thoughts, "I meant you could stay here and develop Tolpuddle House, you could make a healthy living out of it. There are all sorts of possibilities" she added enticingly.

"Such as?" Katie demanded "being a housekeeper and gardener? I mean I've enjoyed it for a few months but I don't think it's my long term ambition."

"No, no – not that" Cliona scoffed, "I can't see you as Mrs Bridges! But it could be a boutique restaurant, or a chic coffee shop with stalls of local crafts people, like we talked about before. I know a good potter if you want one. And you could certainly run a coffee shop – look at all the catering you've been doing since you got here."

Katie looked thoughtful; the idea had obviously hit a nerve,

"But who would come?" Katie pondered out loud, "I mean, to make it pay you'd need a good throughput of customers."

"Well, that's easy" Cliona answered, "we see them all every morning – coachloads of them walking past Tolpuddle House twice, everyday!" she ended triumphantly.

Katie laughed and raised her glass, it was a surprise to her but it was actually a possibility. She had always thought about running her own business, she had always assumed it would be some sort of agency in recruitment or office services but actually, running her own coffee shop, that could be fun and strangely the thought of staying around Laxley didn't seem such a bad idea really, in fact it was becoming more appealing every day, somehow it had snuck back into her heart. Katie knew she had a lot to think about over the next few weeks, but for now there Pinot Grigio!

CHAPTER 23

"LUCY!" Ben bellowed from the kitchen, once again his sister was refusing to surface from her room, "don't make me come in there - I will drag you out of bed - again!" he added with menace. He had no time for Lucy's feet dragging today. He, Charlie and John were due down in Southampton for a couple of days and they wanted to be off no later than 9 o'clock. It was already 7.30am and he still had to make sure Lucy had packed her bag ready to go to Jean's that evening and then drop her off at school.

"LU!" he started again, and broke off somewhat startled as a fully dressed Lucy with overnight bag in hand emerged from her room, nonchalantly pulling her school blazer on.

"Yes?" she asked with her best shot at supercilious.

"Bloody Hell Luce - I didn't realise today was the blue moon!" Ben laughed, "Better keep an eye out for those flying pigs too - they can leave a nasty bruise!"

"Funny - NOT!" she replied and added in response to Ben's quizzical look, "I know today's important so I had a shower last night when you were still at the office so I could be ready quickly this morning."

"Thanks sis" Ben said with feeling, touched by her thoughtfulness - all the more special as it was unusual, "come on then, let's get this show on the road" he added, grabbing his keys and heading out, with Lucy right behind him. Five minutes later he was back, having managed to get Lucy out of the flat on time and to remember her overnight bag, he could be forgiven for forgetting his own! Lucy didn't quite see it that way and tormented him for the entire thirty minute drive to her school. Ben was at the office ten minutes after that and, once settled with a mug of hot, black coffee, he handed Lucy's bag to Jean and tried, once again, to give her some money.

"Look, just take this, get everyone a pizza tonight, save yourself a bit of work," he explained

"A pizza!" Jean answered, in horror, "I'll do no such thing. I have a shepherd's pie sitting in the fridge and that's every bit as good as any pizza. If Lucy doesn't like it then she can lump it – and the apple crumble for afters as well" she added for good measure.

Ben grinned, he knew Jean wouldn't take the money, but he liked to offer, if only to see Jean's reaction. He knew Lucy secretly loved going to Jean's home and sitting round the dining room table with her rowdy family and tucking into hearty, tasty meals from her childhood. And, despite appearances to the contrary, Jean loved having her to stay too, she loved Lucy's liveliness and spirit, and not having a girl of her own it made a pleasant change for her to have some female support at home. Not that either of them would ever admit it, it was all part of the fun to pretend they were putting up with each other!

Five long hours later, and many road works, traffic jams and motorway middle lane hoggers, Ben, Charlie and John had reached Southampton, booked into their cheap, and not entirely cheerful, hotel and had arrived on the site to meet Stewart who had been there a couple of days already finishing all the plans. And a brilliant job he had done too Ben had to say. They were soon all wandering around the site bringing the plans to life in their minds, adding a window here, removing a wall there, but it was clear the whole site had great potential, a whole row of terraced houses that had been allowed to reach such a derelict state it was why BW could afford to buy the whole site, but they were all fixable and would be a lovely little mews terrace when finished with open plan fronts and courtyards to the back and Stewart had been right their potential was evident as was the whole area's which had been very down at heel but already a new housing estate was starting to be built down the opposite end of the main road and the row of shops across from the houses that had been half empty on Ben's last visit now only had one unit vacant, having added a Tesco Express and a coffee shop to their repertoire. All of which would help attract more buyers to the area.

After much wandering of the site they decided to adjourn to the aforementioned coffee shop, as despite their enthusiasm, the day was not the best and the drizzle was starting to seep in through their clothes and settle in their joints! Once they were ensconced in the two large leather sofa in the steamed up bay window of the café, with their own steaming mugs of coffee in front of them, they were soon talking ten to the dozen about the project and even the next one!

"Still, let's not get carried away," John started to add a note of caution, "this is a great job but we need to get this right, the better we do on this with deadlines and sticking to budgets the more seriously we'll be taken next time. We need someone on site the whole time for this one, to make sure it all runs smoothly and to make decisions as they're needed." He looked expectantly at the others.

"I'll be here obviously," Stewart answered, "But I can't manage the building work and the architectural work too – it doesn't work well." They all nodded, it was well known that architects needed reigning in every now and again, not all their bright ideas were feasible, even a brilliant Architect such as Stewart.

"Still, it's quite a commitment to be down here, all week, every week," John continued, "I've done it before so I know – But Claire probably won't mind being rid of me for a bit!"

Ben laughed, "It's our first big project and both you and Charlie have family so it's probably better if I'm the one that comes down," he offered.

"Or maybe, we could take it in turns?" John looked at Ben then Charlie, "Look we all want to be involved and, yes, Charlie and I have family, but so do you now Ben."

Charlie nodded, "Yes, I like the sound of that; I know it'll be hard but I think we should all chip in."

" Well, we don't have to decide just now - we'll start first week in May so let's think about it and make a final decision in a couple of weeks, when you've had time to talk to Claire and Anna" Ben suggested and they all agreed that sounded like the best idea for now. However, as Ben lay down on his rather squashy hotel bed and surveyed the bland wallpaper on the walls of the room that could be in any town in the country, he realised it was time for him to sort out his home situation. He had, he grudgingly admitted to himself, loved having Lucy to stay, despite all the drama's that came with her, she livened up his evenings (and gave him plenty of excuses to pop round to Katie's house, a little voice inside his head added). But it wasn't just his money riding on this project and he had to make it a priority. Ben felt the dread gather in the pit of his stomach. It was time to talk to his mother again!

The next day, when Ben, Charlie and John had got back to BW's office Ben decided to make the call. Unlike many people, Ben couldn't put off an unpleasant task; he preferred to get them out of the way rather than brood on them for days and then still have it to do anyway. He dialled the number of his mother's mobile, strangely the ring-tone sounded quite normal, not the slightly longer, shriller tone you usually got when calling abroad. They must be making them sound the same he thought idly as it rang. Finally on about the twelfth ring, someone answered, "Hello" the familiar female voice drawled. Ben clenched and unclenched his hands to relieve the tension before he answered. "Hello Mum, how are you?" he asked.

"Ben, is that you?" Trudy's vague tones and question immediately got under Ben's skin - who else would be calling her Mum, there was only him and Lucy! Taking a deep breath he carried on, "Yes, Mum, it's me. I was wondering how you are, you know, the inner core, peeling layers and all that."

"Oh, darling, how sweet. I'm very well now; my layers have been stripped to the core and re-layered in line with the universe. I'm at peace, at one with energy," she sighed contentedly.

"Umm, great, great" Ben stammered, "so you'll be heading home soon then, will you? You see, I've got quite a big project on and, well, I might have to be away a bit in the future so it might be best if Lucy were able to come home rather than going from pillar to post" he explained. Trudy trilled with fake laughter and Ben grimaced.

"Oh Ben, how funny you are. When will I be heading home? I'm at home, of course, I've been back for over a month. Where on earth did you think I was?" she asked

"I thought you were where you were last time I spoke to you – as you haven't told me any different." Ben said, through clenched teeth.

"Well why would I, my dear?" Trudy asked, bemused, "we don't usually tell each other everything we're doing."

"Well, it might have crossed your mind as Lucy, your daughter, is staying with me. She might like to have known her mother was back" Ben was fighting hard to keep his temper.

"Oh" Trudy sounded genuinely surprised, as if the idea had never crossed her mind, which, to be fair, it probably hadn't, "I'm sure she's fine with you, anyway Trevor and I needed a bit of space to commune together. Lucy can be quite demanding you know."

Ben made his decision in that instant. He put the phone down without another word and wrote his mother out of his life. He could cope with her forgetting about him and what he was up to, after all he had many years to get used to it, but Lucy was fourteen. Demanding! All she wanted was a bit of attention from her mum, food to eat, clothes to wear, those sorts of things. Lucy deserved much better than their mother was prepared to give and Ben would have to find it for her

instead. He didn't know how it would work but Lucy was going to stay

with him. She was already doing better than ever before at school, and

he wasn't going to abandon here now, though how the hell he was

going to do it he had not a clue – and he had even less idea how he was

going to tell Lucy.

CHAPTER 24

"Just tell her" Cliona stormed, "she'll understand Ben, she knows you're your Mum's like" Ben had just shared his news with Katie and Cliona as they sat round Katie's kitchen table, ostensibly discussing the final details for the fayre but once Lucy had been dispatched with Poppy to start putting jewellery into packets ready for her stall, he'd had to share the recent developments with them.

"Don't you agree Katie?" Cliona looked to Katie for support.

"I think she will, but it doesn't mean she won't be hurt. Mum and Dad used to disappear all over the world and I always had Grandpa and Mo to stay with – and they always told me when they were back but I always felt a bit abandoned if I'm honest – and this is a whole other level. I mean, she's not travelling she just doesn't want her back. God, what sort of woman would do that?" she raged and then added, "Sorry Ben, I know she's your Mum, I just can't get my head around it."

"Don't worry" Ben smiled ruefully, "you're not saying anything I haven't already said many times, but that's me finished with her now. If Lucy wants to stay in touch, that's fine, but I've had it now. I'll look after Luce, one way or another," he added determinedly.

"Of course you will" Katie said, patting his arm reassuringly, "she'll be fine – and you've got plenty of friends round here to help you anytime."

Ben smiled gratefully, he could feel the responsibility on his tensed shoulders but it wasn't something he was walking away from.

"Anyway," he started, "enough of that now, let's talk about something else, like the arrangements for the fayre – which is, in fact, why I'm here!"

Half an hour later they had agreed that Ben and Lucy would come at four o'clock on the Friday to help with the setting up and then Ben would be on hand during Friday evening, Saturday and Sunday with the van to ferry the food from Declan's to the marquee and in between time he could do odd jobs as required by Katie.

"Within reason" Ben warned as he saw Katie rubbing her hands together with glee. "We'll see" was all she said, smiling as she stood up, "So anyone for a cup of tea, I think I've got some apple pie in the fridge if anyone's hungry?" Katie offered

Ben needed no further prompting he hadn't been ready to head home just yet, and not just because of the conversation he was going to have to have with Lucy when he got there. If he was honest he was always reluctant to leave Katie's flat. He found his eyes resting on the doorway where Katie and he had kissed after Cliona's dinner party. After that he had kept his promise to be a friend to Katie whenever she needed one but he couldn't fool himself any longer that that was all he wanted. Still no point dwelling on it he thought, friends she wanted so a friend he would be.

"Er hello - earth to Ben" Katie broke into his reverie, waving a hand in front of his face.

"Sorry" he laughed, "just thinking about something. What did you say?"

Katie decided not to take offence and explained, "I was asking if you're okay to stay on for a bit longer, Mo and Bert are going to drop in soon and they'd love to see everyone - if you've not anything more important to do," she finished teasingly.

"Well, I suppose I can, if there's another piece of pie, I could hang on for a bit longer." Ben countered.

Katie, laughing, cut him another huge slab of pie with a dollop of ice cream which she plonked down in front of him, marvelling at how he managed to eat so much and there wasn't an ounce of fat on him that she could see - maybe there was a lot to be said for a job that wasn't entirely office based! Just as Ben was finishing the last mouthful of pie the doorbell went and soon Mo and Bert were bowling through the door and Mo was already in full flow.

"You've fixed the door Katie" she said accusingly, "Bert nearly ended up at the back of the house when I told him to give it a good push! Just as well it wasn't me - I'd have been back in hospital" she laughed, "so what else have you been doing to Tolpuddle?" she eyed Katie with stern eye, belied by the twinkle in it.

"Well" Katie replied, "We've given the front room a lick of paint - but that's about it."

Mo headed straight back into the hallway and over to the drawing room and flung open the door.

"A lick of paint! You've transformed the room, Katie Kettle - it's even warm in here." Mo exclaimed with delight.

"Yes Mo, I did that" Ben appeared at her shoulder and gave her a bear hug.

"Actually you helped Billy the plumber and swore a lot as I recall" Katie teased, "I'm not sure exactly how much work you actually did!" she added as she took a step back to avoid Ben's playful swipe towards her.

"Well whoever did it - it looks and feels wonderful" Mo said, "and if I wasn't pining for my kitchen table I'd sit in here with my cup of tea, which I'm sure you were about to offer" she looked at Katie expectantly who knew when to take her cue and led them all back into the flat to get the kettle on.

They were soon all settled at the table as Katie made a huge pot of tea for everyone and Mo caught up on all the news from Cliona and Ben, soon Poppy and Lucy came rushing through the door, like exploding balls of dazzling colours, one blonde head and one dark head bobbing up and down with joy and they were quickly hugging Mo and then finishing up the apple pie between them, a spoon each, straight from the pie dish. Through a mouthful of sweet crumbly pastry Poppy asked the question they had all (except Katie & Cliona) been wondering about when Mo would be returning to Tolpuddle. Everyone turned from Poppy to look at Mo expectantly. Mo had been waiting for this moment and always a fan of the dramatic arts she took a deep breath, averted her eyes and said quietly, "Well that's the thing Poppy, I'm never coming back" Mo waited for the gasp and then added before they jumped to the wrong conclusion, "Not to live anyway"

Katie and Cliona looked at the others as the news sank in that they were both already privy to. Although Katie smiled to herself knowing there was more to come, that Cliona didn't know either. Mo, as was her way, was feeding them the line enticingly so that they all bit, just as she wanted, and she wasn't to be disappointed. Poppy was first to react.

"Not coming back?" Poppy repeated, "But why not?"

Mo paused and then in an even tone replied "Well my dear, it wouldn't be right, would it? Me, living here, and my husband living at Cheadle House." Mo was a study of nonchalance.

"No, no, I suppose ..." Poppy started and then stopped, her mouth bobbing open and closed like a goldfish, then she shrieked, "Husband! You just said husband!" she finished accusingly.

Mo chortled as all the faces turned to stare at her one by one in surprise, except for Katie who was greatly enjoying the spectacle.

"Yes, Poppy, I did say husband didn't I? Bert has asked me to marry him and after much persuasion I said yes – so we're tying the knot in May and moving into one of the bungalows in the grounds at Cheadle." Mo explained to her eager audience. The satellite delay soon passed now and in no time everyone was hugging Mo and shaking Bert's hand with the usual expressions of congratulations.

"So when exactly is the big day?" Cliona asked once everyone had settled down again around the table with a fresh brew in hand.

"Soon I would think" piped up Lucy without thinking.

"Lucy!" Ben chided her, "don't be rude" Lucy looked up innocently, unaware why it might be rude. Mo, her own shoulders heaving with laughter, cut in "Ben, she's right dear, at our age we don't want to be hanging around, do we? We thought the Spring Bank weekend in May."

"And that's part of the reason we're here" Bert added ominously, "Mo has a cunning plan to involve you all – don't you my love?"

"I do" Mo confirmed, "and it's no good you all looking in the other direction, you all know me well enough to know I'll get my own way, one way or another so you may as well accept the fact now!"

They all did know Mo well enough to accept that this was indeed true and so they waited patiently for their instructions. As it turned out it wasn't too bad, Mo and Bert had arranged to be married in St Paul's church in Laxley Heath and were planning a fairly hefty knees-up in a marquee on the common afterwards, the original plan of using Cheadle House having to be abandoned as they didn't have the required licence. Katie, unsurprisingly, had been allocated the food – "but we only want a buffet – lots of lovely things for people to nibble on when they want" Mo explained.

Cliona was to be in charge of entertainment, and had carte blanche to do as she wanted, which Katie thought might be a touch rash, but Cliona looked thrilled. Poppy, with Lucy's help, was to decorate the marquee and the tables, nothing too tasteful as Mo succinctly put it! Ben was to organise the transport, which at first seemed a fairly simple job as the church was forty yards from the green, but he soon found out he was also expected to get all the invited residents from Cheadle House to Laxley Heath and back again, hopefully all in one piece – as well as the wedding car to take Mo and Bert to the train station for their honeymoon getaway in Scarborough.

"Ha" laughed Katie as she saw the realisation sink in on Ben's face and his brow crease, "you thought you'd got of lightly didn't you?" she joked.

"Not at all," Ben answered, "I was just about to ask if there was anything else I could do." He said smugly, sitting back and folding his arms in defiance. Mo rubbed her hands together, "Well since you ask Benjamin, my dear, we wondered if you'd consider being Bert's best man? He has a daughter and she feels a bit uncomfortable to do it and she separated from her husband a few years ago so he can't do it, and quite honestly I don't think any of Bert's friends could stand up for more than five minutes. Old buggers!" she mumbled, without a hint of irony. Ben was somewhat taken aback, he had met Bert a few times now and liked him greatly, but being his best man was something else. Bert could see Ben's hesitation and as he hadn't said much until now he decided to add his thoughts, "You see lad, I just need someone to look after the rings, hold me up when the knees start knocking, sign the register – don't worry, you won't have to come on the stag night!" Bert chortled; Ben laughed too, "I'd be honoured to be your best man, Bert, really. And don't be too sure about that stag night either!"

"Excellent" Mo grinned and held Bert's hand, "you could organise it with the hen night if you like - I don't know what Katie's got planned." She added, without expression except a sly wink in Ben's direction.

"Whaaaaat?" Katie demanded, juggling her mug which she was threatening to drop. Once she had settled it safely back on the counter she demanded again, "What hen night? And why am I organising it?"

"Well, it is the chief bridesmaid's job isn't it?" Mo asked

"Yes it is but ...." Katie stopped as the penny dropped, "Chief bridesmaid!" she squealed, "I've never been a bridesmaid before" she added clapping her hands together excitedly.

"So I can take that as a yes then?" Mo asked unsteadily. "Oh absolutely Mo - it will be an honour" Katie engulfed Mo in an enormous bear hug with tears running freely down both their faces.

"But there's one thing I must insist on" Katie added, "we are not having the hen night with the stag do, I'm a stickler for tradition."

CHAPTER 25

April in Laxley Heath was a busy time, preparations for both the fayre and the wedding carried on apace and it seemed that everyone in the village had some job or other that they were responsible for. Whenever Katie was out and about in the village she would see Ted Taylor stringing bunting across the main street or Andy the Landlord stocking up on beer for the tent and she always stopped for a chat and a joke with them all. Katie had never felt such a part of somewhere, it was like every idyllic village as seen on numerous TV shows all rolled into one. Mary Allen waved across from her shop, "Good Morning Katherine" she said, Mary was not one for shortening names, "I'm glad I saw you, how's Ken doing, I haven't seen Mary Clackett for a while and I was hoping he was doing well." Katie was able to confirm that Ken was indeed doing well and that Mary and Ken had actually gone to Southport for a couple of week's holiday before Ken came home for good.

Before Katie knew it, it was the Friday morning of the fayre weekend. It dawned bright and sunny, if a little chilly but no one was going to mind that Katie thought as she sat on her little patio in front of Tolpuddle House, sipping a coffee and watching the first of the day's coach parties march past. "I hope there's somewhere to get a decent cuppa" she heard one of the group saying; "it was like dishwater at the hotel this morning" she moaned to murmurs of agreement from those around her.

Katie knew that, unfortunately, they were doomed to disappointment, The Rose & Crown did do tea and coffee but it was pretty basic and even so it wouldn't be open for another couple of hours when the party would probably be on the way to Burton Manor. Maybe there would be some demand for a coffee shop here Katie pondered as she watched the next coach arrive at the coach park. She had been thinking about the possibility of opening the café more and more over the last few weeks. Helping Mo with the wedding arrangements had made her realise how much she'd missed Mo when she had been cut off in London and her friendships with Cliona, Poppy, Ben and even Hermione had made her realise how important it was to have real friends in your life. A little voice suggested she might want more than friendship with one of them but Katie ruthlessly pushed it aside. Men had been off the menu for four months now and life had been much less complicated, it was probably best kept that way for now, at least until she had decided where her future lay. She wasn't going to plan her future around a man again. She had so learned that lesson now!

Standing up Katie stretched and held her face towards the sun, it could easily warm up through the day and that would bring even more people out that evening for the opening party of the fayre weekend. It looked like she would have a very busy day ahead!

By 11 o'clock that morning she was certainly being proved right. She had collected the day's food from Declan's restaurant and transferred it into the fridges and cabinets in her makeshift kitchen at the back of the main marquee. She had set out the serving counters as she wanted them, making sure the start was where everyone came into the tent and the end was at the seating area. This had been more complicated to achieve than she had thought it would be as Hermione had been insistent about running it the other way round as she was worried about people blocking the entrance as they queued. But with a bit of persuasion and some barrier ropes Katie had created a queuing line that wouldn't block the entrance to the rest of the tent. Katie didn't think queuing of that scale was really likely to be a problem anyway. People were much more likely to come in dribs and drabs she reasoned to herself.

By six thirty in the evening Katie started to realise just how wrong she had been, the queue was starting to snake around the green as the entire village, it seemed, had decided to save themselves the hassle of cooking tea and to get their evening meal at the fayre instead. Katie was filling jacket potatoes, slicing quiches, spooning crumbles into dishes and slicing pizza almost simultaneously. Fortunately she had

Jess, Andy the Landlord's daughter to help her, and she was a godsend. Jess was serving all the people queuing with a pleasant smile and an efficiently quick turnaround in the seating area without anyone feeling they were being hurried along. And when some of the older villagers arrived Jess simply picked up their plates for them and walked along to the table with them, cutting down on the 'chat' time without appearing at all rude. It was clear Jess had done this many times before. At seven fifteen there appeared to be a bit of a lull so Katie sent Jess for a well-earned break and started to clear some of the chaos that surrounded her, though, if truth be told, she wasn't entirely sure where to start!

"Need a hand?" a familiar voice said behind her, "I'm a dab hand at the clearing up" Ben was leaning against the counter with a tea towel in hand.

"God, yes please" Katie grabbed him quickly before he could change his mind. "If you could clear the tables? Most of it can be thrown away, the plates are paper but the mugs and cutlery need to go in these crates and across to the pub. Andy's putting them through his dishwasher – but make sure it's on hot, I don't want them coming back with bits on" she added sternly.

"Aye, aye Cap'n" Ben teased and set about the tables as Katie cleared the kitchen debris, setting the supper items up and serving the odd customer as she went along. She had kept Friday's supper simple so she wouldn't have too much to clear up before Saturday which was going to be the busiest day. She had jacket potatoes in the potato oven with cheese, tuna and coleslaw to go on them, all to be served in boxes so there would no washing up. She also had many cheesecakes, ready sliced and waiting to be plated for those who wanted something sweeter. Katie was just checking the urns were full of water and getting the takeaway cups she was going to use in the evening ready when she heard a strangled cry behind her. She spun round just in time to see Jess sail across the kitchen area and land in a crumpled heap on her right ankle, at which point she let out another scream. Katie dashed over to her and she could see the tears in Jess's eyes as she tried to get up and put some weight on the damaged ankle.

"Here, lean on me" Katie instructed and then led Jess to one of the seats in the café. Jess's ankle was throbbing now and she was distraught.

"I'm so sorry Katie; I don't think I can walk on it at all. Maybe we can put a chair behind the counter and I can serve from there" she offered. Katie smiled and shook her head. "No Jess, I think you need to go and get that ankle checked out properly. Don't worry about me _ I'll be alright, I'm sure I can get someone else to pitch in." she said with more certainty than she felt. Dispatching Lucy to find Jess's dad, Katie soon had Jess patched up and on her way to Accident and Emergency at Rawlinston Hospital. She now had to tackle her second problem of who she could get to help. Lucy had offered but she was already helping Poppy on her stall, and judging by the amount of things she had dropped clearing just three tables it looked like she might be more of a liability than a help!

Just as he was wondering where to turn Ben appeared round the corner of the marquee with two crates of now clean crockery and cutlery. "What's up, Katie Crabsticks?" he asked as soon as he saw her worried face. Katie explained her current dilemma. "No worries" Ben smiled, "I can help, I was always on standby anyway. So if you're okay with it I'll give you a hand." Katie didn't hesitate, Ben had shown himself to be surprisingly useful at the job so she accepted his offer before he had chance to change his mind.

The evening was soon in full swing, the committee had booked a country and western band for the evening with a caller for the dances. The marquee had been decorated appropriately with bales of hay dotted around to sit on, and flagons of ale on the tables. There was an array of checked shirts and denim from those who were dressing for the occasion. The lively ripples of music were proving infectious. Katie looked across the dance floor and she could see Cliona and Declan throwing themselves around with gay abandon. Cliona's hair was flying out and up and down, Declan seemed remarkably light on his feet for such a bear of a man. Then there was Poppy dancing with Guy if she wasn't mistaken, they weren't quite so wild as Cliona and Declan but, none the less, seemed to be enjoying themselves. Katie thought it was probably the first time she had ever seen Guy smile – it improved his appearance no end, as did being with Poppy if Katie was any judge. Even Lucy had left her teenage street coolness at the door of the marquee and was now launching herself into a swirling polka with a good looking boy Katie recognised as Jess's older brother, Dominic. Katie laughed as Lucy's ponytail was flung up and down as if it had a life of its own.

"Wishing you were out there?" Ben whispered over her shoulder, making her jump.

"Oh no" Katie shook her head, "I'd be hopeless at it" she added, looking wistfully at the dance floor.

"Ah but you don't need to be any good – after all they tell you what to do" Ben reasoned, with that he grabbed her hand and ran her to the dance floor before she could protest. They found a gap in the dancing hordes just as the caller announced everyone to take their partner for the Gay Gordon. Soon Ben and Katie were twisting and turning and polka-ing around the floor and, if they were a little inept, they made up for it with their enthusiasm. They made quite a striking sight as they flashed across the dance floor, Katie's auburn hair flying out and her amber eyes shining as she laughed as they missed yet another step and then Ben's tall figure, a head above most others on the dance floor. Cliona thought she had never seen either of them happier and she said as much to Declan.

"Don't go getting any ideas, Clio" Declan cautioned, "don't start meddling – if they're right for each other they'll find it out for themselves."

Cliona pouted, but acquiesced, a little too easily for Declan's comfort but he decided, on this occasion, to ignore his instinct and whisked Cliona back onto the dance floor.

After half an hour of the exertions, Katie and Ben retired back to the kitchen gasping for a drink. It was already nine thirty and the band would be having a break soon, so business was likely to take an upturn. After quenching their own thirst, Katie and Ben soon had the jackets ready to go and copious amounts of cups ready for those in need of a tea or coffee. In no time they had a queue formed but they had become a well-oiled team and they soon had everybody fed and watered, as Mo called it. Katie was just around the back of the kitchen taking the last few potatoes out of the oven as Cliona came up to the counter to grab a slice of cheesecake and a large mug of tea, seeing her opportunity she decided to stop and have a quick chat with Ben. Fortunately for her Declan was chatting to some business acquaintances at the far side of the marquee or there was every chance he would have dragged her away, recognising the look on her face as the one she had exactly before she was about to extract her extremely large wooden spoon and start stirring!

"So you two made a striking pair on the dance floor" was her opening gambit.

"Striking being the operative word" Ben joked, "I think we took out most of the dance floor at some point or another, and ourselves if these are anything to go by" he added, looking at newly forming bruises on his forearms.

"Well you were both well into the dancing anyway – or was it into each other?" Cliona suggested archly and was pleased to see a slight flush in Ben's cheeks not entirely due to his recent dancing so she decided to press on. "You looked lovely together; I'm so glad you're both getting on, Katie needs someone good in her life now – after that idiot in London."

"It's a bit soon for that isn't it" Ben asked intrigued, despite himself, "she's probably sworn off men at the moment hasn't she? That's what women do when they've been disappointed isn't it?"

"Disappointed!" Cliona roared with laughter, "Have you just dropped out of a Jane Austen novel? Let me tell you, we're not disappointed, we're usually bloody furious or totally broken hearted but not disappointed Mr Wilson!" Ben laughed, "Okay, okay, I get it but still I don't think Katie's looking for anyone else just yet."

"Well I wouldn't be so sure" Cliona said, as a parting shot, leaving Ben wondering if maybe she was right. There was no denying it - he liked Katie a lot but had always told himself that it wasn't an option; she was only looking for friendship so that was what he had given. But if it could be more ....

CHAPTER 26

Ben was just pondering this intriguing new thought when he heard Katie bellowing from the back of the kitchen area

"Wilson, get your backside in here – the job's not finished yet, you know, everything's still to be washed and gotten ready for tomorrow. Don't think a quick trip round the dance floor gets you off the hook" Katie stood, hand on hip, waving a fish slice in as menacing a manner as could be fashioned with a plastic implement.

"Alright, I'm coming, for God's sake, you're a hard task master Katie Crabsticks, I'm not even getting paid for this – I'm doing it all out of the goodness of my heaaaaaaaart!" Ben howled as his legs slipped from under him on a blob of cream that had been dropped on the floor, and he landed with an enormous smack on his back!

"Oh my God" Katie screeched, "are you okay?" she added running over to him. Ben groaned and Katie started giggling, "Sorry, sorry, I don't mean to laugh, it's just I keep seeing it in my head and you looked so funny." She finished on another bubble of laughter, "I'm sorry, sorry. I'm okay now – are you? Does it hurt anywhere?" she asked with concern.

"It's my back" Ben said so faintly that Katie had to lean right down next to him to catch his words.

"Where, where does it hurt?" she asked.

"Just here" Ben said, grabbing her hand and catching her off balance so she fell down on top of him.

"Not so funny now eh?" Ben teased and wrapped his arms round her as she tried to get up, "There's no escape" he added, but Katie had stopped struggling. She didn't feel like escaping and simply lifted her head to look Ben straight in his clear blue eyes, his eyes darkened as he met her gaze and started to pull her gently towards him, just as their lips were about to touch Lucy's voice sounded from the counter out front

"Is there any cheesecake left? I'm starving"

Katie sprang up guiltily just as Lucy appeared in the kitchen ready to repeat her question when she noticed Ben on the floor. "What are you doing down there Ben? Did Katie knock you out?" she asked. Katie thought she heard him say 'sort of' but it was swiftly followed by a groan as he pulled himself up so she might have been mistaken.

"I slipped on that" Ben explained to Lucy, pointing to the offending blob of cream now spread across the floor, "and Katie thought it was most amusing too – isn't that right?" he asked looking at Katie who felt her colour rise.

"Yes that's right" she admitted, "but I defy anyone not to laugh when watching such a comedy pratfall as that"

"Oh right" said Lucy, losing interest quickly now that Ben seemed to be okay, "so is there any cheesecake left?" she returned to her original question.

"Yes" Katie replied, rolling her eyes, "there's a couple of slices on a plate in the back there, take it through for you and Poppy." Lucy was gone before Katie had finished speaking, leaving Katie and Ben staring awkwardly at each other. Ben cleared his throat, "Umm, so was that the last of the cheesecake?" he grinned suddenly, forcing Katie to relax.

"Actually, it was, and I was really looking forward to a piece of it – Nevermind, I can probably rustle up some toast and jam if that'll do?" she offered.

"Well it'll do for now but how about we do it properly on Sunday night? Let's have dinner at Angelo's, after all, the last thing you'll want to do is cook something and we can talk properly then with no interruptions" Ben said as he looked her directly in the eyes so that she wouldn't misunderstand him. Katie couldn't think of anything she'd rather do on Sunday night but settled for saying "Okay then that'll be really nice" Ben smiled, "Great, it's a date then – and I won't have to wash up!" he added.

"Maybe not" Katie answered in a mock stern voice, "but you'll still have to tonight so we'd best get a move on."

Ben groaned - again!

CHAPTER 27

Saturday morning dawned even brighter and sunnier than the day before and with the sun came much more warmth than the day before. Katie raised her face to the sun as she walked up the main street to the marquee for day two of the festivities. It was only seven o'clock in the morning and already it was warm enough to just be wearing a T-shirt, although Katie had tied her cardigan round her waist just in case it grew colder during the day. Not that it was likely it would ever be cold in the marquee if yesterday had been anything to go by! The kitchen had been extremely busy and extremely hot, but to be fair, Katie thought, that might have had something to do with the dancing too. In fact the thought of it now was bringing on a flush! Katie bounced happily up the road, she hadn't felt this happy or positive for a long time, long before Marcus, long before London and she knew in her heart it wasn't just down to the fine weather, but that was a great start and she was looking forward to spending a bit of time relaxing in it later in the day. What a vain hope that turned out to be!

It transpired that Katie was not the only one who wanted to enjoy the weather and the fayre had been thronged with visitors, villagers enjoying their annual festivities and coach loads of tourists, who spotting the event on their way to Burton Manor, had all stopped and were busy exploring the delights of the craft stalls, rooting for bargains in the antique shops and playing on the coconut shy and hook-a-duck! "Even the church is bursting at the seams" Cliona told Katie as she dropped by for a cold drink, "I haven't seen the vicar this happy since he had two chalices of communion wine to finish." And, of course, all these people were paying a visit to Katie's café. Tea, coffee, scones, pastries, cakes, biscuits and squash were flying off the counter. She and Ben barely had time to say hello before the first group of thirty pensioners had arrived and there hadn't been a lull since. At eleven o'clock Katie had to send Ben for extra supplies as all the cold drinks had gone. When he returned the lunch time trade was starting and Katie was soon barking out more orders to him. Are the quiches ready? Can you clear those tables? Were all the cold drinks put away? she demanded.

"Yes, they were" was Ben's calm reply, "and could you pass me that brush to put where the sun don't shine and I'll sweep the floor at the same time" he added with a grin.

"Don't tempt me" Katie said ominously.

"No? I was going to try and do that tomorrow evening" he said with a wink that brought the colour immediately to Katie's cheeks.

"Oh Katie, my dear, you look flushed, you must have been very busy doing all this by the look of all this lovely food" a voice said from the

310

other side of the counter, just in time to save Katie from her blushes. Katie spun round to see Mary Clackett standing there, beaming from ear to ear.

"Mary, how lovely to see you. How are you? How's Ken doing?" Katie asked.

"Well, my dear, why don't you ask him yourself? He's sat at the table over there" Mary pointed behind her. Katie dropped what she was doing and ran over to Ken giving him the biggest hug.

"Ken, I'm so happy to see you, you look so well. How are you feeling?" she asked.

"Well, lass, I'm doing right well now, we've had a few weeks at the coast with Mary's sister and I'm right as rain now – and that's mainly due to you and this young man here." He said, tipping his head towards Ben who had appeared with tea and scones for them all.

"I never got the chance to thank you properly" Ken continued, "and I'm not sure if I can, but me and my Mary will always be grateful that you two were there when it happened." Ken shook Ben's hand and kissed Katie on the cheek as Mary's eyes welled up with tears and she nodded her head so vigorously it looked like it was on a spring.

"Yes, yes, I don't know what would have happened if you weren't there" she added.

"It's alright, Mary, love" Ken said, patting her hand, "don't get upset, it's okay now and I've been given the all clear to go home."

"Oh Ken, that's wonderful" Katie exclaimed, giving him yet another hug, "so when are you coming back to Tolpuddle?"

"Well, that's the thing, lass, Mary and I have decided not to come back to Tolpuddle House. You and young Ben here might not always be around and if something else happens we need to know someone is nearby. So we were chatting to Mo and Bert the other day and they told us all about the bungalow they're moving into at Cheadle House and that there's another one vacant, so we went to have a look around it - and loved it. So we're going to move in there - it's all arranged" he finished happily and held Mary's hand like two teenagers just falling in love not two septuagenarians who had been together fifty years. As Katie had wistfully put it when she was telling Cliona over a quick coffee the following day. Saturday had flown past after the Clackett's visit with barely time for a sip of water and Katie had returned home to Tolpuddle at half past eleven and gone straight to bed, barely even having the energy to even get undressed. She had returned for the final day of the fayre flagging a little and by late morning Ben had gone off in search of some real coffee for a proper caffeine boost, rather than the instant stuff that Katie had. Cliona had popped across for a quick chat before the church service finished at eleven thirty when numbers would pick up a bit.

"How sad is it" Katie moaned, "that I'm now officially jealous of seventy year olds' romantic lives, compared to mine"

"Well, from what I can see, it looks like yours is picking up a bit. Where is Ben by the way?" Cliona questioned, none too subtly.

"He's finding some real coffee - we needed a shot of proper coffee to get us through the rest of the day and the clear up." Katie answered as smoothly as she could, not wanting to give any indication she had heard Cliona's 'subtle as a sledgehammer' hint.

"Hmm, fetching and carrying for you, pandering to your every need, I'd say you've got nothing to worry about on the romantic front - Ben isn't always this helpful, you know. Last time I asked him to help at the Aromatherapy and Herbal Remedies Convention he said, and I quote, 'I'd rather stick needles in my eyes and chew off my own arms than spend ten minutes with the crazy, mad women you know Cliona'" Cliona recounted with twinkling eyes.

"Yes, but that is a bit different to the village fayre - to be fair" Katie laughed.

"Maybe, maybe not. I just know Ben Wilson of old and serving tea and coffee to the grey army has never been top of his to do list before." Cliona finished archly and disappeared back to her stall.

Katie was still laughing to herself as she started to slice the last of the quiches.

"Katie, Can we talk?" a deep voice, so well-known to her stopped her in her tracks and she swung round nearly dropping the quiche that was in her hands.

"Marcus!" was all she could manage in response, shocked by the sudden appearance of him. He was as handsome as ever, if a little less smart and a little more drawn in his face. His expression of uncertainty was new too. Katie had only ever seen him decisive and certain. Gathering her thoughts, Katie managed to ask, "What do you want Marcus?"

"I want to talk to you, Katie. Please, I'm sorry I know I've hurt you and I wanted to talk to you, to explain" he pleaded, "Please just talk to me." Katie could see people starting to stop and watch the little scene developing and the last thing she wanted was to play it out in front of the whole village. Quickly she realised she needed to get Marcus away from the marquee. Putting on her best smile, as if delighted to see him, she said brightly, "Marcus, sorry, you surprised me. I'm so happy to see you after all this time. I'm due a break; let's take a walk round the green. We've so much to talk about." And with that she put down the quiche, threw off her apron and grabbed Marcus's hand and almost ran out of the marquee with him as if she couldn't wait to be alone with him. At least that's how it appeared to Ben, who Katie hadn't seen, as he had arrived in the back of the kitchen just in time to see

her gaily throw off her apron and grab Marcus by the hand and run out

with him. Nor did Katie see the look of sheer pain etched on his face as

walked through the marquee, got into his van and drove away.

CHAPTER 28

Katie dropped Marcus's hand as soon as they had gotten out of sight of the marquee and its many pairs of curious eyes and turned immediately on him,

"What the bloody hell do you think you're doing here?" she stormed, wrong footing Marcus completely as he had been taken in as much as Ben by Katie's 'happy to see him' act.

"I'm sorry" he stammered, "I wanted to see you, to talk to you."

"Oh I see now, four months later you need to talk to me – so you just turn up out of the blue, without a by your leave, not a phone call, email or even a text and you expect me to drop everything and talk to you, to make you feel better." Katie stormed at him.

"I know, I'm sorry but I thought if I rang, you wouldn't answer or you'd refuse to see me. I thought if I just turned up at least you'd speak to me – or shout at me at least!" he smiled ruefully. Katie smiled, despite herself.

"Well, you got that right at least!" she said begrudgingly and sighed, "What do you want to say Marcus?"

"I want you back, Katie"

Katie knew what poleaxed felt like now. After all these months Marcus wanted her back. She thought how desperately she had wanted this happen. How often she had dreamt about it. Marcus turning up, begging her forgiveness once he had realised he couldn't live without her. And now it was happening, right in front of her, so why wasn't she jumping for joy, throwing herself into Marcus's arms like the final scene of a really cheesy afternoon TV film.

Katie looked into his face, he was trying to look uncertain, as if he wasn't sure if she'd take him back, but Katie knew his face of old, from all the deals she had sat and watched him work on. Once he knew he had the upper hand he always tried to look as though he didn't – he thought it wrong-footed his opponents, made them careless. Katie looked Marcus straight in the eye and asked, "Why now?"

"What?" Marcus jolted, he hadn't really been expecting more questions, he was now vaguely conscious this might not be going the way he had planned.

"Because I miss you, sweetheart. I don't function properly without you – I need you" he answered as smooth as the perfect roux!

"But why don't you function without me? What do I have that your wife doesn't? Only four months ago she was all you wanted. You didn't even give me a backward glance as you raced out of the boardroom" Katie continued, a little bitterly.

"But Sarah's left now – we couldn't make things work anymore, and I realised I needed you. You make things work. I need you at the office too; nothing is how I like it. I want you back, my darling. I know how wrong I was - please let's not fight anymore and let's start our future together." Marcus explained with a flourish.

Katie realised it was a day for sayings to come true as she literally felt the scales drop from her eyes and saw for the first time, the real Marcus Chamberlain. A weak, vain, good-looking man who thought the world revolved around him and who could see no wrong in what he was saying.

"So Marcus, did Sarah leave you or did you leave her?" Katie asked, knowing full well what the answer was.

Marcus answered in his persuasive lawyer's voice, "Well technically, she left me but it was only a matter of time until one of us left. What does that matter now?" he held out his arms to Katie waiting for her to fall into them.

"You're right you know" Katie suddenly grinned, "It doesn't matter at all to me, other than that I don't blame her one little bit!"

"What?" Marcus looked dumbstruck.

"I said, I don't blame her one little bit, you treated her appallingly, so did I, but at least I wasn't married to her. So now she's seen the light and binned you, you thought reliable, efficient Katie would be a good back-up did you? Thought you'd pop up to see her in the sticks, declare you're undying need and I'd be straight back to London with you, making your life nice and easy again." Katie stood hands on hips, challenging Marcus to deny it.

As this was pretty much exactly what Marcus had thought he had absolutely no idea what to do or say next. Fortunately, Katie had no such problem – for the first time since breaking up with Marcus, she knew absolutely what she wanted him to do and what she wanted to do herself. The realisation filled her with excitement about the future but firstly, she needed to dispatch the past.

"Just go now, Marcus," she told him, "I'm not coming back to you. I don't want to! I don't love you anymore, if I ever really did. I'm staying here in Laxley with real friends and I'm going to run my own business not prop up someone else's, a beautiful coffee shop and craft market and I'm going to be responsible for my own happiness."

"You're going to stay here?" Marcus replied incredulously, "here? But it's so far away."

"Yes, Marcus, it is" Katie answered happily, "and that's one of the many reasons I love it!" With that she turned on her heels, not Jimmy Choos anymore, but she didn't care about that now, and she headed back into the marquee, leaving Marcus with nothing to do but walk back to his top of the range Mercedes with as much dignity as he could muster and head back to London as quickly as possible where he wouldn't feel so out of place.

As Katie entered the back of the kitchen she looked for Ben, exhilarated after dispatching Marcus so comprehensively and she wanted to share the news with him straightaway. Now she had even more reason to celebrate that evening! Katie saw that Lucy was behind the counter serving up one of the last quiche salads as Katie walked over to her.

"So, where's Ben? Skived off for a break and left you to hold the fort eh? I can't turn my back on him for a minute" Katie joked

"Something like that" Lucy grumbled, "he had something come up at work urgently and he had to go, he rang me on my mobile to tell me I had to help you" she added somewhat ungraciously.

"Oh" Katie felt the disappointment fill her momentarily, "well, work is work – can't be helped. But look, Luce, I'll be fine here now, everything is slowing down. You go back to Poppy and help her pack up" she suggested. Lucy didn't need telling twice – her apron was off and she was across the tent before Katie could turn round.

It was a shame Ben wasn't here, Katie thought, but, still, she could tell him all about it that evening when they had dinner. She checked her phone but there were no messages, he'd probably ring her a bit later to arrange things. With that Katie made sure her phone wasn't on silent and put it in her pocket before she set about the mammoth task of

clearing everything up!

By five o'clock when she had finally finished washing all the crockery

and cutlery, clearing the rubbish and counting up the money she still

hadn't heard from Ben. She had checked her phone so often Cliona had

asked if she was expecting some news.

Everyone was finishing up now and going over to the Rose & Crown for

a well-earned drink, including Cliona and Declan who were insisting

that Katie go with them. Katie decided to send Ben a text to let him

know where she was then he could either join them or let her know

what time and where to meet him.

CHAPTER 29

"So did anyone hear from Ben last night then?" Katie asked as casually as she could when Cliona had joined her for coffee the next morning. They were meeting to start the planning of the café and craft business at Tolpuddle House but Katie was still feeling a bit miffed, and a little upset, though she wouldn't admit it, that Ben had never responded the evening before and their promised dinner date had not materialised. So she wanted to get to the bottom of it before they started on the designs for the business.

Cliona was not so easily fooled by Katie's attempt at casual, she could see that Katie was upset that Ben hadn't shown up the previous evening and Cliona had also noticed how many times she had checked her phone for messages or missed calls. Unfortunately Cliona didn't have any good news for Katie.

"Well he sent Declan a brief text saying something important had come up at the Southampton project and he was heading off down there" she explained

"Oh - did he say for how long?" Katie asked, somewhat deflated, despite her best efforts to be indifferent.

"Well, not exactly, but he said Lucy was off to stay with Jean for the week so at least that long, I suppose. Why - did you need him for something?" Cliona could never resist prodding for a bit more information.

"No, no, I just never got to say thanks for helping me out over the weekend. It would have been a nightmare on my own. But nevermind, I can tell him next time I see him – next weekend maybe." Katie said stoically, "now, let's start the planning, that's what we're here for" she said, grabbing her pad and pen and the first lay out option.

It wasn't the next weekend or, indeed, the couple after that. Lucy came to visit during the following week and by the look on her face Katie knew she wasn't happy. "He's not coming back until Mo's wedding now – apparently there's all sorts of problems with the Building Inspector and the plans or something so he can't get back and I've got to stay at Jean's house!" Lucy clearly wasn't entirely happy with this arrangement.

"But I thought you liked staying with Jean?" Katie said

"It's okay, but she never lets me out later than nine thirty, even at the weekends. I can usually wangle another hour out of Ben, hour and a half if he picks me up." Lucy grinned, "Jean's not quite so persuadable!" Katie laughed too; Lucy had changed a lot over the last few months since she had been living with Ben. She still had a wild streak but she was much less defensive and rebellious – being wanted and not being passed from pillar to post had done wonders for her, and she was still only fourteen so she was entitled to few teenage grumbles.

"Well, if it's okay with Ben and Jean, maybe you could stop here next weekend – it's the one before the wedding so we're having Mo's hen night here on Saturday. Don't think it'll be wild one, although I can't say for certain with Mo!" Katie added.

"Oh please! Anything's better than another weekend at Jean's – I may as well become a nun!" Lucy said with a little too much feeling for Katie's liking.

"It'll be all girls here too, so don't be expecting Brad Pitt or Johnny Depp" she chided.

"Urghh! They're way old!" Lucy sneered, making Katie feel every one of her twenty nine years.

"Well whoever it is you have your eye on, they certainly won't be here but none the less, you're welcome to come and stay if Ben and Jean say it's okay." Katie said.

"Cool" Lucy answered, pleased, "but where will I sleep?"

"My spare room, I suppose – it's warm and cosy in there" Katie decided.

"But what about your fella - won't he mind? Or will he be out of the way?" Lucy interrogated.

"My fella?" Katie was bemused, "what 'fella' would that be?"

"The posh one who came to the fayre, quite good –looking – a bit old though." Lucy dismissed Marcus in a sentence.

"He's not my fella," Katie laughed "he was in another life but not anymore – I'm young free and single these days" she declared and put a hand over Lucy's mouth as she was about to say something rude about the young bit!

Katie shared this gem with Cliona that night as they went through more plans and applications for the conversion of Tolpuddle House.

"Why on earth did Lucy think I was with Marcus? She's a cheeky mare – but I can't help liking her. Still, I've no idea why she thought I was back with him."

Cliona kept her own counsel, she had a fair idea where Lucy had got the idea from and if she was right it would explain Ben's sudden disappearance and the increasingly lame excuses he was making to avoid coming back. Cliona felt it was time to help things along a little, after the hen party; she'd be making a quick call to Southampton to straighten out any misunderstandings!

CHAPTER 30

The best laid plans, even of Cliona, sometimes go wrong, and the call to Ben in Southampton never got made after the hen party. Declan had had an accident in his car and although he wasn't badly hurt, his fractured ankle was enough to keep him off his feet and for Cliona to be extremely busy running him back and forth from the restaurant and hospital appointments. Ringing Ben slipped completely from her mind and so it was the night before the wedding Ben had rung Mo and Bert with his excuses, another emergency on site, he wouldn't be able to make it, he was so sorry but everything was arranged for them and Declan would stand (or sit) in as best man.

Katie was beside herself with rage, (brought on largely by disappointment but she wasn't about to admit that), and she was raging to anyone and everyone who would listen. Lucy, with remarkable diplomacy, who had been one of the many Katie had offered her frank opinion of her brother too, decided to slip outside when her mobile rang and she saw it was Ben calling!

"Alright Bro, are your ears burning?" she started

"No" Ben sounded confused, not unsurprisingly, "Why – should they be?"

"God, yes – you haven't half upset Katie. She's calling you all the names under the sun now you're not coming to the wedding tomorrow. Why aren't you coming?" Lucy asked curiously as she was a little disappointed that her brother wasn't coming back too, but Ben wasn't listening to her question, he was already in full flow.

"I don't know why she's getting so angry. I've organised everything I was supposed to and Mo and Bert were fine about it!" he stormed.

"Well, I think she was worried some things might get missed or something" Lucy answered diplomatically.

"Well if I have missed anything I'm sure she can sort it out – or her boyfriend can" Ben said bitterly.

"Huh" Lucy grunted but didn't get chance to say anymore as Ben continued his rant.

"Anyway she won't be doing that once she's back in London - will she? Mo and Bert will have to fend for themselves then – won't they? Or will she expect us all to pick up everything for her." Ben paused for breath and Lucy took her chance.

"What are you on about Ben? Why will Katie be in London? She's got all the renovations at Tolpuddle to do. I don't think she'll have time for going to London." She explained.

"Renovations – what renovations?" Ben queried, "So she's selling Tolpuddle House is she?"

"No" Lucy answered, slightly exasperated, rolling her eyes, "she's not selling it, she's turning the front half into a coffee shop and a craft centre and knocking through to the flat at the back."

"Oh yes" Ben said knowingly, "so he's moving up there is he? The city lawyer in the sticks"

"Huh – who?" Lucy said again, this conversation was going very strangely, very strangely indeed.

"The lawyer, Marcus, Katie's boyfriend" Ben explained

"But she hasn't got a boyfriend – oh you mean the posh bloke from the fayre, you said that was who he was before." Lucy finally caught up with conversation

"Yes – Katie's boyfriend, as I said" Ben said as if talking to a child, so Lucy responded in kind

"But-he's-not-her-boyfriend!" Lucy said slowly, "She told me the other week. She told him to take a hike; she wasn't remotely interested in him anymore." Lucy finished.

"Oh shit!" That was the last thing Lucy heard as the line went dead. She shrugged, she loved her brother but he was bloody weird sometimes!

CHAPTER 31

The wedding day dawned, bright and sunny, little wisps of white fluffy clouds followed each other across the blue sky slowly, as if keeping an eye on the proceedings below. Katie got up early and after enjoying her own mug of steaming hot coffee to fortify her for the day ahead, she woke Mo up with breakfast in bed. Two slabs of toast and honey and a pot of tea with a china cup and saucer.

"After all, it is a special occasion" Katie said, as she placed the tray on Mo's lap. Mo's eyes were shining, she looked radiant, just as a bride should, Katie thought, and quickly shoved to one side the little pang inside her that wondered if she would ever get to have that feeling. Today was about Mo, and Bert of course, and Mo deserved this happiness – she'd always put others first and it was time she was centre of attention. Katie had a little surprise for her now whilst they were still on their own. Soon Poppy and Lucy would be descending on them and then they probably wouldn't have a chance. Katie pulled the little box out of her dressing gown pocket and put it on the tray in front of Mo.

Mo looked up

"Is that for me? But I'm supposed to get you something, you're the bridesmaid after all," she said.

"Well, we're doing things differently today. You've done enough for me over the years, Mo, so I wanted to get something just for you, so you know how grateful I am and how much I love you." Mo squeezed her hand and picked up the little box and carefully opened it. Inside was a small silver heart shaped charm to fit onto Mo's bracelet, but when she looked closer she could see it was in two parts. Katie looked at Mo as she examined the charm.

"One part is for me and one part for you – that way we always have a part of each other, if that's okay" Katie explained.

Mo looked up with her eyes glistening with tears, "Oh Katie, it's beautiful, of course it's okay" she said, picking up one half of the little heart and handing it to Katie, "I can't believe you sometimes, Katie Kettle. I swore I wasn't going to cry today and I haven't even got out of bed and I'm blubbing like a baby –I bet you did it on purpose" she added in her more usual tones. Katie laughed and bobbed a kiss on Mo's head and winked at her.

"Hairdressers' will be here in an hour so we'd best get a wriggle on." She said as she headed out to the kitchen.

Katie was absolutely right that that was the last bit of peace they would have. Ten minutes after Katie left Mo to have her breakfast; she had laid out a selection of breakfast cereals, fresh bread with honey and butter, croissants with strawberry jam and an extremely large pot of coffee, and ten minutes after that Poppy and Lucy had bounded

through the door, full of excitement but not affecting their appetites in

the least. Hairdressers, florists and photographers had swiftly followed

as had the chauffeur arranged by Ben, Katie noted, still not ready to

forgive him. The chauffeur drove them slowly down the main street to

the church and it seemed like all the village had come out wave and

send their best wishes to Mo. At eleven o'clock exactly they were stood

outside the church as the organ struck up the first chord. Mo gripped

Katie's arm a little tighter but was she was ready to go and they made

their way down the aisle to the accompaniment of the organ, played a

little haphazardly but enthusiastically by Joseph Stillington, who had

been playing the church's organ for a little under 83 years! In no time

they were at the front of the church beside Bert and Declan (and not

Ben, Katie thought bitterly) and Father Foster began the familiar

phrases of the wedding service.

In forty five minutes they were all outside the church again in the

sunshine, voices laughing, children running around and cameras

snapping away. Katie looked at Mo and thought she had not seen her so

happy since Grandpa had died, still she hadn't seen much of Mo at all

for the last four years but Katie was determined that would all change

now. She was in Laxley to stay and Mo would be only ten minutes away at Cheadle. It sounded absurd but she had forgotten how much she loved Mo and how much she loved being with her, it had taken being forced to come back for her to realise all this. If a little voice was nagging at the back of her mind saying how much she had loved being with Ben too, she chose to resolutely ignore it! Katie came out of her reverie with a snap as a giggling Lucy came running up to her. Lucy was dressed in the same deep purple satin as Katie as she had been designated third bridesmaid after Poppy and herself.

"Katie, there's a problem" she announced, followed by a reel of giggles, "something to do with moving the tables out of the marquee onto the grass. They need you to go and talk to someone about it."

"Moving the tables?" Katie said incredulously, "moving them where?"

"I don't know" Lucy shrugged, "something about having some on the other side of the bridge as it's a nice day" Lucy stifled another giggle, Katie wondered if she had managed to get to the champagne already!

"I think they want you to go over and have a look where they want to put them" Lucy continued, a little more seriously. Katie sighed, this was the trouble when you organised everything yourself – you couldn't take the day off. She may as well go and have a look; they'd only send someone else after her and all the guests were going to be taking photos for a bit longer yet. "Ok Luce, I'll head over there now. Let Mo know where I am will you? I won't be long"

"I wouldn't count on it" Lucy whispered under her breath as Katie set

off towards the green. Lucy typed a text and sent it; it only had one

word – 'SORTED'.

Then she set off screeching at the top of her voice "Poppy, Poppy,

you've got to hear this!"

Katie walked towards the bridge at the end of the green, remembering

once again the daydreams of her childhood and how the prince was

waiting at the other side of the little stone bridge, sword aloft, hair

flying in the wind, ready to whisk her away on his white stallion.

"Huh" Katie thought, "princes just aren't what they used to be, there

was never one around when you needed one." She had reached the top

of the small slope of the bridge now and she stopped to look over the

side into the stream below. The water was so clear she could make out

her own reflection in the water. The sun was warm on her back and

Katie closed her eyes, enjoying the sensation. She felt some of the

tension slip away from her shoulders and she allowed herself for the

first time to accept why she was so angry with Ben for not coming to

the wedding. Of course, she was bothered that Mo and Bert would be

upset but once Ben had sorted everything out he had not left them in

the lurch at all. No, the real reason she was so upset was much closer

to home. She had been waiting to see him, aching to see him really.

Katie realised how much she had missed being a part of Ben's life, being close to him. She had fallen in love with him. She couldn't quite put her finger on when it had happened, but there it was, clear as day, she, Katie Crabsticks, loved Ben Wilson with all her heart and now she thought it might break in two all over again now he hadn't turned up to the wedding, she had to face the fact that he couldn't feel anything for her or he wouldn't have missed this opportunity to be with her, no matter how busy work was.

Sighing deeply, Katie reluctantly opened her eyes and peered back into the crystal waters below and started suddenly when she realised hers was not the only face peering back at her!

Ben smiled slowly as recognition dawned on Katie's face about whose reflection was looking back at her. Katie felt a slow flush rise on her cheeks as she felt Ben must know everything she had just been thinking, feeling vulnerable and exposed by Ben's sudden appearance Katie went of the offensive, turning round to him and stormed, "So you've decided to put in an appearance after all – and take your commitments seriously then?"
Ben was stopped in his tracks momentarily; this wasn't quite how he'd seen this reunion going.

"Er what?" he managed articulately.

"I said you've decided to show up after all. I assumed you had more important things to do, people to see" Katie answered, indignantly, tilting her chin up and swishing her hair in what she thought was an imperious manner. Ben smiled and then grinned,

"No one is more important than you" he said simply. Katie looked at him, taking a breath to hit back at him, assuming he was about to accuse her of being self-centred, when Ben added very quietly, "Well, at least to me"

Katie felt like someone had punched her in the stomach. "I'm sorry?" she stammered, not daring to look at his face. Ben gently put a finger under her chin and lifted her face to look at him.

"No, I'm sorry Katie, I'm sorry I left without speaking to you. I'm sorry I haven't rung you and I'm sorry I let you and Mo down, but I couldn't help it. It would have hurt too much to stay." Katie leaned against the bridge looking into Ben's handsome and earnest face, feeling uncertain and shy.

"But why?" she asked, "What was going to hurt you?"

"You were" Ben silenced Katie's response with a finger on her lips. Katie felt a ripple of desire run through her body.

"I saw you leave with Marcus, you looked so happy I thought you were going back with him. I thought you'd been waiting for him to come. I couldn't have stayed and watched you with him." Ben whispered. Katie could hear the agony in his voice and hope started to rise in her but she didn't dare let herself believe it yet.

"But why would that have hurt you?" she asked for reassurance. Ben looked deep into her eyes, locking her to the spot and leaned one arm either side of her on the bridge so she could feel his breath, warm on her face.

"You know why Katie" he groaned and in movement pulled her to him and kissed her ruthlessly and completely. As they pulled apart Ben looked down into Katie's amber eyes.

"I love you Katie Crabsticks. I have since I was nine, I think. So if you're staying in Laxley then so am I – no arguments" Katie sighed and kissed him again. This was one argument she didn't want to win!

THE END

Printed in Great Britain
by Amazon